THE
GREEN
CHILDREN

A SYCAMORE MOON NOVEL

DOMINO FINN

BLOOD &
TREASURE

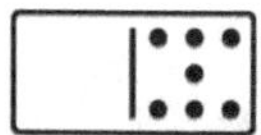

Published by Blood & Treasure, Los Angeles
First Edition

Front Cover by James T. Egan of Bookfly Design LLC.

Print ISBN: 978-0-692-61822-6

DominoFinn.com

THE
GREEN
CHILDREN

Act 1 - The First 48

Chapter 1

Ongoing lives, no matter how interesting, trended toward routine.

Diego de la Torre's time in Sanctuary had been anything but ordinary. Fistfights, shootouts, wolves, witches—and a body count larger than the eighteen months he'd lived here.

But lately, things for Diego had been business as usual. The tow business, specifically. He was now a biker-turned-blue-collar. A clock-puncher.

Diego's company truck rumbled along Interstate 40 on the way to another suit with a flat tire. His third job this year wasn't the most glamorous, but it wasn't the crappiest either. It was honest work, dealing only in breakdowns and emergencies. None of the scams the tow companies in Detroit pulled that preyed on hardworking people. Diego didn't do cold tows. The open Arizona land had no demand for them. There was something to be said for that.

The open road appealed to him too, but it wasn't

enough. Driving a rig was simply too low key. Sure, there were errant threats from disgruntled drivers and arguments over distance and money, but those were nothing more than bluster. There was no real danger anymore. That fact never stopped Diego from secretly hoping the next call would be the one where somebody threw a punch or pulled a knife.

Hey, there was nothing wrong with a respectable disagreement once in a while.

But Diego considered the bright side. It was a beautiful spring. It was a legal paycheck. He hadn't been shot at in nine months. Life always offered the hope of something more, with the caveat that the best of times were often the most bland.

The old days he longed for... They weren't bland. An ex-service man, an ex-biker outlaw—Diego had lots of stories. He wanted to regain that source of adrenaline. Changing tires and charging batteries wasn't cutting it.

So when a frantic woman lunged into the highway in front of his speeding truck, Diego once again felt that spark.

He jammed the brake pedal to the rubber floor mat. The six tires smoked and scraped against the asphalt, causing the rig to swerve dangerously. By the time it came to a stop, the tow truck took up both westbound lanes.

Luckily, traffic was light this morning on account of it being Easter Monday, the day after the holiday and the cap of a long weekend. No vehicles rear-ended him. Diego swiveled his head searching for the woman.

A fist pounded his window and made him jump. The woman had somehow circled his truck.

"You've got to help me!" she screamed. "Help!"

Again Diego scanned the area. The dense forest on either side of the highway cut down visibility, but aside from the crazy woman in the middle of the Interstate, nothing appeared amiss. She yelled again to get his attention.

"All right. All right," he said, shifting his rig into reverse. He backed up over the wide shoulder and didn't stop till his back wheels were in the dirt. It wasn't a graceful parking job, but it wouldn't cause any accidents.

"What the hell do you think you're doing?" he demanded as he kicked open his door. The woman clutched at him like glue.

"My daughter," she rasped. "My eight-year-old daughter is out here."

And then Diego immediately understood the mad look in the woman's eyes, the shimmer of sweat on her skin despite the crisp breeze. She wasn't crazy. She wasn't a tweaker. She was a mother living her worst nightmare.

"Slow down," he said, grabbing the woman by the shoulders. She was slender. Thin nose, narrow lips—everything about her was fragile except for her wide, gaping eyes.

She shook against his grasp. Her long brown hair, almost black, swung wildly as he held her.

"You need to calm down for a second," urged Diego. "Look at me."

"She's out here."

"Look at me."

She turned to him and brushed the hair from her face.

Her light-brown eyes met his and relaxed for a moment. He glimpsed them in their normal state, at ease, welcoming. Kind. The woman had a natural beauty that was elegant and soft.

"What happened to your daughter?"

She took a breath. "We were hiking in the woods. Just ten minutes ago."

"Where?"

"Up there," she sputtered, pointing north to the trees. Besides the access road, the area was heavily wooded. The Sycamore forest, they called it.

"She came to the highway?"

The woman became exasperated again. "I don't know."

Diego searched up and down the 40. The only clear sight lines were along the road. He hadn't seen any pedestrians before pulling over. If the little girl was only a few minutes away, she wasn't on the street.

"Okay," he said, grabbing the woman's head to lock into her eyes again. "Don't worry. We'll find her." She returned a slight nod.

The biker climbed into his truck and reached for the CB.

"Hey, Harry. You there?"

It took a second to raise the man, but he answered.

"Diego? What's it look like?"

"Uh, I'm not there yet. I might be a little late."

Harry's voice immediately grew coarse. "You better not be. Not again."

"I'm serious, Harry. Call up Chuck to cover for me."

"I'm not gonna call Chuck 'cause I've got you."

Diego hissed. "There's a missing kid out here. This is an emergency."

"It's always an emergency with you, Diego. Can't you—"

The biker switched off the radio. He didn't have time to deal with his boss.

"Take me to where you last saw her," said Diego with comforting confidence.

The woman smiled at him. There was something alluring about a smile from a stranger. Not a business smile like a cashier might flash, but an earnest one from the heart. Maybe the appeal was in what came next. In the desire to get to know the person better. In the possibilities ahead.

Diego remembered that smile because he realized he might never see it again.

Chapter 2

"Julia Cunningham. That's two Ns, right?"

Julia nodded and wrapped her arms around her body for warmth. For two hours she had been numb to the cool air. Now, back at her cabin suite with the fire running, her adrenaline was spent.

"And your daughter's name is Hazel?"

"Yes, Detective."

Diego sat on the arm of the couch, trying not to be a nuisance. He'd taken over the search for the missing girl and assumed he had a good handle on things. Coming up empty felt like his fault.

"My daughter and I were hiking this morning," began Julia. "Not too far. She's only eight. She was running back and forth, looking for the perfect sticks to make magic wands. I called for her, but she didn't answer."

The Coconino County detective nodded but kept his eyes on his small notepad. He looked like a pro, in his early forties, smooth, clean features except for worry wrinkles on his forehead and by his mouth. His hair receded at the temples forming a sharp V at the top of his head. Average all around, except for his bright pink tie.

"Why did you think to run straight for the Interstate?" he asked pointedly.

Julia shook her head and paused. "I don't know. I had last seen her in that direction. I thought I heard her singing. I just kept running until I was on the highway."

"Do you have any other friends or guardians in town?"

"No."

"What about a husband? A boyfriend?"

Diego wasn't sure why these questions were being asked, but he found himself interested in the last answer. Julia shook her head absently.

The detective stopped writing and focused on the woman. "And you're sure Hazel went to the Interstate?"

Julia twisted her face in frustration. "What? No. I told you I'm not sure. I was just looking for her."

The detective seemed to frown. He considered the mother for a moment before speaking. "Chances are she didn't cross the street. Most likely she's still in the woods somewhere, closer to the campgrounds than we realize. She might be hurt or scared, but I'm organizing a search party. We'll cover the area and find her. I'll have someone posted here in case she manages to wander back."

The detective glanced at Diego. The biker looked away. He felt like an interloper, intruding on this woman's most vulnerable moment. Diego examined the business card in his hand to keep busy. Detective David Harper, Coconino County Sheriff's Office. The man seemed capable enough, but he was distant. Disconnected.

"What about your home address?" asked David. "Does she know it?"

"Yes," answered Julia. "Why?"

"It's possible a car picked her up and she got a ride home. Williams is close. She could already be there. It's probably best if you returned just in case."

"No," said Julia firmly. "I'm not leaving. Hazel will be right back. I know it."

Detective Harper sighed. "Ma'am, if you knew that, then why'd you call the police?"

Diego stood up. "I called. Don't give her a hard time, okay? She's just trying to be optimistic." Diego moved beside Julia and put his arm around her back. She looked so fragile, but she was trying to be so strong.

"Oh my God," she cried. "What if someone picked her up?"

"Let's not get ahead of ourselves," said the detective. "There's absolutely no reason to think that. It's a possibility we're aware of. We'll put out her description statewide. We're going to need some pictures of her, Ms. Cunningham. The quicker we get those, the better. That's another reason I suggest you let one of my deputies take you home."

David Harper moved to the front door and opened it. He waved in a young woman wearing a sheriff's uniform: a dark brown hat, tie, pants, and a tan button-up.

"Deputy Garza will see to everything." The woman stood by the doorway and gave a firm nod.

"You're not coming?" asked Julia.

Detective Harper frowned. "I have a few things to finish up here. I'll be over as soon as I can." As he spoke, he marched everyone outside.

Quiet Pines was charitably labeled luxury camping. The reality was far from roughing it. Most of the campers stayed in expensive cabins or their own RVs. Full amenities like electricity and water were available at every site. But it was a clean taste of nature, and the weather was just getting nice. The combination packed the grounds with visitors, many of them locals.

"What about you?" asked Julia, turning to Diego. Her hands clasped his shoulders. "You'll come with me, at least?"

Diego balked at the request. He didn't know how to answer. He didn't belong here. "You sure?"

"I don't want to be alone."

The biker relented and slowly nodded. He was getting himself deeper, but he didn't have a choice. Before he could speak, he noticed a man with a white panama hat approaching from the office building. Like the Coconino detective, Maxim also wore a suit, more stylish with a modern cut, but also more worn and neglected.

Diego's expression turned apologetic. "I need to talk to the friend I told you about. He'll help us. I'll swing by right after. I promise."

She was disappointed despite his reassurances. It worried

Diego to see the empty look on her face. He wondered if Julia would ever be happy again. Deputy Garza escorted her away, leaving him with the Coconino County detective outside the cabin.

"Sorry I'm late," said Maxim, joining them. "I had to finish some things up." He eyed David Harper. Maxim brushed the left side of his jacket away to reveal a gold badge on his belt. "I'm Detective Maxim Dwyer from the Sanctuary Marshal's Office."

The other detective raised his eyebrows. Sanctuary was a small town ten minutes away; the marshal's office had no jurisdiction here. "This is a county matter, Detective."

"I know. I'm not here officially. Just as a favor to a friend."

David turned to Diego and understood. "I see. I'm Detective Harper. We're still searching for the girl. I don't suppose you have any knowledge that can help?"

Maxim shook his head. "Not at all. I'm just getting here. Are you organizing a search?"

David grimaced slightly. "Of course, Detective."

"I'd like to be involved. I can offer the manpower of my department and drum up civilian support in Sanctuary."

Begrudgingly, the county detective agreed.

Chapter 3

Maxim recoiled and shook the insects off his feet. The crumpled, rotten log beneath his shoe was infested with them. Termites. Maybe something else. The eerie shine of his flashlight's beam on their wings, the unnatural hive of movement... It was unsettling. Especially in the middle of the night in the woods.

It was all the reminder Maxim needed that he wasn't much of an outdoorsman.

The detective was still wearing his suit. That was strike one. His shoes weren't made for hiking either. As he pounded the last of the bugs from them, he made a mental note to throw them away.

Maxim raised his Maglite to his flank. Twenty yards to his left was Clint, one of the bikers from the local motorcycle club and the best hunter of the bunch. To his right was another civilian. Flanking them would be others, spread out in a wide formation, attempting to get as much coverage of the dense wild as possible.

Maxim had made good on his word to David Harper. He'd gathered support in Sanctuary to find the missing girl and was currently leading his own leg of the effort. After a harrowing day, Hazel Cunningham had still not turned up. The sheriff's office had been forced to broaden the search area, but the damage was already done. The little girl might be spending the night lost.

Maxim hopped over the ruined log and hurried to keep pace with the others. He swept his light back and forth, looking for anyone hiding or sleeping among the trees. Sycamore—the wild to the west of Flagstaff, bordering Sanctuary. The land built for outdoorsmen.

Sycamore was an imaginary place. The name wasn't on any map, and it was bigger or smaller depending on who you talked to. Some denied the place existed. Coconino and Yavapai Counties were enough designation for the unincorporated forest and desert, not to mention the many townships that dotted the landscape.

But for those that lived in the wild, the concept was very real. The Sycamore woods were different than other forests. Not the oaks and pines and sycamores, themselves—it was a matter of the whole. The beauty of the landscape attracted a strange sort. Wild men. Those distrustful of society and government. Not the south but the southwest. It created a lawless mentality in the area, a foreboding that seeped into the bark and the leaves and the dirt. Sycamore didn't *feel* like a normal place.

On reflection, Maxim wasn't sure if the miscreants

created the atmosphere or if the atmosphere attracted the miscreants. It was a chicken-and-egg problem, but one thing was sure: everyone out here belonged, in their own twisted way.

The detective checked his cell phone. Reception was getting spotty, sometimes dropping out altogether. Of course, he thought. Just another sign that the woods were fighting him. Just another sign of a sentience beyond his understanding.

It was late. Late at night, sure, but late for the girl, Hazel Cunningham. Whether a victim of accident or design, she'd been missing nearly fifteen hours. The chances of serious danger increased as each hour passed. While Maxim had started the afternoon optimistically, he couldn't help but doubt himself now.

The girl was only eight. Cute, judging by the pictures he'd seen. He didn't know anything about kids, but he imagined she was a good one. The mother only had nice things to say.

The situation forced Maxim to ponder his own loss. His wife had gone missing some years ago. He'd been hopeful in the face of that tragedy as well, right up until he discovered her grave. These relationships, these attachments, they tugged hard at his soul. He couldn't imagine being a parent. He couldn't imagine ever wanting to be one.

In the far distance ahead, Maxim thought he saw a light. It was bright but contained—a minor glow that didn't illuminate the surroundings. Maybe it was a cell phone.

The detective checked both men to his flanks again. The

beam of his flashlight caught each of them in position, moving within their lanes. None appeared to notice the flare ahead.

Maxim studied it. For a moment it wasn't there, but then he found it again. It was turning, sometimes facing away from him, nearly invisible, and sometimes shining back at him with a gentle sway.

"Hello?" Maxim called out. He shined his Maglite ahead.

The glow continued its movement as if riding a midnight current.

"Is anyone there?"

The strange light dimmed, and Maxim picked up his pace. He was afraid of completely losing sight of it. He turned off his flashlight and the glimmer grew in strength, still spinning in a dizzying pattern. He was getting closer to it.

But a part of him swore the beacon was moving away from him.

Maxim crunched over the brush. After hours of searching, this was the break they'd been waiting for. Twigs clawed at his face as he pushed ahead. The glow spun in a circle. It blinked and faced him, then danced away.

Whoever it was, they were definitely avoiding him.

"There's someone over here!" he called out. The detective surged forward, sliding between the thickening trees. As he neared the source of the blaze, it didn't grow larger or clearer. Whoever carried it seemed to hover just out of sight, moving silently—but as quick as lightning.

Maxim abandoned caution and charged. With his

Maglite shut off, that was a bad move. After several paces, his knee crashed hard into something that bowled him over. He thudded face first to the ground.

His head spun only for a moment, and Maxim recovered quickly. He heard the branches snapping as someone converged on him.

"You okay?" asked Clint. The biker had seen the commotion and abandoned his path. Maxim looked up and a flashlight shone directly into his eyes. He turned away quickly. "You hurt?"

"Nah," said Maxim, waving off the help.

"Then what the hell is all the racket about?"

Maxim pulled himself to his feet. He was tender above the knee where he'd run into the object and nearly blind after Clint's light in his face. His eyes had trouble adjusting to the darkness again. He scanned ahead, but couldn't see the small gleam again. "Where's my flashlight?" Maxim pawed at the ground until he found it, but it didn't help. He illuminated the forest ahead, but the bulb of light was gone.

"What's going on?" asked the biker.

"There was a light up there." As he spoke, the old man on his other flank approached. "I don't see it," Maxim added, rubbing his eyes. "Where'd it go?"

The old man stopped and shook his head.

"We didn't see no light, man," said Clint. He shined his flashlight around until he finally fixed the beam on a point behind the detective. "Ouch," he said.

Maxim focused on the object he had tripped over. A metal bumper from an old truck was nestled in the grass, rusted out and abandoned. It didn't make any sense for it to be in the middle of the woods. The detective turned away in disgust. When he moved toward the last place he'd seen the light, he couldn't do it without limping.

"I saw something out there," he repeated with conviction. The others didn't respond. They just followed him silently.

He tried, but he couldn't find it again. Maxim cursed himself for tripping. For getting distracted. He trudged ahead, determined not to lose whatever opportunity was left. The detective was slower now, but the pain in his leg subsided the more he pressed on. It was certainly nothing compared to a lost little girl.

Searching the area ahead turned up nothing. He was sure this was the place he'd last seen the light. Pretty sure, anyway. The woods all looked the same, just an oppressive army of pillars in what was otherwise a wasteland.

Maxim noted the flashlights of the rest of the search party in the distance. He'd gotten turned around for a minute, but he righted his path. The other two men stuck loosely to his trail. It annoyed Maxim that they were checking up on him.

The bad feeling returned to his stomach. Sadness for the world. Half of Sanctuary was searching the woods north of the Interstate for Hazel. He didn't know what bothered him more—that times of trouble like this existed at all, or that so many people could become invested in what was sometimes, ultimately, a lost cause.

Maxim had long ago learned that answers often brought

more pain than absence.

Just as the detective was about to check the time again, he really did see something. At first he figured it for a deer, but the silhouette pushed away from a tree. Maxim shone his flashlight over it.

It was a person. A child.

Maxim limped forward. As he neared, he saw her, the little girl with long, disheveled hair. She was pale and weak—malnourished. She wore a pretty blue dress that was frayed and tattered on the ends, and long streaks of dark eyeliner dribbled down her cheeks.

Did eight-year-olds wear makeup? Honestly, Maxim couldn't say.

"Hazel!"

The girl stood still, unresponsive to Maxim's voice, not even affording him a glance. She stared past him, above him, into the trees.

"Hazel, can you hear me?"

Maxim kneeled in front of the girl and clasped his arms around her. She was cold, her arms and legs exposed to the night air. He pulled off his suit jacket and wrapped it around her shoulders.

Maxim heard the others approaching from behind. He withdrew a whistle from his pocket and blew it several times. The line of flashlights from his search party all converged on him.

He checked the girl's vitals. She was in shock. Her limbs were scratched up. Her feet, absent of shoes, were bleeding. She'd probably panicked and stumbled around the forest in a daze.

"It'll be okay," said the detective, picking her up in an embrace. She breathed heavily, which he took as a good sign. Wherever she was, she was coming back to him.

Short, stuttered coughs escaped her lips. They were like muffled cries. As a swarm of flashlights waved around him in the air, Maxim clutched the girl more tightly.

"It's gonna be okay, Hazel," he assured her once more.

The little girl seemed to notice him for the first time. She watched him with troubled eyes. "But my name's Annabelle."

Chapter 4

"We need to get her to the hospital," stressed the paramedic.

Maxim chewed his lip and considered the little girl. She was wrapped in a blanket now, sitting in the back of the ambulance, doors open, feet on bumper. "She's okay, isn't she?"

"Looks that way, but it's standard procedure. She needs to be examined, treated, fed—"

"I understand that," said Maxim. "But I need some time with her."

"I don't know."

"Listen, man. That girl is not eight years old. She said her name was Annabelle. That means there's another little girl out there. This one can wait a little longer if it means finding the other one."

The paramedic winced under the pressure. Nobody wanted to deny Hazel Cunningham a chance. The man averted his eyes. Maxim took that as agreement enough. He approached Annabelle and waved away the woman unsuccessfully trying to get her to drink a hot chocolate.

Annabelle hadn't said a word going on fifteen minutes. Without proper identification, Maxim couldn't figure out her story yet.

Looking at her now, it was obvious she wasn't Hazel. Annabelle was a little older, taller. Her long hair wasn't as dark and had curls in it. This was another little girl that had been lost in the woods, probably longer than a day judging by the condition of her clothes and level of exhaustion.

The only problem was, why hadn't anyone been looking for her?

"Are you ready to talk to me now, Annabelle?"

The preteen was catatonic. Her baby blues gazed downward, not at the ground but low enough to avoid eye contact.

Maxim sighed. He noticed the paramedic watching him and knew he needed to make headway soon or they would take her away. He sat beside the girl, feeling the soothing hum of the truck's engine.

"Can you tell me your last name?"

No answer.

"Or, at least, what you were doing alone in the woods?"

The girl's eyes fluttered as they registered a thought. She was definitely listening to him, perhaps deciding whether to speak again.

"You know," said Maxim, "a lot of worried people are outside right now. I don't know how long you've been out there, but there's another little girl who wandered away from her mom this morning. She's out there somewhere. Right now. She's younger than you, just a kid. And she's probably cold and scared. And Annabelle?" Maxim leaned forward to get a better view of her face. "I think you can help her."

The girl's lips stretched tight. She was upset, he saw now. The shock had worn off but maybe she was still distraught. Traumatized. Maybe Maxim did need to leave her alone.

"Three days," said Annabelle suddenly.

"What?"

The girl stared ahead. "I was out here three days. And I wasn't alone. I was with my friends."

Maxim took in a breath. "Which friends? Did you see Hazel?"

Her face was devoid of emotion, but she considered the question. Then she simply shook her head.

"Okay, Annabelle. What about adults? Were there any grown-ups with you? Did they take you anywhere?"

The little girl paused, then turned away. "You're the one that took me."

Maxim was taken aback by the statement. But the girl wasn't accusing him of anything malicious. It was just a statement, perhaps a way for a passive-aggressive child to be clever. Before he could follow up, Maxim heard a commotion on the other side of the vehicle. Deputies from the sheriff's office attempted to contain the situation.

"Where's my daughter?" a woman demanded. "Where is

she?"

Maxim frowned and stood. Walking around the ambulance, he saw the deputy holding back Julia Cunningham. Diego was next to her.

"It's okay, Deputy. Let them through."

Julia immediately charged him and ran around to the back of the ambulance. "Where's my da—" She froze, confused and frightened.

"Ms. Cunningham, we're still looking for Hazel."

Diego came around and saw Annabelle. "She's the wrong girl."

"I don't understand," said Julia.

Maxim spun Julia away from Annabelle. "I'm sorry if you'd gotten your hopes up. We found another girl wandering in the woods, but we don't know anything else yet."

"So that's it?" asked Diego. "You're done looking for Hazel?"

Maxim set his jaw and focused on the woman. "The search for your daughter is ongoing, Ms. Cunningham. A lot of good people are still looking. You two should continue assisting them. I need to stay with this girl and see what I can find out. It could be a lead."

"This is bullshit," exclaimed Diego. "Half the search party went home because they thought we found Hazel."

Maxim glowered at the biker and raised his voice. "It's getting late. We can pick things up tomorrow, but for now I'd suggest helping who's left. We're focusing on the area where we found Annabelle."

"She's not there," said the girl suddenly. Everyone turned to her. The words were cold, detached. "You'll never catch them."

"What does that mean?" asked Julia, looking to the detective before addressing the girl. "What do you mean?"

Maxim caught the woman by the shoulders before she advanced on the girl. "Deputies!" he called out. Two men were immediately at hand. "Get them out of here."

Annabelle spoke now, in a whisper. "I'll never catch them."

Before they could drag the frantic mother away, Diego put his arms around her and whispered. He pulled her away gently and shot Maxim a hard glare. The deputies escorted them from the area.

"What are they doing here?" came a voice from behind him. Maxim turned and saw David Harper approach. He must have just pulled up after calling off one of the search parties.

"Detective. You done for the night?"

Harper nodded. "We can't see shit out here anymore. We'll start again when the sun's out. I heard you found another possible victim."

"This is Annabelle," he said. "She was out there for three days."

"Thank you, Detective. That will be all."

Maxim jutted his chin out. "Actually, I'm still questioning her."

The other detective brandished a smug look. "This is my case, remember? Finish up here. I'm taking the girl to

County."

"I'm not—"

David Harper banged a fist on the side of the ambulance. "Let's go people," he yelled. The paramedic returned and helped Annabelle into the back. The truck had been running already but the red strobe lights came on.

"Where are we going?" she demanded.

David Harper returned a relaxing smile. "We're going to the county hospital in Flagstaff, honey."

She pulled away, suddenly having a fit. "I don't *want* to." The detective boxed her into the back of the ambulance. "I want to go home!"

"Wait!" said Maxim, pushing into the truck and past Harper. "Where is home, Annabelle?" He grabbed the girl by the shoulders and kneeled beside her, speaking gently to calm her down. "Where is home?"

She faced him straight on, deflated. "Sanctuary."

Maxim turned to Harper with a challenge on his face. "That calls it. She's not going to Flagstaff—she's going to the clinic in Sanctuary. The marshal's office is now actively involved in this investigation."

Chapter 5

The headlights struggled to illuminate the dark road ahead. It was an old car—the brakes squealed and the engine rattled in its frame. It was almost as loud as Diego's motorcycle but without any of the thrill.

The biker sighed and snuck a peek at Julia, in the passenger seat of her own car. Diego had stuck with her the entire day. He'd left his bike at her house and they'd driven to the search together.

"Maxim's a good detective," Diego insisted. "He's a friend."

Julia's tears had long dried, but that didn't mean she was doing well. Her lithe body was curled with worry, struggling against the oppressive burden. It was a weight under which she would eventually collapse.

"But it's not his case," she said. "That other detective is in charge."

"I'm sure he's good at his job too, but Maxim will still

help us out. He was out there all night with us."

"He's looking into that other girl."

"It could help—"

"In the meantime, Hazel's still out there. Alone. Scared." Julia shook her head. "How am I supposed to sleep tonight knowing she's lost?"

Diego remained silent for a moment. The questions she asked didn't have good answers. He wished he could help. He wished the world didn't have to be so shitty. "We're not any good to Hazel unless we're well rested. She's probably curled up somewhere safe herself, sleeping. We can start over fresh in the morning, when she comes out."

Julia sniffled. "You mean that? You'll help me tomorrow?"

Diego pulled off the highway, remaining silent all the way through the turn onto the city street. "Of course."

Her breath stopped. He could feel the woman staring at him. Diego ignored it, not wanting to look at her for some reason. He occupied himself with remembering the way back to her house.

"Why?" she asked. "Why are you doing this? No one else cares."

"That's not true."

She wasn't satisfied with his stock answer. "Why do *you* care so much?"

Diego swallowed. He didn't know what he was doing. He didn't have a plan. But he did have a reason. "Sometimes you have to be strong for other people."

He finally risked a glance her way, and he saw something

he would never forget. Despite the worry that wracked her features, Julia was a beautiful woman. He felt undeserving of the kindness he saw in those eyes, directed at him. It made him vulnerable. He turned away.

"You know why I first moved to Sanctuary?" he asked, turning down a residential street. "It was my younger sister. She got mixed up with some bad people. I had always protected her. I was always strong for her, you see, so I followed her here from Detroit."

"Detroit? You don't seem like a big-city boy."

Diego smirked. "I am, through and through. But the wild out here spoke to me. It made me feel alive. I was happy she led me out here. And I helped her, as big brothers must."

Julia watched him again, biting her soft lips. "Where is she now?"

The biker sighed. "I let her go. Also as big brothers must. She moved on again. Calls me once every few months. She's doing fine, but it's because she's strong by herself now."

Julia's reverie ended. Her interest faded and the lost look returned to her eyes. "Hazel isn't strong by herself."

"I know, Julia." Diego pulled into the woman's driveway, cursing himself for suggesting the turn in conversation. He came to a stop beside the house, next to his shiny Triumph Scrambler. He spun in the seat to give Julia his full attention. "That's why we both need to be strong for her. Right now, tomorrow—as long as it takes to find her."

She frowned. "What if we never find her?"

Diego leaned over and put a firm hand on her knee. "No," he said. "We can protect her from this world. You need to believe that."

If the biker was good at one thing, he liked to think it was protecting others. It had been his sole mission back in the Commissioned Corps. But today was a different time for him. If he was truly honest with himself, he didn't know if that was him anymore. It had been a while since he carried a gun.

She fell into him and nuzzled her face on his shoulder. It was a brisk night, and the sudden warmth sent a tingle up his back. He wrapped his arms around her and clasped tightly. He yearned for the contact, but he couldn't let this lead anywhere. Not under these circumstances.

Diego pushed her away and stepped out of the car.

He was attached to this now, he knew.

Chapter 6

A sound jolted Maxim awake. His body jerked more than usual because it wasn't well supported in the chair. In a moment he realized he was in the Sanctuary clinic on the second floor of the marshal's office. Even though he swore he heard someone say something, he was alone—besides the little girl in the hospital bed.

Annabelle appeared at peace. Eyes closed, deep breathing. Sunlight crept through the blinds and cast her in a warm glow. The girl had been cleaned up a bit. Her face held a pinkish hue and her light-brown hair had been brushed. It was good to see her sleeping so soundly.

Last night had been a different story. Annabelle had been through an ordeal in the woods. She was severely undernourished. After the paramedics and nurses took over, Annabelle became increasingly agitated until a panic settled in. It must have been scary for her, to be probed and prodded. Admittedly, Maxim added to that burden.

He'd questioned her as much as he could, but the girl stopped talking. It got to the point that the doctor didn't appreciate his presence, so the detective had gone to his desk downstairs and gotten some research done. With only a first name and the inability to appeal to the public in the middle of the night, he didn't turn up much.

Annabelle was a mystery. Just a girl who'd appeared out of nowhere in the forest. Three days, she had mentioned before getting in the ambulance. Three days in the woods. Three days, yet nobody had reported her missing.

"I'll never catch them now," came a cool voice. Maxim almost jumped. Annabelle's baby-blue eyes were open now, affixed to him. Her words were calm. Difficult to read. Not a trace of sarcasm or pain.

Maxim Dwyer cleared his throat. "Don't you worry about that, Annabelle. I'll be the one doing the catching. You just relax."

His words were meant to soothe. To create sympathy with her as a victim. But the girl just blinked plainly at him.

"Do you feel like talking?" he asked carefully.

Annabelle's face tensed. "I don't have anything to say to you."

Maxim nodded, acting as if he understood. She didn't trust him, and it would be difficult to get quality information from her if he pushed too hard.

"Are you mad at me, Annabelle?"

She turned her head and stared at the featureless ceiling. "I don't have anything to say to anyone."

Maxim realized he was leaning forward, gripping the

armrests of his chair. Over eager. He relaxed backward and composed his words before speaking.

"I'm a detective with the Sanctuary Marshal's Office. I need to ask you some questions about where you've been and what you've seen."

Annabelle refused to face him. "I can't tell you."

"This is important."

"I don't remember. It's all like a dream. Even right now."

"Annabelle," he said patiently, "this is very real."

Her eyes narrowed. "I mean everything's foggy. It's all behind a sheet of plastic, you know?"

Maxim tried to hide his puzzlement. He knew the doctor had prescribed some medication, but he wondered if illicit drugs had been involved before the hospital.

Annabelle jerked her head from side to side. "Where am I?"

"Shh," he said. "It's okay. You're safe now."

The girl noticed the restraints on her wrists and ankles. They agitated her more and she began to buck and twist on the bed. "Where am I?" she screamed.

Maxim stood and secured her shoulders. "You're safe now," he said over her struggling. "You're safe now in Sanctuary."

A nurse peeked in the open door and called for help.

"Annabelle," urged Maxim. "Calm down."

It was no use. He easily overpowered the young girl but she refused to relax. The nurse came and held her down. Soon, the female doctor entered and did a brief examination.

"She needs to be sedated," she concluded. "She's still awfully weak. You're working her up."

"I'm sorry," said Maxim.

"Yet you're still here."

"I need to know what she knows."

One of the nurses returned with a syringe. Annabelle thrashed. The nurse injected the medication into her IV. Maxim held tightly until the girl calmed. After a moment, the nurse helping restrain her was satisfied and let go. Annabelle looked up, at them but no one specifically, without focus.

"I don't want to be in Sanctuary," she said.

Maxim's brow furrowed, his confusion evident this time. Something was clearly troubling the girl, but she wouldn't tell him what.

The nurses exited the room at the doctor's insistence. She crossed her arms over her chest and arched a wicked eyebrow at Maxim. "You too, Detective. You're riling up my patient."

Maxim had a moment of indecision as his eyes locked with Annabelle's. He saw them losing their clarity as she grew drowsy. But she still had enough power to speak.

"If you cared about me, you'd let me go."

The detective was speechless. He became aware of his hands, still on the girl's shoulders, bracing her against the bed. He released her but didn't step back, still intent to capitalize on her last minute of consciousness.

"I *do* care, Annabelle. Please. Just tell me where you live. At least tell me your last name."

Her soft eyes closed. He heard a sharp hiss from the doctor's direction, and he knew he was wearing on her patience.

"Tell me your last name," he repeated, still leaning over the bed.

The girl's breathing slowed and became regular.

"Hayes," she whispered, with melancholy.

As she drifted to sleep, something about the girl's sadness latched onto him.

Chapter 7

Maxim pounded on the door again. It was heavy wood, Spanish style, with a decorative grate over the small window. The yard was teeming with such old-world accents: a rooster weather vane, a brick gate, a lawn jockey. The centerpiece of the entry was a large, two-tiered stone fountain. Water streamed into the air and splashed into the top tub where it dribbled from fish mouths into the bottom. The lawn was well tended, the house paint crisp and clean. It was like standing in the American Dream.

Maxim had expected nothing less. Sanctuary wasn't big enough to have real neighborhoods, but this was definitely the nicest street in town.

"Mrs. Hayes," he called out, knocking again. It was early, not yet 7 a.m., but he knew this couldn't wait. "Mrs. Hayes!"

The lock clicked and the large door swung open. Maxim wasn't prepared for what he saw.

The woman was in her early thirties, with a stylish blonde bob still soaking wet from a recent shower. A bathrobe hung loosely around her shoulders, Her exposed skin, still glistening, had the tan of a woman who'd just come back from a tropical vacation.

"Mrs. Hayes?" asked Maxim, struggling to remain professional.

"Yes." She answered with annoyance. This was an interruption for her, not a curiosity. Her face was pretty, even when upset.

Maxim cleared his throat. "Yeah. I'm Detective Maxim Dwyer, ma'am."

"It's early," she said bluntly. "Don't you think we could've done this at a better time?"

The detective chewed his lip and offered an inquisitive look.

"The Land Rover," she said. "You came about the vandalism."

Maxim sighed. "Can I come inside, Mrs. Hayes?"

"It's Ms. I've been divorced going on seven years. You might as well call me Olivia." The woman let go of the door and let her shoulders sag. The bathrobe fell open slightly and Maxim caught a glimpse of her chest as she turned around and led him inside.

"Sheesh," whispered Maxim, unsure if he should enter.

The robe she wore was plush, but it couldn't hide her slim figure. The woman had the confident walk of the hottest girl in the bar. She had no idea what was about to hit her, but at least Maxim's news was mostly good.

She led him to a large living room and pointed to the couch. "Well, you might as well sit down. I can make you some tea or coffee or—"

"I'm here about your daughter, Ms. Hayes."

The woman froze with her jaw open. The gears turned quickly, but Maxim saw her expression switch from confusion to horror. "Annabelle?" she asked softly. Then she strode up to him. "What happened to my daughter?"

"She's fine," he said. "Please don't be alarmed. She's okay. We found her in the woods last night, lost."

Olivia was incredulous. "What do you mean, lost? Where is she?"

"Annabelle's at the clinic on Main Street. She's a little malnourished and received treatment for minor bruises and scratches, but there's nothing serious to mention. She was lucky."

"Lucky?" she asked with disdain. "Why wasn't I notified immediately? I want to see my daughter right now!"

Maxim had only known Olivia for a few minutes and already her bossiness overwhelmed him. This was a woman used to getting what she wanted.

"Slow down," said Maxim firmly. "You daughter was near catatonic when we found her last night. She didn't tell us much, not even a last name. I had no idea who you were until thirty minutes ago, which is why I interrupted you so early."

Olivia nodded and was about to say something but Maxim spoke over her.

"And your daughter is currently medicated and getting

some sleep. Rest is the thing she needs most right now. So we'll get you right over to the clinic to see her, but I need you to answer a few questions first. Is that okay?"

Olivia drew her lips taut and nodded.

"Annabelle is twelve, is that correct?"

Olivia nodded again.

"And she lives here?"

"Yes."

"When was the last time you saw her?"

The woman trembled. She dried her arms against the bathrobe and pulled it tighter around her. "Her father had her for the long weekend. Annabelle's school has holidays for Good Friday and Easter Monday, so she was supposed to be back today. I was going to pick her up from school."

"And the last time you actually saw her?" he asked patiently.

"Friday morning. I dropped Annabelle off with her father in Bellemont."

Maxim nodded. The town was just off the Interstate and the closest civilization to Sanctuary. "I'll need his name and address before I leave. Do you know what activities they had planned? Was this a special occasion for Easter?"

"Not really. Annabelle sometimes visits him for a couple days at a time, but with the holiday she wanted to extend it."

For all of Olivia's bossiness, when Maxim had asked her to cooperate for the sake of her daughter, the woman had complied. Her concern appeared genuine.

"Did her father warn you that anything was wrong?"

Olivia hissed. "Not at all. He should've called me about

this."

The detective grunted in agreement. "And what about you? Do you think anything was wrong?"

The mother was taken aback. "What do you mean?"

"With Annabelle. Was there anything strange about her behavior when you dropped her off?"

Olivia put her hands on her hips and scoffed. Again the bathrobe fell open slightly. Maxim wanted to look away but didn't. "Just what are you implying about my daughter, Detective?"

"Nothing," he answered, turning to face the room, strangely turned on and feeling guilty about it. He gazed down the hall and saw the grand wooden staircase and realized they were alone in the large house. "It's just that Annabelle was awake for days. She was exhausted but overly tense. Is it possible she was abusing alcohol or drugs?"

"No." The sharpness in Olivia's voice commanded Maxim's attention. Her face was flushed, and thankfully the bathrobe was tied tightly around her waist now.

"What about any medication?"

"Annabelle is perfectly healthy," insisted Olivia. "What happened to her, Detective?"

Maxim softened his voice. He had to ask these questions. It would be negligent not to. But he knew: of all the lenses to view a person through, a mother's eyes were the most stringent. The mere mention of impropriety, however likely, always caused offense.

"We're not sure yet," he said. "Some minor exposure to the elements. It doesn't look like she was hurt or... anything else. But she's been mostly sleeping since we found her so it's hard to say. There's another child that went missing yesterday, close to the same area. She was staying at a campsite between Bellemont and Williams. The Coconino County Sheriff's Office is looking into it, but I'm heading up Annabelle's case. We'd like you and your daughter to cooperate. When she's healthy, of course."

"Of course," returned Olivia, nodding. "Annabelle and I will answer any questions you have. But talk to Gulliver first. That bastard. I bet he had something to do with this."

"Your ex-husband, ma'am?"

The scorn in her expression was confirmation enough. "He should have told me something was wrong."

Maxim recorded the man's address on his smartphone and put it next on his mental to-do list. He hated when spousal disagreements endangered children.

"What did you say your name was, Detective?"

"Maxim Dwyer."

"Maxim," she repeated in a distracted tone. "I hope you won't object to me putting some clothes on and seeing my daughter at the station. I can tell you anything else you want to know then."

The detective put his phone away. At this point, the immediate concern was the father. Anything else from Olivia Hayes could well wait.

"Of course," he said. "But there was one more thing. When you first saw me you mentioned something about a vandalized Land Rover?"

"Yes," she said, dismissively. "I called the police last

week. I usually park in the garage, but I was in a rush last Wednesday and left the car outside. Someone had thrown a brick through my window." Olivia headed for the stairs.

It was clear, given the circumstances, that the incident was now an afterthought.

Chapter 8

Maxim hadn't yet reached his car when the call came in. It was the marshal himself, probably expecting a progress report.

"Hello, sir. I just spoke with the mother, but it looks like Annabelle Hayes was in the custody of her father when she went missing."

"I see," he said with a measured tone. "Where is he?"

"Close. He lives in a condo in Bellemont."

Marshal Boyd jumped quickly. "So the Coconino County Sheriff's Office would've responded to the missing persons call. They should have notified you."

"That's if the disappearance was reported at all," countered Maxim. "According to Olivia Hayes, the husband never contacted her."

Maxim could hear the marshal's disappointment. "We're still dealing with too many unknowns."

"Not for long," said Maxim, slightly annoyed at the

marshal's impatience. Boyd asking about the case was harmless enough, but Maxim hated not having the answers. Frankly, it surprised him that Boyd was on top of the case this early in the day. Usually the dawn hours were Maxim's time to be alone. "I'll see you at the station after I pay him a visit."

"That needs to wait," asserted Boyd. "I need you in the front office to address the press."

The detective stopped outside his personal car, an Audi TT coupe. "The reporters can wait until we have a bead on this. A 'no comment' should do for now."

"It will not, Detective. I've already scheduled the press conference. It's in half an hour."

"What?" Maxim thrust his head into his hand. "Annabelle's barely said ten words to us. I just now talked to the mother. This case is only a few hours old."

"Perhaps Annabelle's involvement is, but Hazel Cunningham already has traction countywide. This is a hot button in the community right now. An Easter weekend tragedy. The discovery of Annabelle Hayes only makes this more newsworthy."

Maxim grimaced. "Can't we let Coconino handle the press for now?"

"This isn't just a county concern any longer. Now that the Sanctuary Marshal's Office is involved, we need to put a face on it. We need to let the public know that our office is doing everything it can for our children."

It made perfect sense. Marshal Boyd was a politician. Managing appearances for his father the mayor was his primary concern. Sometimes Maxim feared it was more important to the man than solving the crimes, that the semblance of preserving the peace trumped actual peacekeeping.

"So you want a two-minute fluff job. 'The marshal's office is putting its full weight behind this.' That sort of thing."

Boyd didn't answer immediately. He lived in a world of bullshit, comfortably padded by its confines. Stripping it away made him feel naked.

"Yes."

"Fine. But I need to keep it quick. Wrapping up Annabelle's involvement will be a piece of cake, but it isn't the only matter here. Hazel Cunningham is still out there."

"I am confident you can manage," returned Marshal Boyd. "You're my best detective."

Maxim snorted. "I'm your only detective." Then he hung up the phone.

Chapter 9

Diego sat on his bed wearing nothing but an old pair of jeans. He leaned forward, elbows on tattered knees, fists clamped together in front of his face, waiting in silence.

It was a meager apartment, barren of all the little things that made life a joy. Devoid of color and personality save for a single picture of his sister Angelica; to Diego, the space was just a few rooms with a kitchen and a bed.

It suited him because he hated being cooped up inside. Riding his motorcycle on the open road was his thrill, his escape from the ordinary. Now, that's what his life was. Ordinary.

Diego had been awake for a while, but his thoughts paralyzed him. A series of wild memories had turned into a series of dead-end jobs. Leaving the service, abandoning Detroit, landing in Sanctuary—it all seemed so far away now. Worse, it all seemed so pointless.

It wasn't easy to think about, but he forced himself. So

he sat there, unmoving. Taking stock.

Diego knew he was on the edge of something. He knew he had a choice. Julia Cunningham needed him. He'd promised he would help her. But even if he kept to his intentions, he wondered what good they were.

He swiped his phone from the nightstand and dialed Maxim. After a few rings it went to voicemail, and he slammed the phone down in disgust.

Diego hopped to his feet and nervously paced the room. This wasn't him. Mulling over options.

Thinking.

That realization gave him a chuckle. The biker was at his best when he simply acted. He often paid the price for his rash decisions, but at least the pot got stirred. At least he took action.

So why did he doubt himself now?

He trudged to the living room and flipped the TV to the local news.

Diego jumped when he heard a knock on his door. His alarm turned to excitement and he hurried to answer. To find more answers. To see a clear path.

Still not fully dressed, he swung the door open to see Henriette glowering at him.

She was a cold woman, in her fifties, with buzzed gray hair. She spoke deliberately, as if to assert her superiority. "Rent's late after the third," she said sternly.

Diego sneered. Henriette wasn't the problem, but she wasn't the solution he'd been seeking. He rolled his eyes and shuffled to the kitchen bar. He picked up the check and handed it to her.

"I'm sorry. Yesterday—"

"Is this one going to clear?"

Diego pulled back and feigned a polite smile. "That last time was just a mix-up. This check's good. I included the twenty-dollar late fee."

The woman eyed the check as if it were a window directly into his bank account. She accepted it while remaining dissatisfied. "If you have trouble remembering the first of the month, you should write a note and tape it to the inside of your door."

Diego stared blankly at her. "That's a good idea." He pained another smile and nudged the door closed. The woman acted like his mother, but he knew it was his own fault. All he had to do was drop the check in the deposit slot on time and he would never have to see her again.

He leaned against the door with a deflated sigh. He'd been in Sanctuary a year and a half now. He never figured he'd blow through his finances so fast. It wasn't an issue when he rolled with the motorcycle club—they had money coming in from their extracurricular activities—but now Diego was on the straight and narrow. And on his own. That was really dawning on him for the first time.

The volume of the TV carried over a familiar voice. Diego approached the flat screen and saw Maxim Dwyer standing in the marshal's office entryway, speaking to reporters.

Chapter 10

Maxim cleared his throat.

"It's important to keep in mind that this is an ongoing investigation. Annabelle Hayes is safe and under medical care. There's no evidence of an actual crime yet, but it's our duty to look into the matter."

The Sanctuary Marshal's Office didn't have a press room so they handled these situations with as little pomp as possible. Maxim Dwyer stood outside, in front of the station doors. The marshal and patrol sergeant were behind him at each side. There was no podium, just a gaggle of reporters pressed together at the base of the steps, shoving cameras and microphones forward.

"Is this connected to Hazel Cunningham?" one of them asked.

"Not necessarily," he answered. "We are, of course, exploring that possibility, but at the moment these are separate cases. The Coconino County Sheriff's Office is running that investigation, and we are assisting them in the matter. In the spirit of cooperation, I'd like to take this opportunity to reach out to the public, see if anybody knows anything. Homeowners should search their properties. Everybody should keep an eye out in the parklands. If anyone sees anything, please call 911 and the proper authorities will be dispatched immediately."

"It's been more than twenty-four hours. Is it already too late for her?"

"Certainly not." Maxim smiled in practiced patience. His plan was to focus on Sanctuary's case and deflect attention from Coconino's, but he had to do his part for the still-missing girl. His small mention would need to be enough for now. "But I'll leave the questions about the Hazel Cunningham case to the sheriff's office."

A woman spoke up. "Isn't it irresponsible to allow Annabelle Hayes time to recover while another child is still in danger?"

Maxim studied her. The black woman was the only reporter of the bunch he didn't recognize. She was shorter than everybody else but had a personable face. That meant she could ask the serious questions without appearing to be on the attack. But she was. Her question was loaded.

"As a detective," he stated with detachment, "I need to defer to the insistence of the medical staff, but that doesn't mean the investigation is at a standstill. It is the duty of our office to be thorough and expedient for the people of Sanctuary. We are doing everything we can for Hazel Cunningham, but it doesn't help her to jump to conclusions and assume these cases are linked."

The reporters asked questions all at once. One man's deep voice rose above the others. "But you're not dismissing the possibility of a serial abductor?"

Maxim sighed. The media's MO was to stir up panic first then get the facts later. Half the reason for these press conferences was to assure the public that the world wasn't ending. "There's absolutely no evidence of that at all. We're not discounting any possibilities, but neither are we entertaining dangerous speculation."

"What about the autistic girl?" asked the mystery woman. "Alice Radford?"

Maxim blinked plainly into the cameras. He hadn't heard the name before. "Can you elaborate?"

The reporter raised a single eyebrow. "Alice Radford went missing in Williams last year. She wandered back home a day later."

Yes. Maxim remembered now. The autistic girl had been eleven years old. She'd gotten separated from her parents during a local parade. The county had been on full alert until she returned, unharmed. He'd understood the girl wasn't highly functional and was lucky to have found her way back.

Maxim nodded to present the cameras with calm confidence. "Yes. Unfortunately, situations like these are not entirely uncommon. Sycamore—excuse me—Coconino County has sprawling forests and flatlands. The territory's too large to cover easily and slows down rescue operations. That's why it's important we don't panic and assume the worst when we lack immediate results. Nine times out of ten getting lost is just that: getting lost. It can still be a dangerous matter but we should temper our conclusions. In the case of Alice Radford, there were no signs of foul play, but as that is under the jurisdiction of Williams PD and the sheriff's office, you should contact them with further questions."

Maxim stared hard at the woman. She didn't appear satisfied with his answer, but that was normal with reporters. His expression dared her to continue, but she didn't have a follow-up question.

Another reporter: "Are Annabelle's parents being investigated? Why didn't they report their daughter missing?"

Maxim considered. It was bad form to immediately attack the parents in cases like this, but it was par for the course. Once children were found, if their cases didn't add up, the questions pointed more sharply to the parents. Now that Annabelle was okay, it was open season.

In truth, detectives often had the same suspicions.

"The marshal's office is still reviewing all available information. As of now, no charges have been filed against anyone."

"Isn't it negligent of them to not know where their twelve-year-old daughter was?"

Maxim glanced at Marshal Boyd before he answered. "That hasn't been determined yet." His answer was curt. It obviously displeased the reporters.

The woman spoke up again. "But isn't it true that

neither the mother nor the father had seen Annabelle since Friday? Who was responsible for her for three days?"

It surprised Maxim that she knew that much. The reporters were well versed in the case. Because they were doing background as soon as Hazel Cunningham had been reported missing, they essentially had a day's head start on him. Maxim wondered what outlet the woman worked for. She didn't wear any obvious branding.

"All I can say at this time—"

She interrupted him. "Is it true that Annabelle Hayes was camping in the woods over the weekend with her friends?"

Maxim paused. He wasn't prepared for this. He flashed the marshal an I-told-you-so expression but Boyd stoically faced forward.

The detective didn't know anything about camping in the woods. He hadn't spoken with the father yet. This was exactly why he hadn't wanted to hold this press conference yet.

"We can't comment on specifics at this time," said Maxim firmly. "All avenues are still being investi—"

"Should we alert families not to go camping for the time being?" asked someone else.

More hysteria. But the woman in particular seemed to know specifics. She had a source of real information, possibly the father. The detective had a lot of catching up to do.

Maxim cleared his throat again. "As always, minors should be under the supervision of a parent or guardian."

Another outbreak of voices competed for his attention.

Maxim put his hand up to quiet them. The woman ignored his request. "What *can* you tell us about what happened to Annabelle Hayes?"

The detective pouted. This had been a mistake. How could he project confidence to the media if he didn't even know what he was investigating?

Before he could speak, Marshal Boyd stepped forward. "That's all we have for you at the moment," he said, putting his hand on Maxim's shoulder. "Detective Dwyer has pressing business. As the case develops, we will share more information."

An uproar consumed the small crowd. The sergeant opened the door to the marshal's office and Maxim stepped backwards into the station. Boyd turned to look at him, his blue eyes crystalline daggers.

So far, this hadn't been Maxim's best day.

Chapter 11

Diego switched off the TV and threw the remote down. At least the press conference explained why his friend hadn't answered his call.

Diego had asked the detective to look into Hazel's disappearance, but he was mired in another family's problems now. Maxim would be playing catch-up with Annabelle's side of things. It may very well resolve Hazel's situation, but Diego couldn't sit idle in the meantime.

Julia needed him. Hazel needed him.

The biker paced back and forth between his living room and bedroom. Eventually, he made it into the bathroom and shaved, sharpening the edges of his mustache and goatee. Dark circles lined his eyes. He splashed cold water on his face to give himself a jolt, but he still looked worn out. He was tired from the long night and the sleepless morning.

He wandered back out to the main room and picked up his keys from the kitchenette bar. Beside them was a school photograph of Hazel Cunningham. Bent and worn from a day in his back pocket, it was the only image he had of the girl. He'd seen other pictures at Julia's, but this one had been the subject of his stares. This one had been burned into his mind.

Hazel was a cute kid. Brunette hair that matched her mom's, light skin with just a hint of freckles. Her eyes were darker, though, yet full of joy. There was something about childhood that prompted adoration from others. Hazel's smile was wide, with slightly crooked teeth, but something about it felt out of place in her expression. Diego studied it at length but couldn't glean any further insight.

A shake of his head helped throw off his stupor. There wasn't time for this. He pulled on a white T-shirt and grabbed his phone again.

"Pendle," answered the gruff voice on the other end of the line.

"Harry, it's Diego. I'm not gonna make it in today."

The biker could easily imagine the look on the man's face.

"This is some kind of joke, right?"

"I'm sorry, man. It's not a joke. It's personal stuff."

"This about that kid?"

"Yeah."

Harry's voice softened. "Yeah, I saw that. It's a fucking shame, I tell you. On Easter, too."

Diego waited with a frown. He didn't know what to say and he hated being beholden to his boss. Harry Pendle wasn't a bad guy. He owned the company and struggled to make ends meet. The tow business wasn't easy.

"You were out there when they found the other kid last night?" he asked.

"Yeah. We searched all around the campgrounds. East and west along the Interstate. North closer to Sanctuary."

"Those woods are huge. It could take a week."

Diego sighed. "That's what I'm saying."

Harry considered for a moment. "Look, Diego, it's a horrible thing. I mean, I hope to God they find this kid, okay? But is this woman your wife or something?"

"Hmm?"

"I mean, what's the deal? Is this your kid? I can understand the Good Samaritan thing, but you have real responsibilities. Be neighborly all you want, but do it on your own time."

"That's bullshit, Harry."

His boss scoffed. "I'll tell you what's bullshit. This is your third job this year, and it's barely April. I took you on because you told me you were a hard worker."

Diego rolled his eyes. "What do you want from me?"

"I want you to put in a full shift four days a week without asking for favors." Harry waited for a response but didn't get one. "Otherwise," he continued, "you'll be looking for your fourth job."

The biker swiped at the air in frustration. He strolled over to the window and peeked through the mini blinds. The sun was out in full swing. Visibility was perfect. The sky was clear, the wind was blowing—it was a nice day to be outside.

Diego thought of his past experience with outlaw bikers. "Cage" was the word they used for cars. Today, if Diego had to sit in the tow truck all day, he really would feel captive.

"I'm gonna be looking for a little girl," said Diego. "You can fire me for that if you want."

His boss laughed. "Oh I can, can I?" he asked mockingly. "Can I? Thanks for giving me that ability, Diego. I wasn't sure if I had that power *as your boss.* I wasn't sure if I could fire you for not doing your fucking job."

"Thanks for keeping the big picture in mind," said Diego. "Just do what you need to do."

The biker hung up the phone. He didn't know what he needed, but it definitely wasn't this hassle.

Chapter 12

Diego parked his Triumph Scrambler outside the camping office. His bike was a sleek roadster, black and chrome and sixties inspired. A shotgun holster attached to the frame rubbed against his right leg as he dismounted. In his outlaw days, Diego carried a Benelli M4 semi-auto shotgun. He had a thing for guns, and it was a sweet weapon, but he hadn't been able to replace his lost one yet. After the tragic events of the year before, he didn't know if he wanted to. Now the holster was an empty reminder of pain and loss.

The biker wasn't completely unarmed, of course. He still packed a trusty knife that had kept him safe on many occasions. Whenever Diego went into the wild, the blade was always sheathed to his forearm under the sleeve of his riding jacket, but for now he left it on the Scrambler. It had its own spot, a custom slot built into his exhaust, hidden in plain sight.

Diego wandered the grounds with a suspicious eye. He

hoped he wouldn't need to use any weapons to get Hazel back, but he would if it came to it.

Quiet Pines was a large, multi-use luxury campsite. Deluxe wood cabins took up a third of the property. Lacquered to a smooth glaze and ornamented with high roofs, the cabins had all the comforts of a fine hotel. Full electricity, plumbing, spa tubs, porch swings. It was about the furthest thing from camping that Diego could imagine, but the area was littered with pine trees and the air had the healthy smell of nature.

Individual sections were available to less extravagant campers as well. Cars and trucks parked adjacent to picnic tables and tents. Each site had its own fire pit, and each large section had its own facilities building with bathrooms and showers.

Finally, a row of RVs had their own parking spots, complete with full plug-ins. Power, water, waste management—it was all available to paying customers.

Whatever happened to sleeping bags and campfires?

At the end of his tour, Diego returned to the office where he'd parked and headed inside. A large man sat at a desk crowded with paperwork.

"Which lot are you?" he asked.

Diego furrowed his brow. "Sorry?"

"What's the lot number of the campsite you're staying in?"

Now Diego understood. "Oh, no. I'm not camping actually. I'm here about the girl that's missing."

The sweaty man peered at Diego and nodded. "I

remember you now. You were with the police yesterday."

It was lucky the manager remembered him. The biker bowed his head and exaggerated his South American accent. "Diego de la Torre. Nice to meet you."

The office manager didn't raise his hand to meet Diego's. "But you're not a police officer yourself," he said matter-of-factly.

So much for his good luck. "Not exactly, but I'm working with them. And with Julia Cunningham."

"Poor lady. You know something like that's never happened here? We run a very safe site."

"You can't control everything. It's not your fault."

The man nodded and leaned back in his chair, finally giving his full attention to Diego. "I'm Charlie Charles. Twice the name, twice the fun."

Diego's eyes widened. "I can see that."

"Twice the girth, too!" Charlie cracked into a boisterous laugh and Diego hoped the man was referring to his belly. "Sit down, sit down."

Diego took a seat and decided to get through this quickly. He didn't feel like listening to bad jokes while an eight-year-old was lost.

"I checked around the grounds," started Diego. "Everyone looked pretty normal. Was there anyone staying here who felt off to you?"

The office manager chuckled. "We're in Sycamore, son. Nobody would be here if they weren't just a little bit different."

Diego tilted his head and waited for a real answer.

Charlie waved his hand dismissively. "The police interviewed everyone yesterday. Since you're working with them you should have that info." The man gave Diego a wink.

"I'm more concerned with whether the police could have missed anything. Did they account for everybody?"

Another chuckle. "There's not much place to hide. The cars and RVs are all parked by their lots. I know for a fact the deputies talked to every renter. I went site-to-site with them, giving them the names of each guest."

"You have contact information for every single person on the grounds?"

Charlie shook his head. "Just the renters. The ones paying me the money. We have a limit on the number of guests in each lot, but we don't make them register or anything. I trusted that follow-up to the police." The man's face darkened. "I wish there was more I could do for that girl. I have two daughters myself. Can't imagine what the mother is going through."

Diego's thoughts fluttered to Julia. He'd spoken with her on the phone this morning but was hoping to avoid seeing her in person until there was better news. Perhaps it wasn't realistic, but the thought of seeing her smile again was all he thought about. First he had to free her from this terrible burden.

"You are helping by cooperating, Charlie."

"Well, I don't know what to tell you. I know a lot of the locals, the repeat customers, but it was so busy and my memory's not that great."

"I saw quite a few empty lots out there."

Charlie slapped his desk. "Something about a child abduction in broad daylight that'll kill business. Besides, it's Tuesday. Easter weekend is over and it's back to the grind. Not all of us outdoors folks are the types with nine to fives, but plenty of normal families come out. Trust me, it was a full house this weekend. Six cabins, ten hook-ups, and sixteen sites. All thirty-two lots were occupied. I even had to deny an RV entrance. Can't remember the last time that happened."

Diego perked up. "When was this?"

"On Easter Sunday, late at night. We're staffed twenty-four seven. I was there that night. Red came by looking for a plug-in, but I had to turn him away. We were full."

"Red?"

"He's a regular. An old man. I see him two or three times a year, maybe. He lives in his motor home hereabouts. Moves around as it suits him and visits the local campgrounds to resupply and use the facilities. Most of these guys do that. It's not a problem as long as they pay."

"Do you have his name and address?"

"Sure," said Charlie, "but it's a waste of time. Like I said, Red was in and out that night. I don't know where he ended up, but he was long gone before that girl went missing."

"I'd still like the address."

Charlie sighed and lifted his heavy frame from the chair. He plodded over and opened a file cabinet. "I didn't get his information that night on account of turning him away, but I'll have some paper on him somewhere." The office manager leafed through months of documents and chatted to pass the time. "The old man's a character. A little loopy, but likes to keep to himself. He'd probably be a true hermit if he could, but electricity and plumbing are too damned convenient. I know he stays by Williams a lot. They've got a few RV clubs by the train station." Charlie shook his head and chuckled. "Red likes trains or something. Always going on about them. A bit embarrassing for a grown man. Ah. Here it is." He dropped the paper on his desk.

Diego grabbed a nearby pen and notepad and copied down the information. "It just says 'Red.' And this is a PO Box."

Charlie shrugged. "What do you expect when his house is an RV?" The heavy man leaned forward and planted a finger on the address. "You see? Williams, Arizona. I bet he's train-watching as we speak."

Diego sighed. He could probably tap Maxim to run down the information, but he was hoping for something he could move on immediately. Once again, he pictured Julia's smile.

"How will I know if I've found him?"

The office manager laughed again and returned to his seat. "He's easy to spot. He's an old man with a metal leg." Diego shot the man a curious look and he explained. "It's not really a metal leg, but one of those braces, you know? Clamps to the thigh and calf and bends at the knee. It's for support. I figure he was in Vietnam or something but never asked. He seems a little self-conscious about it."

Diego nodded, hoping for something more. "Okay, so

the police have thirty-two names of people they've interviewed, and Red makes thirty-three. Anyone else?" The biker wondered if Maxim had access to that list.

"Well, actually," said Charlie, stumbling on his words, "there were thirty-one groups interviewed."

"What do you mean? You said this place was full."

"Yes. It was, Easter night. But first thing in the morning one of my campers packed up his tent and checked out. Lot twenty-four." Charlie shook his head. "Damnedest thing. He'd given a down payment on one more day but left first thing Monday morning. Said he needed to leave immediately. He didn't even argue when I said I couldn't give him a refund on such short notice."

Diego almost jumped from his seat. "Did you tell the police about this?"

"No. I guess I should have, but it slipped my mind. I was swamped. But again, this young man checked out at sunup, 6 a.m. or so. He looked like he was in a hurry, but it didn't have nothing to do with that girl. I saw her and her mom leave their cabin hours later."

Diego rubbed his hand through his hair and pondered the timeline. Charlie noticed him struggling and leaned forward.

"Looky here. If the police don't think it was any of my campers, I don't think it was any of them. The mother and daughter hiked into the forest, outside my grounds. I understand you're trying to be thorough, but I don't want you badgering all my guests. It's bad enough they were here when it happened. And many of them aren't the type that like the police, or whatever you are. And those other two? They were long gone. It couldn't have possibly been them. And I'm telling you, nobody strange was hanging around the property."

Diego hissed in frustration and looked out the window. Scattered groups of campers wandered the grounds, readying for hikes or loading up their cars.

"Was the early riser alone? He'd been staying here, so you should have his name and address, right?"

The office manager sighed heavily. He stared forward at his desk as if he was having second thoughts about his unconditional assistance. "Are you sure you're working with the police?"

Diego's black eyes bored into the man. "Just think about eight-year-old Hazel Cunningham out there. We're probably passing the twenty-four hour mark right now."

Charlie pressed his lips together and winced. It wasn't long before he reached for a clipboard on his desk. He found the man's name on the second page.

"Jason Bower. It was just him, alone. That's normal for the mountain men, but you could tell this one grew up in the city. He asked me questions about how to pitch his tent and wasn't prepared for the cold. He had to buy extra blankets from me." Charlie raised his eyebrows as he read the address. "Well, look at that," he said, sliding the clipboard to Diego. "He's a local too. He lives just ten minutes away, in Williams."

Diego clenched his jaw. Both men the police hadn't interviewed were just down the Interstate. That suited the biker just fine. He had a tank full of gas and knew how to track people down. And if they didn't talk, well, he knew how to do other things as well.

Chapter 13

Bellemont was the town closest to Sanctuary. On the south side of Interstate 40, Maxim passed it every time he went to Flagstaff. There wasn't usually much cause to actually stop in Bellemont, but Maxim knew it well enough. That was unfortunate because it allowed the detective to drive on autopilot, which left him brainpower to ruminate on the disastrous press conference.

Maxim was relieved when he finally pulled into the parking lot. He was confused, though, and even went so far as to double-check the address. He was in an old complex, three large building strips with connected condominiums. The paint was faded. The grass was brown. After seeing Olivia's cushy living situation, it was hard for Maxim to imagine her ex-husband somewhere like this.

But then, she'd intimated he was a deadbeat.

The detective had trouble finding the condo because the number had fallen off the door. Even after he decided he found the right one, he took a few minutes to check the neighbors to make sure. By the time he finally approached the door to knock, it opened by itself.

A man in jeans and a T-shirt eyed him with a smirk. "Knew you'd be coming this way," he said.

Maxim did a double-take. The man was in his forties, at least, and had a pocked face from years of smoking. He was balding but had thick brown hair on the sides of his head and a mustache to match.

"Sorry?"

"I saw you on the news. Bang-up job you did there. I'd be surprised if you could find your own asshole, much less my daughter."

The man's clothes must have been ten years old, but he wore a shiny green pair of cowboy boots. Maxim wasn't sure what he'd expected, but this couldn't have been Olivia's ex.

"Gulliver Hayes?"

"And they call you a detective," he said with a smirk. A baby cried in the background and Gulliver stepped outside and closed the door halfway. "What do you want?"

"Aren't you going to ask me how your daughter is?"

The man shrugged. "They said on the TV she was okay. They didn't lie, did they?"

Maxim shook his head. "They didn't lie, Mr. Hayes. You can visit your daughter if you like."

"Can't," the man answered. He leaned to the side and spat in the sorry excuse for bushes. "I've got a haul to Palm Springs today. She'll be here when I get back."

Maxim lifted an eyebrow but didn't say anything. He

wasn't a family counselor. Obviously, this man's marriage had broken down for a reason.

"Can we step inside while I ask you a few questions about Annabelle?"

The baby inside cried louder. Gulliver turned inside. "Leta!" he screamed. "Shut that baby up!" Then he closed the door and returned his attention to Maxim. "In case you haven't noticed, I got my own baby to take care of."

"Yeah, you're father of the year."

Gulliver sneered. "It's a nice day. You can ask me your questions right here."

The baby inside quieted. Maxim peered through the window but couldn't see past the glare. "Okay then. First of all, can you tell me where your daughter was this weekend?"

"The question to end all questions," said the man. "According to the TV, she was camping with her friends."

"Well I want to hear what you know, Mr. Hayes."

"That *is* what I know. Annabelle wasn't here this weekend. I got six angry voicemails from my ex-wife before I woke up this morning and finally talked to her, so I turn on the TV and see you tripping over your own balls. Then I hear that reporter lady doing your job for you."

Maxim fought off a frown. He had no idea why Olivia would've married this guy, but he definitely knew why she'd left him.

"You're saying you never saw your daughter at all this weekend?"

"That's right."

"But Olivia claims she left her with you."

"That was on Friday. Friday's not the weekend."

Maxim fought off his urge to slap the man. "Fine, Mr. Hayes," he grumbled. "Let's talk about Friday then. That was the last time you spoke with Olivia before this morning, correct?"

"Well, let's see..." Gulliver squinted as if he were solving a differential equation. "Shit. I think it was over a year and a half ago that we actually talked. That's a pretty good streak for me."

Maxim took a breath. His patience was wearing thin. Maybe a slap wasn't enough. Just one well-placed head butt.

The man chuckled, softly at first, then exploded into laughter. "Detective," he said, shaking his head. "Let me tell you how it is. Annabelle was a good kid for a spell, but she's been poisoned. Turned against me by her mom. Now my own daughter hates me. She only talks to me when she needs something, and she definitely don't want to spend Easter weekend here. But none of that will stop her from using me as an excuse to get outta town."

Maxim stepped forward. "Out of town? For the weekend?"

"For good," he said. "Run away. She's done it before."

"Annabelle's tried to run away before? Olivia didn't—"

"That woman lives in a bubble," he said. "Always has. She thinks if she ignores problems long enough, they'll go away." Gulliver paused and lowered his voice. "What is Annabelle now, twelve? Where do you think that girl's gonna be by the time she's seventeen? I may not be a man of means, but I would've raised her right. All that black eyeliner and lipstick." Gulliver made a whooshing noise with his lips. "Discipline's important."

Maxim couldn't believe what he was hearing. If Gulliver was telling the truth then Olivia definitely withheld important information from him.

"I'm gonna need you to be clearer about your interaction with your ex-wife and daughter on Friday, Mr. Hayes."

Gulliver shrugged. "This is the way it works, Detective. What happens is, Annabelle tells her mom she has plans with me. Olivia wants the girl outta her hair, so she drops Annabelle off by the street." Gulliver pointed past the other buildings to remind Maxim where the road was. "I open my door, she sees Annabelle walk inside, and she drives off without so much as a wave in my direction. The whole thing happens without me and her ever talking, and to be honest, it suits me fine. 'Course, what Annabelle says to me is different than what she tells her mom. She told me she was going to a concert in Flagstaff that night. She has a friend, Bryan, that lives here in Bellemont. So she wanted to have lunch with me until the boy and his parents picked her up for the night. She was never supposed to sleep over. She was never supposed to spend the weekend with me. For all I knew, she was back at home with her mother by the end of the night. I never knew she wasn't supposed to be there, so I couldn't rightly know she was missing. But I'm sure that didn't stop Olivia from putting the whole escapade on my shoulders."

Gulliver huffed after his long speech. He wasn't a likable person, but it seemed to Maxim he was being truthful. As with the media this morning, Maxim's focus was on the parents, and it was swinging back towards the mother. Olivia Hayes should have mentioned her daughter's attempt to run away before.

"I worked hard for that woman," said Gulliver with a touch of sentiment. "As soon as her aunt died and left the whole estate to her, she wanted a divorce. Suddenly a truck driving salary wasn't good enough for her. I had to start over with a new family, and excuse me if I can't give everything I have to my ungrateful daughter. But I'm happier now that I'm away from that woman. Annabelle probably would be too. You've got to ask yourself, why does she keep trying to run away?"

"I don't know," said Maxim, before he realized he'd answered a rhetorical question. "So, just to follow up, did you see Bryan's parents?"

"Huh?"

"Bryan's parents. When Annabelle was dropped off with you, you said Olivia watched the hand off. So when you handed off Annabelle to Bryan's parents, did you watch?"

Gulliver scratched the back of his head. "Musta been busy. That girl gets excited and runs off. Not my fault. And speaking of which..." The man retreated into his house and left Maxim at the step for a minute. He returned with a heavy key chain and handed it to the detective. "That's hers. She musta left it here on Friday."

Maxim studied the jumble of interconnected key chains. There were only three keys—the key rings and ornaments made up the majority of the bulky item. It clanged and jingled against itself as he turned it in his hand. There was a car alarm or garage opener fob, a mini flashlight, and some kind of skeleton face pendant.

"You didn't think she'd need these to get home?"

The man shrugged. "Just found 'em yesterday. I did think it was weird that I hadn't heard about it. Then again, Annabelle's a weird girl."

Maxim was starting to think they were a weird family.

Chapter 14

Jason Bower was a deadbeat. Perennially out of work and associated with bad company, he was always either on the giving or receiving end of various hardships and criminal enterprises. The forty-something led a sad life, alone, and had been jailed for multiple drug offenses. He'd inherited his mother's modest house when she died of lung cancer, which was just as well, because her son was the biggest disappointment of her living days.

You can learn a lot by talking to the neighbors.

Not a single one liked him. They didn't know him, not really, but they all knew he was a blight on the neighborhood. Williams was an industrial community, an enduring ghetto that wouldn't exist without the Interstate. A crossroads of sorts where travelers and industry passed through. Those who actually lived here were not of great means, but many were good people who strove for fulfilling lives.

Jason wasn't in that category. He'd allowed his mother's house to fall into disrepair. He was responsible for recent car break-ins. Police had visited his house three times over the last year. Every neighbor had a lot to say. But none could tell Diego where Jason was.

They hadn't seen him in days, they said. Which made sense, given that the man had been at Quiet Pines. But he'd left the campgrounds in a hurry Monday morning—he couldn't have disappeared into thin air. Yet there was no activity in the house. No car in the driveway. The only thing for Diego to do was wait.

The outlaw-turned-tow-truck-driver sat beside his Scrambler a couple of houses down. He knew the shiny bike stuck out in the old neighborhood so kept it positioned behind a parked van and hoped people wouldn't see it. When the waiting became unbearable, he walked to a market down the block, picked up some cigarettes, and headed back. He was on his third when he spotted Jason Bower.

He didn't know what Jason looked like—Diego didn't have a photograph—but the man slinking along the street was definitely him. Scraggly tan hair, a wrinkled plaid shirt over faded jeans, and his head on a swivel looking for danger. Diego de la Torre watched as the man crept towards his house, in broad daylight, and snuck into the backyard.

Jason was hiding from someone, and doing a poor job of it. Diego wondered if the police were already searching for him.

Ten minutes later, Jason peeked out from his backyard, checking up and down the street before emerging. He held a large plastic shopping bag, stretched into a massive ball, stuffed with items that resembled laundry. As Jason scanned the block, his eyes passed over Diego, who immediately turned away.

The biker acted casually and tinkered with the engine of his Triumph. Jason didn't seem to think much of him because he moved on at a normal pace. Diego flicked the ashes of his smoke and watched his target make his way towards the same market Diego had come from. The biker decided to follow him on foot.

Jason Bower was obviously concerned about being seen, so Diego kept a good distance between them. The man turned the corner without looking back. When the biker arrived at the cross street, he spotted Jason further down the block, past the small strip mall. Diego continued through an empty lot until he saw where the man was headed: a tattered husk of a building with an unlit cocktails sign. A dive bar.

Knowing Jason might take another quick look around before entering, Diego ducked behind a bus stop advertisement. Next time he checked, Jason was gone.

The man hadn't been home all morning. Something had happened at the campsite that caused him to leave in a hurry, but he obviously didn't have anywhere to go. While trying to avoid his home, the best he came up with was a local bar down the block.

Jason was certainly being evasive. He had something to hide, no doubt. The fact that he'd been in Hazel's vicinity before she vanished gave Diego confidence he was onto something.

As the biker approached the entryway, he imagined what could be within. It was unlikely Hazel was inside—while the bar was probably empty this early in the afternoon, an eight-year-old would readily stand out. That meant the girl would be at another location.

If Jason didn't have her, who did?

Diego realized he didn't know where Jason's car was. His driveway was empty, likely to convince anyone interested that he was out of town. The biker wondered if Jason was stupid enough to park in the bar's corner lot. Diego passed the building and checked. There were only two vehicles, a pickup truck and an old Volkswagen Beetle. Both were clearly empty.

To the bar, then.

Diego stepped inside. A large Samoan man frowned at him. Defensive line, thought Diego. Maybe made it to college, maybe didn't, but he had to have been a hell of a high school player. Now all his frame was good for was intimidation, and it worked on Diego.

The biker pressed passed the obstacle. The bartender squinted against the sunlight that invaded his lair. He was an older man with a brittle demeanor. Surprisingly, the small space had several patrons: two tables' worth and a few at the bar, all men of course.

Jason Bower was at the bar alone.

The man picked himself up and headed into the back hallway, leaving his shopping bag and a backpack on the floor. Jason didn't look his way. It was perfect. Diego went for the back.

"The bathroom's fer payin' customers," said the bartender in a voice that held more weight than he did.

"That's fine," answered Diego, barely slowing his stride.

"What'll you have then?" he barked.

Diego stopped when he realized the bouncer had taken notice. He pulled a couple of bucks from his wallet and slapped them on the counter. "Get me a root beer with a straw." Then he continued into the back.

The hallway made the dingy bar area feel like a hospital. It was darker, dirtier, and smelled like a sewer. Diego held his breath and pushed open the door to the men's room. It was a single, tiny stall. Diego didn't even think there was enough square footage to accommodate the Samoan. A dirty urinal was tucked beside an even dirtier sink, and the toilet was empty save for being covered in piss.

Diego skipped out and went to the women's room next. It was locked. Diego checked up and down the hall and didn't see anywhere else to go besides the emergency exit, which a sign warned would alarm on opening. The biker pounded on the bathroom door.

"Occupied," grumbled a man.

"Open up," commanded Diego, banging harder.

The door swung inward to reveal an angry, bald man missing half his ear. Behind him, a trashy woman with torn stockings sat on the toilet seat. She didn't even bother looking up. Instead her attention was fixed on the line of coke on the sink.

"What the fuck?" demanded the man.

Diego just put his arms up and backed away.

The exit. Jason Bower had used the exit.

Diego bounded through the exterior door. No alarm sounded. The harsh sun blinded him. At the last second he noticed a quick movement to his side. Something smashed him on the head and his vision changed from white to black. Diego slammed to the floor and threw his arm up to block the following blow, but it never came. Jason Bower retreated back into the bar.

The biker reeled on the asphalt. The padded arm of his riding jacket supported him, shards of glass embedded in the leather. Half of a jagged Miller bottle rolled to a stop next to his head.

Diego shook his head and came to his senses. He picked himself up and lurched back inside.

His senses were being put through the ringer. Light, dark, light, dark. He was disoriented and still not fully in command of his balance. But he saw Jason leaving the bar with his bags slung over his shoulder.

"Stop," commanded Diego.

Jason broke into a sprint, and Diego lunged ahead. The biker picked up an empty barstool and spun his body around, sending it flying into the man's back. Jason tumbled to the floor and Diego pounced on him.

Everything was going according to plan, more or less, until the bouncer got involved.

Chapter 15

Maxim kneeled beside the teenager. The boy sat on the couch, head down, staring at his fidgeting hands. His father, a well-muscled but short man, stood over them both.

"You won't get in any trouble, Bryan," promised the detective.

"Speak for yourself," said the father. He eyed his son harshly. "Bryan, you're grounded no matter what you do, but you'd better tell this police officer everything you know right now. If I find you left anything out, I'll send you to your grandmother's for the summer."

"No, Dad!" he cried. "Please!"

The urgency in the boy's voice caused Maxim to smirk. The old lady must've been a real hag.

"Okay," said the boy. "I was with Annabelle. But only at first. The whole thing was like a prank."

The father huffed and tensed his crossed forearms over his chest. Maxim nodded reassuringly to Bryan.

"What was a prank? The disappearance?"

"No, the whole thing. The camping." Bryan glanced fearfully at his dad. "You know, she's always talking about leaving town for good. Hitchhiking to Los Angeles. Living off the streets if she needed. So a few of the guys thought, you know, it's a long weekend. Grady's parents were out of town, and he convinced Allison and BT to go. We all kinda thought it would be fun to run away for the weekend."

"Run away my ass," said his father, shaking his finger. "You charged seventy-five dollars to my credit card, and you're gonna work every penny of that off. With interest."

"*Okay*, Dad. I'm sorry."

Maxim bit his tongue. As a minor not charged with a crime, Bryan was only talking to the detective at his father's pleasure. Maxim didn't like the man interrupting his progress, but he was wary of getting on the father's wrong side. So far, they both were cooperating completely.

"Did you stay at Quiet Pines?" asked Maxim.

"No. No campsites. We wanted to be off the grid. To prove we could live off the land. That we didn't need our parents."

The father scoffed.

"It was just for fun, Dad."

Maxim nodded again. "So where did you stay?"

"BT knew a place just south of Sanctuary. A tree that got hit by lightning last year."

Maxim knew the place. As with Hazel Cunningham, Annabelle had last been seen north of the Interstate, although Quiet Pines was fifteen minutes to the west.

"And you never went into Flagstaff for a concert?"

"No, I never heard anything about that. All I knew was, she was cool for the weekend. But Annabelle's always lying to her parents like that. They don't care."

The kid may not have been far from the truth. Maxim glared at the boy pointedly. "So what happened to her?"

"Man, nothing! We just kissed a little. If she says anything else then that's a lie!"

"I'm talking about her disappearing, Bryan."

"Oh," the boy said meekly, glancing at his father. "Everything was fine Friday night. We slept in separate tents and everything. When we woke up the next morning, she was gone."

"Why didn't you tell anyone?"

"'Cause we didn't do anything," he insisted. "We figured she just chickened out, you know? Walked back to Sanctuary. Her tent and bags were gone, so it was obvious she left by herself. And then BT noticed his wallet was missing. He thought maybe she went through with it and hitchhiked to California. But I didn't think so. I mean, Annabelle likes to talk a lot. She acts like she's an adult, but she's not. I knew she was still around."

"So that was the last any of you saw of her?"

Bryan nodded.

"If I talk to Grady and BT and Allison, they'll all say the same thing?"

"I swear."

Maxim chewed his lip. He wouldn't take the kid's word for it, of course. Half his job was confirming mundane information. It was in the little discrepancies that the lies revealed themselves.

"Look at me, Bryan," said the detective, locking his eyes on the boy's. "Did anyone do anything to Annabelle to make her leave? Do you know why she would have left you?"

The boy didn't answer immediately. His lip quivered. "No."

"Bryan," intoned the father.

The teenager stared at his lap again. "I—she might have been a little drunk."

"What?"

"Grady brought some wine coolers. I only had a taste."

His father snorted. It didn't take a detective to see through that lie. Maxim put his hand up to calm the man.

"Listen to me, Bryan. This is important. Did Annabelle say anything that night about what she wanted to do? Where she wanted to go?"

He shook his head. "Just Los Angeles, man. She wanted to be a singer. She was always recording herself, singing new songs and stuff."

Maxim frowned. "And if she didn't go home, if she didn't see her mother or father or any friends from school, where else would she have gone?"

Bryan thought for a moment but nothing came to him. The ringing of Maxim's phone interrupted them and he backed up to retrieve it from his jacket.

"Is that what you spent my seventy-five bucks on?" demanded the father. "Alcohol?"

Maxim stepped away as the two argued. He didn't recognize the phone number but answered anyway. "Detective Dwyer."

"Detective," came a familiar voice. "This is David Harper. There's an incident that needs your attention."

"What is it?"

"Your friend, Diego de la Torre—he's in police custody. He deserves it, to be honest, but he's asking to talk to you."

Maxim winced. "What did he do?"

"He followed a man into a bar in Williams and attacked him. Security grabbed him and a local uniform responded. Diego insisted this was related to the kidnapping so the deputy notified me."

Maxim tensed. "Related how?"

"That's the problem. It's not. Your friend is getting himself into trouble over this." David Harper assumed the same smug tone of superiority Maxim had come to expect. "Listen, this looks like a misunderstanding. The victim doesn't want to press charges and I realize your friend is worked up over recent events. As a favor to you, I'd be willing to let him walk, but you need to come down here to pick him up."

Great, Diego was getting into his usual trouble and cashing in a get-out-of-jail-free card. The last thing Maxim needed was a distraction. Even worse, he would now be in debt to a cocky detective from another department.

But he had no choice.

"Give me the location."

Chapter 16

Maxim parked on the side of the road behind Detective Harper's unmarked car. Unlike Maxim's silver TT, it was a government vehicle. In the house's driveway was a Williams Police Department cruiser, with the familiar Shamu black and white coloring.

Diego de la Torre had garnered the attention of three agencies.

Speaking of the biker, as soon as Maxim exited his coupe, he spotted the outlaw handcuffed in the back of the police car, surprisingly calm. The biker turned to Maxim and smiled. The detective simply shook his head and continued past.

David Harper waved from the front porch and met Maxim halfway.

"Thanks for this," said Maxim.

The other man nodded. "It's not a problem." The Coconino detective appeared spent, but Maxim didn't see any anger on his face. Perhaps Harper really was making a kind gesture.

"This is what went down," he said. "Your friend got a name from the manager of Quiet Pines. That man, Jason Bower, lives at this residence. He actually wasn't on our list. According to Diego, we missed him at the scene because Jason checked out before the girl went missing. You with me so far?"

Maxim sighed and glanced back at Diego. "Yeah."

"Okay. So far, so good. Not a bad piece of information, actually. But then your friend decides to confront the man himself. Bower, being followed by a biker, is naturally afraid for his life. He clocks Diego with a bottle and they get into a brawl at the local watering hole. Except, this isn't the best neighborhood. They keep a bouncer on at all times, even in the morning. And you should see this guy. He's a grizzly bear."

"Got it," said Maxim impatiently. "How much trouble is he in?"

Harper raised his eyebrows and paused for dramatic effect. "None. Jason's sorry for what he did. Diego only got physical in response. It's funny how easily a large Samoan can appeal to a man's reason. Your friend decided he was fine with the authorities handling the rest."

Maxim chuckled. "Neither wants to press charges?"

"Nope. As long as everyone cooperates. I'm gonna call this a wash."

A police officer in blues exited the house. He nodded at Maxim, who returned the gesture.

"Sorry about all this," said Maxim. "And thanks. Can we get Diego out now?"

The officer shrugged. "I was waiting for you."

"By the way," said Maxim before they moved to the car, "where are you on the camper?"

Detective Harper stretched his shoulders and yawned. "Jason Bower? He says he never even saw the girl. He let us search the premises, and a phone call confirmed that he left the campgrounds three or four hours before Hazel went missing."

"What was the fight about?"

"Guy owes money to some bad people, apparently. He says he's been in hiding over the weekend, avoiding any unpleasant confrontations. That's why he went to Quiet Pines. Get this. He had his hopes on the Final Four. Only Saturday's game doesn't go his way and he needs to wait for the championship on Monday."

"But he's still hiding out today so it looks like he missed his payday."

Harper shrugged. "We both know how that goes. Bower panics while deciding how to climb out of his deepening hole, sees your friend, and thinks he's a scary gangster."

Maxim chuckled. "He's not far off."

Both detectives waited for the other to say something, but that was all there was. A funny story, as long as you weren't Jason or Diego, but nothing more. The lead on Bower had triggered false hope. Still, Maxim couldn't help but wonder what else Diego had on the man.

"Okay. Let's get Al Capone out of the car."

Chapter 17

Diego grew impatient as they neared the vehicle. It didn't make sense. He'd been detained for over an hour already—what difference did another minute make? But Maxim was sure as shit taking his time getting him out of this cage.

Cage. Diego again thought of the biker word for cars. He had just wanted to avoid being cooped up in the tow truck today. He never figured the term to be so literal.

As his freedom teased closer, all he could see was the photograph of Hazel Cunningham, still in his pocket but etched into his synapses, like an afterimage forever burned into a TV screen. Diego needed to get out, shake things up, change the picture again.

Maxim, as if reading his thoughts, paused outside the car door. He shot Diego a familiar stare, half warning, half threat. It instructed Diego to behave. To act rationally.

To not be himself.

Diego fumed and wanted to curse but held back. If there

was ever a time to check his temper, it was while in police custody. As he knew it would, the door opened just seconds later.

"Proud of yourself?" asked Maxim.

Diego sneered. "How about you give me the guilt trip later, after Hazel's safe?"

Maxim backed away and spread his hands in surrender. The detective was good like that. He was a cop, for sure, but his priority was always the victim.

Officer Bagley approached to help Diego exit the car. The biker shrugged away the assistance. He gladly turned around and accepted the uncuffing of his hands, though.

"Today's your lucky day," said the cop. "But Arnold doesn't want you in the Gold Room again."

Diego rubbed his sore wrists. "I like my bars with a little less puke anyway."

The officer smiled and shut the door.

"So are we done with this?" asked Detective Harper. The man crossed his arms and stood tall. "You promise not to harass Mr. Bower anymore?"

"I promise," said Diego. "Just a conversation, if I can."

The detective shook his head and turned to Maxim. "Is this guy serious? He—" David stopped himself and stepped into Diego's personal space. "No. Listen to me. Mr. Bower's had a long day. And he's in a world of shit already without you. He sold his car today to cover a gambling loss, and might need to sell the house."

"That's his problem," replied Diego. "If you really gave a shit you could put a protection detail on him."

David Harper laughed. "I *don't* give a shit, man. As long as I'm not dragged away from my work. He could dig his own grave for all I care. So can you. But you're not talking to him again."

Diego's face must've gone red. He wanted to tell the cop off even though he'd just done him a big favor. That consideration made him pause. Thankfully Maxim cut in.

"Actually, I don't want to step on anyone's toes, Detective, but if you're done with Jason Bower I'd like to chat with him for a few minutes."

The next few seconds were filled with silence. Diego's friend had done exactly what he expected, and he didn't see how he wouldn't get his conversation now.

"Fine," said David, scowling. "You do whatever you want. But don't expect any more favors, Mr. Torre. You've been warned." The detective swept his hands together as if he washed them and addressed Maxim. "He's your responsibility now." David Harper made his way to his car. He sat inside, started the engine, and rolled down the window. "Officer Bagley," he called out. "You might be inclined to wait here until their interview is done, to keep things civil."

The young police officer stammered like a deer caught in headlights, but composed himself. "Sure."

With one last shake of his head, Detective Harper drove off, hopefully gone from Diego's life.

Diego moved for the house but Maxim put his arm across his chest.

"I don't need to ask if you're done throwing punches, do

I?"

"Just words."

The detective nodded. "Okay. How about I start things off? You can come in only if he has no objections." Maxim beat the biker to the porch and knocked softly. Jason Bower must have expected some follow-up questions because he opened the door and let them inside without a word. Officer Bagley remained by his car.

"I'm Detective Dwyer, from the Sanctuary Marshal's Office."

"I'm not in any trouble, am I?"

"Not besides running out of college ball games to double down on. I just want to ask some questions. Maybe Detective Harper already asked you some of the same things, but please bear with me."

Jason glanced at Diego while he considered, then nodded at Maxim. "You're the one that found that girl up there."

"I am."

"Yeah, man, I'll answer whatever I can. Shit like this shouldn't happen."

Although the man was cooperating, he hadn't invited them to sit down. The three of them huddled by the door.

Maxim cleared his throat. "Mr. Bower, you told Detective Harper you saw Hazel Cunningham right before you left?"

"What? No. I didn't say that."

Diego realized Maxim was setting Jason up, coming at him with skewed questions to catch him in a lie.

"When did you see her last then?" asked Maxim.

"I didn't. Not really. I mean, I may have clocked the family the day before. No offense, but that's one hot mom." Jason flinched away from Diego's glare and cleared his throat. "But I woke up at dawn Monday morning, took off before anyone was up and about. Didn't really see anyone."

"Who did you see?" asked Diego.

The man shrugged. "No one, I guess. There was a couple walking a dog. And Charlie, the office manager."

Maxim pulled out his phone and casually referenced some notes. "No one else?"

"No."

"No one or nothing that looked strange? Out of place?"

Jason swallowed. "It was just morning, man. There was nothing."

Maxim sucked his teeth and nodded, scrolling through some documents. "Mmm hmm. What kind of dog?"

"Huh?"

"The couple walking the dog—what kind of dog was it?"

The man shook his head dismissively. "It was like a German Shepherd I think."

The detective nodded again but remained silent. Diego didn't want to stomp all over Maxim's interview strategy, but his friend was missing the point.

"Why'd you leave Quiet Pines so early?" demanded the biker.

Jason practically jumped at the question. Maybe he didn't feel safe around Diego, even with a police detective in the room. Something about that satisfied the biker.

"I just woke up early," said Jason.

"Horseshit. You left suddenly and prematurely. Charlie said you put down a deposit on another night." Maxim lifted an eyebrow at the news. Diego smirked. "You're not the only one who can ask questions." The detective acknowledged the statement with a tilt of his head and turned to Jason expectantly.

The man's gaze fluttered around the room. He took a step back.

"Hey," said Maxim, snapping his fingers in Jason's face a few times. "It's not a good idea to lie to me. You assaulted a man with a deadly weapon today. I want the truth."

The man's indecision paralyzed him. Diego took a step forward and Jason threw his hands up. "Okay! Okay!" He backed up a few steps and crossed his arms over his chest. "I'm not really into camping, you know? I mean, I like the woods and hiking and all that, but sleeping in a tent isn't my idea of a good time. You know the woods around here. Shit gets creepy at night."

What the man said was true, but that wasn't enough for Diego. "You're trying to tell us you bailed first thing in the morning because you're scared of the dark?"

"I know it sounds stupid," Jason countered, "but listen. I know this area. I know there are dangerous things out there. Animals. Outlaws. Hermits. It's not exactly normal, but it's never been like last night."

"What did you see?" asked Maxim.

"I... It's hard to say. I don't know what I saw or heard. You guys are gonna think I'm crazy."

Maxim clenched his teeth. "What did you see?"

Jason's gaze shifted between both men. He was nervous. If it was an act, it was a good one. But he let out a deep breath and decided to trust them.

"I heard crying," he said. "Like a little kid crying."

"A girl?" asked Diego.

"I don't know. It was hard to tell. It was far away. But this was all the night before. I was jonesing for a smoke so I got off my ass and went for a walk."

Maxim and Diego listened quietly. Jason paused his story and went for a pack of cigarettes on the coffee table, as if the mention of smoking required him to feed his habit. As he lit up, Diego thought about doing the same, but he didn't like the idea of being a slave to it.

"I heard soft crying," he continued after a drag. "But it wasn't coming from the other campsites. It was further into the forest. I went out, just a little mind you, but someone *was* crying. It probably wasn't my business, but I figured I would at least check." Jason put his cigarette to his lips and puffed.

Diego couldn't breathe. "And?"

"I don't know. I heard them and—"

"Them?" asked Maxim.

Jason shrugged. "I guess. There was talking. Whispering. Singing. It was fucking weird."

Maxim stopped him again. "You think a few rebellious teenagers could have done this?"

"These weren't teenagers, man. They were little kids. At least that's how they sounded. The thing is, even as I went deeper into the forest, the voices never got louder. Like, I heard the singing, but I never got closer to it." The man became agitated and took another drag. "I started to think some kids were fucking with me or something."

"How many kids?"

"I can't really say. Could've been two, could've been ten. All I know for sure is there was more than one, because I heard singing and crying at the same time."

Maxim and Diego traded glances.

Jason rubbed his eyes as if he could scrub away the vision. "I know this is gonna sound stupid, but I was pretty wired. It was late, man, and that tree cover blots out the moon. I followed slowly, not sure which way to go, and then I stumbled on a shoe."

Maxim leaned forward. "A shoe?"

"Yeah, like a little kid's shoe. One of those shiny black ones with a big buckle on it." Jason stopped talking as if he'd made his point.

"What did you do?" asked the biker.

"What do you think I did? I booked it back to my tent. That shit creeped me out. I don't know if someone needed help or not, but I wasn't gonna die alone in the woods."

Diego saw Maxim's face grow solemn. "It was just a shoe," said the detective.

"Look," said Jason, hands raised to plead his case. "I owe a lot of money to a couple people. Had to sell my car on the cheap to buy some time, but I gotta look over my shoulder just the same. It's dangerous for me to hang around town, is what I'm saying. But out there, in Sycamore, the fear was something else, man. *Something* was out there. It tears me up to think about where that little girl might be, but I've got my own problems."

Diego rubbed the scruff on his chin. He didn't know what to make of the man's story, but he appeared to believe what he said. One way or the other, something scared him out there. That would explain why he'd left in a hurry. It also meant Jason Bower was likely innocent. Maybe he knew something that could help, maybe not, but he wasn't involved. Diego couldn't blame the guy for taking off, either. He hadn't known a little girl would go missing hours later.

Maxim might think differently. It was his job to go after stuff like this. Like Jason, Diego had his own problems too. But he wasn't the same man. He'd made a promise to Julia, and as the look on Jason's face sent a shiver down his spine, Diego was going to keep his word.

Chapter 18

It was dark out by the time they left Jason Bower.

"A whole day wasted," complained Diego. He lit a cigarette and blew the smoke out with a hiss. The biker headed to his Scrambler across the street and was slightly annoyed that Maxim followed. He sighed and leaned on the chain-link fence. "Let's get this over with, then."

The detective put his hands in his pockets and watched the brooding biker.

"Well?" asked Diego.

Maxim smirked. "Okay. I understand what you're trying to do here. I know you want to find Hazel Cunningham. Hell, I know *you*, Diego. Act first, plan later."

"Saves time."

"It also wastes time. You pulled me and Detective Harper away from our investigations to bail your ass out."

"He's an asshole." Diego blew smoke from his nose. It enhanced his temper.

Maxim nodded. "Yeah, he is. And he did you a huge favor today."

"He did *you* a favor."

Maxim ignored the correction. "And his job is to find Hazel Cunningham. Sometimes you want an asshole to do these kinds of jobs."

"So what do you guys know then?" asked Diego, pushing off the fence and pointing at the detective, cigarette in hand. "After today it'll be two full days that she's missing. What do you think her chances are?"

Maxim held his tongue, but his eyes betrayed the truth. "Annabelle was found after three days."

"And she's fucked up because of it. That little girl's traumatized to all hell. If she was trapped somewhere and escaped, she needs to talk about it. It's irresponsible not to talk about it. You wanna do something useful, Maxim? You get that little girl to talk. You find out where she was."

A sigh. "I'm on top of it."

"Really, bro? I saw your press conference, Maxim. Excuse me for my total fucking lack of confidence in the police. You have no idea what went down."

"Fine," barked Maxim, getting heated himself. "You're right. I wasn't there. I don't know where Hazel is any more than you do. That's how these things work, Diego. You can't let emotion drive you in these moments. This kid deserves our very best. We act professional. We share information. We catch a break. I can't promise that we'll save her, man, but I will get to the bottom of it."

Diego's words caught in his throat as he processed the

detective's last words. There it was. The implicit reality that he hadn't wanted to acknowledge. The fact that this might not have a happy ending. Julia would be crushed, a little girl would be destroyed, and whoever was responsible might even get away with it.

Diego and Maxim had been through a lot together. Was it possible their best wasn't good enough this time?

The burning ash of the cigarette flared as Diego pulled on it. The men were silent. Across the street, Officer Bagley pulled his cruiser out of Jason's driveway and disappeared down the street.

Maxim moved to Diego's bike. "You brought a gun?"

The detective had noticed the shotgun holster. He walked around the motorcycle and Diego explained the obvious. "It's empty."

"I can see that. Where is it? You didn't lose another firearm, did you?"

Diego's eyes narrowed at the reminder. "Of course not. I don't own any guns right now," he admitted. "I've been saving up." The biker didn't mention the real reason. He didn't know if he could trust himself with a gun anymore. Besides, rent was more important.

Maxim chuckled. "So why strap the holster? Afraid of losing your outlaw charm?"

"That's in my heart, brother."

Maxim studied the biker. "Look, Diego. Doing things on your own is fine. Just keep your actions above board. The lead on Jason Bower was a solid one. It was good detective work. But you need to share any information you get with

Coconino. It's their case. I'll do everything I can to press them—you know that—but this only works through cooperation."

The biker nodded silently. He wasn't so sure going after Jason had been a mistake. He didn't get what he wanted, but the strange story about the kids was a curiosity. It gave them something else to think about, at least.

And there was another thing. Diego had another lead. Red, the old man who'd been denied entry into Quiet Pines. He was a loner. A hermit. He still needed to be cleared.

"So is there anything else?" asked Maxim. "Anything you want to tell me?"

Diego tossed the cigarette butt to the ground and stomped it out with the toe of his boot. "Nothing," he said, straddling his bike. "Just talk to the girl, Maxim. Get her to tell you something. Anything."

Chapter 19

"More wine?"

Olivia Hayes poured an extra glass of red without waiting for Maxim's answer. It was an earthy Syrah, she said. All he knew was it went down easy and left a tingle on his lips. Those were good things that led to him drinking more. But that wasn't the whole of it. Not only did the woman know her wines, but she looked sharp in her casual blouse and jeans. And somehow, her blonde hair had the perfect accidental styling that only belonged in the movies.

"It's good," he said, waiting for her to sit down first. She did, on the plush sofa, next to her daughter Annabelle. "Sorry again for the late hour."

"I'm gonna have a fit if you apologize again, Detective. Us girls like our nights."

Olivia smiled, but her daughter wore a vacant expression. She was all prissed up: light brown curls, tender pink skin, a long dress. But it was superficial. Just a coat of paint.

Annabelle was somewhere else, maybe not in body, but in soul.

Maxim sat down on the second couch. "How are you doing, Annabelle?"

The girl's blue eyes fell to the floor, but she was otherwise still.

Olivia ran her fingers through her short hair. "Go on, dear," she said nervously.

Annabelle simply nodded.

"Is it okay to talk?" asked Maxim softly.

The girl barely glanced his way. It wasn't nervousness as much as apathy. She wasn't afraid of talking—she simply didn't see the point.

"Oh, before I forget," added Maxim, fishing into his pocket. He pulled out Annabelle's key chain. "You left this at your father's house."

The girl's head darted to her keys and she snatched them. She twirled them noisily in her hand.

"That's not for a car, is it?" he asked, pointing to the key fob. He noted there wasn't an actual car key on the key chain, however.

"Oh that," said Olivia, shaking her head dismissively. "Kids. She's always leaving that thing around."

Maxim didn't know what Olivia meant, but Annabelle smiled at him.

"Thanks."

The detective nodded. It wasn't much, but it was a start.

"You mind if I show you a picture, Annabelle?" The girl watched silently as Maxim settled on a photo on his smartphone. He turned the large screen around so she could see. "This is Hazel Cunningham. She's not as old as you. She's only eight."

Annabelle affixed her gaze on the picture. Maxim couldn't tell if she recognized her or not. Annabelle was sullen and tough to read.

"Have you seen this girl before?"

She nodded. "I saw her on the news."

"Annabelle!" chided her mother. "You know I told you not to watch those programs."

"But they're talking about me, Mother."

Olivia pouted and shook her head in disapproval. "Dear, you'll never get over this if you continue to wallow in it."

Annabelle seemed immune to her mother's words. She nodded to acknowledge them, but it was for show.

"What about besides the news?" asked Maxim gently. "In real life. Have you seen her?"

The girl shook her head.

Maxim put the phone away. "Did someone take you out into the woods?"

A dark expression enveloped her face. "I was alone."

"I know that's not true, Annabelle. I spoke with Bryan. And Grady, and BT, and Allison. I know you went camping in Sycamore with them for the long weekend."

Olivia almost coughed up some wine. "What's this?" She turned to her daughter, who again faced the floor.

"They were just pretending," said the girl. "I went out to the forest with them, but they just wanted to drink. They didn't really want to go."

"Drink?" asked Olivia, incredulous.

Maxim leaned forward. "Annabelle, they didn't want to go where?"

The twelve-year-old began to close up under the weight of their attention. The detective moved to the girl and took a knee, placing his hand on her shoulder.

"Annabelle, were you trying to run away again?"

"What?" Olivia scoffed and put her glass of wine on the side table. "My daughter did *not* try to run away. She's a victim here. It was that brat, Grady, and his friends. Isn't underage drinking against the law? Can't you do something about that?"

"Olivia, I had a talk with the families—"

"A talk?"

Maxim sighed. "I can't arrest some teenagers for drinking a few days ago. Besides, your daughter participated. It's better to focus on—"

Olivia's face went blood red. "My daughter does not drink."

The detective backed away from them and snorted. This lady was living under a rock. Maxim didn't know anything about raising kids but he knew that much.

"If your daughter ran away then I need her to talk about it. Where she went. What she saw."

"Detective," said Olivia, standing up, "I think you should go now."

"What?"

"I will not have the police badgering my daughter after her ordeal."

"I'm not trying—"

"Her psychologist doesn't want her dwelling on it. He says keeping her distracted is the best thing for now. She needs to learn how to feel comfortable again before she can confront it."

Their disagreement escalated into an argument. Annabelle sat still, brooding. Maxim worried about her, but as hands-off as he'd been thus far, he couldn't afford to give them more space, more time.

"An eight-year-old girl is lost," he pleaded. "If your daughter knows anything of material value, we need that information."

Olivia was about to explode. "Can't you see she doesn't like these questions?"

And then, finding an unlikely lull in the yelling, Annabelle spoke.

"The only way not to be sad is to be happy."

Both adults stopped long enough to focus on the girl.

"What's that, dear?"

"The only way not to be sad is to be happy. Gulliver said that once."

Olivia's shoulders heaved and her breathing slowed. "I wouldn't take anything your father says too seriously."

"I know," said Annabelle. "I don't. But he was right that time. I want to be happy. I want to live out there, in the forest."

For a moment, Olivia's jaw was frozen to the ground. She watched her daughter with an expression that was a mix of horror and shock. Then she jutted her chin forward and shook her head. "You're not going outside again."

"You can't stop me, Mom. I'm old enough now. I don't need to be babied."

"You weren't eating anything, honey." Olivia turned to the detective and shook her head as though her daughter was being silly.

"I don't need food," protested the girl.

Her mother did a double-take. The severity of the situation began to sink in. The words weren't just combative —they had deranged implications. Maxim wondered how she hadn't noticed before. Suddenly, Olivia changed her demeanor.

"You're tired, Annabelle. You should go to bed."

"But I'm not tired, Mother. I hate sleeping."

"Go to bed!"

The ire in Olivia's voice had reached a dangerous pitch. The woman was trembling. At her limit. There was no room in her tone for an appeal, and the girl, as troublesome as she was, filed up the staircase silently.

When they were alone, Maxim studied Olivia Hayes. The poor woman was on edge and didn't know what to do. She bobbled between pacing, taking sips of wine, and staring out the window. For a while, instead of saying anything, Maxim ran the events over in his head, focusing on the words, making sure nothing slipped by.

Then he realized Olivia was crying.

He stepped softly to the window. "Are you okay?"

The woman's back was to him. Her short blonde hair hung over her slender neck, leaving her shoulders bare.

When she didn't answer, he softly touched her back.

Olivia Hayes spun around and buried her head in his chest. Her hands clasped tightly to his back, and he could feel her nails digging into his suit jacket. Her cries turned into a sob, and Maxim put his arms around her slender figure and waited for her.

Women like Olivia Hayes didn't open up much. Maxim didn't know her. He didn't know if the money had changed her, or the divorce, or the daughter. He didn't know what Olivia had done to get where she was, but he knew she was tougher than most mothers he'd met. She was always on the offensive. Always looking ahead.

Soon enough, she brushed her tears away, but she still clung to him. Still leaned her head on his shoulder.

"She's acting strangely," she mumbled. "Different, somehow."

The detective darted his eyes to the staircase to make sure they were speaking privately. "She's traumatized. That's natural. It's good that you got her a therapist."

Olivia tensed for a moment in his arms. "She's saying crazy things."

"At least she's talking now."

Olivia pulled away and playfully slapped Maxim on the shoulder. "Be nice," she warned. He couldn't help but smile.

"I understand this is difficult, Olivia. I really do. But you and Annabelle, you're the lucky ones. She made it back safe. You guys have each other, even if the relationship is strained right now."

Maxim suddenly felt awkward, still half-embracing the

woman while playing detective. He released her. There was a lot of tension between them, he realized. Too slowly. Olivia, taking his cue, let her smile wane.

Maxim continued. "There's another mother in Flagstaff who's crying every night wondering where her daughter is. She might not be lucky enough to ever see her again. Just try to talk to your daughter, okay? Just try to get her to open up. I need to know if she saw anyone out there. I need to know if she had help."

Olivia Hayes frowned and wiped her eyes. Her tough exterior crept into her features again, and she straightened up.

Chapter 20

Diego put his last cigarette to his lips. He hadn't chain-smoked like this in years. It was a minor comfort, at least, that he didn't kill the pack in a single day.

It was now Wednesday morning. Two days after Hazel Cunningham disappeared. The first forty-eight.

Diego thought of the TV show and wondered if that was really a thing. Was there actually a forty-eight hour threshold that drastically reduced the chances of a murder or abduction being solved? For the girl's sake, he hoped the police wouldn't move on so quickly. He knew they'd get answers eventually—they were methodical like that—but his main concern was the behemoth of bureaucracy moving at a snail's pace.

Diego? He had his own way of doing things. A way that got results. Right now that meant sitting on his Scrambler outside a post office and lighting a smoke at ten in the morning.

He didn't know why he hadn't mentioned the lead to Maxim. Or mentioned Red. The thing with Jason Bower had turned into a clusterfuck, but it worked itself out. Diego was okay. They had at least a tiny bit more understanding of the situation. Well, maybe knowledge was a better term, because Diego de la Torre had no understanding of what a crying kid in the forest meant.

A Williams, Arizona PO Box. That was all Diego had to go on now. An old man who'd been turned away from Quiet Pines the night before anything happened.

Except that wasn't entirely true anymore. Jason's encounter occurred that night. Something strange *had* happened the night before Hazel went missing. It just hadn't involved the girl or Julia. That was the one promising sign that silenced Diego's doubts. Why he told himself he could easily waste another day doing this, when he feared deep down the smart play was to make an appearance at the tow yard and apologize to Harry Pendle.

No, Diego pushed the cowardly thought from his head. There was a link here. Finding Red would get him a step closer. And he wouldn't get the police involved until he could prove that.

So it was nice when Diego finally had a turn of luck.

Well, it wasn't entirely luck. The outlaw's skill set consisted of brawling, tracking, and shooting people. He always had a puncher's chance when his task involved one of those three. So when he saw a red-haired old man limping down the sidewalk, wearing an old iron brace on his right leg and holding some sort of cane as tall as he was, Diego smiled confidently.

So much for another pack of smokes.

Red was an old man, impressive in both his frailty and his hardiness. Diego couldn't tell his age from this distance, but the man was skinny and pale, hunched over his staff of a cane, with a head of bright red hair and bushy eyebrows to boot. He was dressed plainly, just a white undershirt and overalls, but it was his frame that made an impression: he was tall and had oversized arms, thin but lengthy, except for hands that were the size of bear paws. Despite the leg brace, he walked with an even gait and long stride, and had he stood up straight and been in the prime of his life, Diego knew he would be witnessing an intimidating figure.

Diego smoked his cigarette and waited as the man disappeared inside the post office. He would need to play this one differently than Jason Bower. Be more discreet. Less direct. He wasn't sure if Maxim would extend him another favor if he got into trouble again so soon. At any rate, Williams PD and the sheriff's office were different beasts.

Ten minutes and a stick of gum later, Red emerged from the building empty-handed. He shielded his eyes from the harsh sun and made his way back the way he came. It was likely he just checked his mail. Diego considered following on foot, but there was no telling how far the old man was going. Besides, the Triumph was illegally parked.

The biker waited until Red was nearly out of sight before starting his Scrambler. He lowered the black face mask on his gold helmet and idled forward a couple of blocks before parking again, making sure not to get too close. Strangely enough, Red didn't turn down any of the residential back streets. Instead, he headed into an industrial section.

That made Diego's job more difficult. Fewer pedestrians meant he stood out, but he managed to block the old man's line of sight by hiding behind a parked truck here or there. Eventually, Red turned onto a set of train tracks, moving along them, out of Williams.

The biker considered what little he knew of the man. Red lived in the Sycamore wild. Away from the bustling towns, even those as small as Williams. He was a loner who liked his privacy and freedom. That made him strange to the conformist crowd. Suspicious, even.

The man began to hobble on his bad leg. Some combination of rough terrain and failing endurance caused him to lean into his crutch more. He appeared older.

Diego gave him ten minutes. Red was a speck in the distance before he needed to move. The tracks leaving the city didn't have a real access road, just a worn dirt path. The passage cut through the wild, with thickening trees on either side. There was no way for Diego not to stick out, so he settled again on distance.

Thus far, Red hadn't glanced back a single time. This was a man who was used to being marginalized. Ignored. It worked in Diego's favor now.

The biker rode the black Scrambler along the tracks, moving as slowly as he could. It wasn't a good plan—it wasn't even a plan at all—it was just action. Implementation. That's what he did best. He would save the elaborate deceptions for Maxim.

Unsurprisingly, like all poorly conceived strategies, it was destined to come with a hitch. This happened when Red, perhaps hearing the low rumble of Diego's motorcycle, searched behind him.

There was no way to hide and no point in trying. Instead, Diego continued forward at a solid pace, faster than before, so as not to appear peculiar. The old man trudged ahead some more, then stopped and leaned on his crutch, watching Diego advance.

The biker—helmet on, face mask down, head forward—drove right by Red. His appearance was a curiosity, maybe, but it wasn't overly suspicious. They were just two men who crossed each other's paths. Furthermore, it was impossible for Red to get a good look at him.

To keep up the ruse, Diego continued ahead. He forced himself not to look back. Besides, Red was clear in his rearview mirrors. The old man struggled ahead on uncertain footing, but Diego left him in the dust soon enough.

When Diego de la Torre was far enough ahead that Red was out of sight, he slowed down again and lifted his face mask. He cursed. Maybe he should have followed Red on foot. But his plan hadn't been a complete failure. He had made progress. Even if Red's destination was uncertain, the old man was a compass, pointing him closer to his goal.

The biker idled ahead, scanning both sides of the tracks, hoping for any signs of activity. Any sign of Hazel. This slow pace continued for a mile until he noticed a clearing to the north.

He'd almost passed it because it wasn't especially visible from the railroad tracks. Surrounded by trees, the clearing was shaped like a flag lot, with a thin path heading into it before it widened. But it was the trees that ultimately caught Diego's attention.

Dead logs, with no apparent cause for their condition, lay haphazardly in the open area. The space was barren of actual growth, leading him to believe it had been caused by a fire or other event.

Without another thought, Diego pulled his Triumph past the clearing and parked within the tree line. The old man had to be at least a twenty-minute mile behind him. Maybe twice that. Leaving his helmet and riding gear on, Diego crept through the brush and to the dry land. Brown grass, black logs: the spot was a bubble of death cutting into the predatory life of Sycamore.

In the center of the clearing, obvious to any curious enough to look, was a faded yellow and brown RV.

Act 2 - Hell on Wheels

Chapter 21

Diego was alone in the clearing, but he instinctively ducked. Something about the surroundings creeped him out. It wasn't the type of thing that was easy to explain—it happened at a subconscious level—but the combination of isolation, dead foliage, and the worn vehicle made his skin crawl.

This was it: Red's RV. The man preferred to live in the wild, just off the tracks, alone but within easy walking distance to town for supplies.

Train tracks weren't like streets. They cut through the wild without civilizing it. No cars pulled over here. No passengers or pedestrians busied themselves in these woods. The iron horse would announce its presence from a mile away and cause the earth to rumble, but it would roar past and allow the land to settle. Until the trees were cleared and man paved over the dirt, this forest would be wild. But, like a lot of Sycamore, it was a national forest. Protected.

Conserved. Ruled by a natural order.

Fallen trees were the only natural features of the clearing. The grass was barely there, dry, dead. For whatever reason, the healthy trees yielded a few hundred feet of space before their dense walls resumed.

Diego glanced back toward the tracks, barely visible through the brush. Maybe Red thought this was a good place to park. The clearing allowed the RV easy access to the dirt road. The wheels of the heavy vehicle wouldn't get caught in thick brush. It was possible the clearing even kept scavenging animals at bay.

Taking maximum advantage of the cushion, the old motor home was parked in the very center of the area. It was a large vehicle, once white but now yellowed by age. A brown stripe ran the length of its boxy frame over the wheels. The front windshield and grill was flat like a bus, but slanted at a slight angle. The whole thing looked like a slightly aerodynamic shipping container with windows, all tinted black except for the front cab area.

Spray painted on the visible left side were the words "Keep Out."

Diego didn't know anything about RVs, but he knew this one was old. Its style screamed the seventies, at least. Small sections of paint were chipped away, a tail light cover was missing, and one of the windows had a flat piece of particle board drilled over it. As decrepit as it appeared, however, it was obvious the vehicle was road ready. The tires were fairly new and it had updated Texas plates.

Some of the surrounding items didn't appear as well

kept. An old sofa sat against the back of the RV, half of the faded fabric ripped away revealing the wooden frame underneath. There were no cushions except what was built in, and much of that padding was torn open and exposed. Various bottles and gallon water jugs, some filled, some not, littered the area. A stack of wooden pallets formed a makeshift table. A broken-down gas generator sat beside it. A plastic blue rain barrel waited to collect water. Another barrel, this one metal, served as a fire pit. It contained ash enough to evidence a year's worth of heat.

Red was a survivalist, then. An old man who'd had his fill of society. He'd made the choice to break away and live by his own rules. That made the man an outcast, but Diego could understand the outlook. He'd run away from the Commissioned Corps when he couldn't take it anymore. He'd joined the motorcycle club and quit when he didn't belong. Tightly regimented service had a way of squeezing away the excess. Red's sentiment wasn't so far off. As long as he still respected the rules of society.

As long as there wasn't a little girl inside that RV.

"Hello?" Diego called out.

Immediately, he regretted making the noise. His instinct was that, if someone was watching him, saying "hi" would ease suspicion. Now that he thought about it, though, he figured if someone had kidnapped a little girl, a stranger poking around would always be viewed as a threat.

Still, no one answered, and Diego heard no sounds. The biker wasted no time and peeked in the windows.

A black film lined the inside glass. As bright as it was

outside, the tinted windows might as well have been opaque. Even cupping his hands to his face against the glass, Diego couldn't see a thing.

He circled the vehicle looking for a weak point. Only the front windows of the long RV were clear, and peeking in them didn't reveal anything out of the ordinary. The passenger seat was used as a shelf, holding a small stack of *Field & Stream* magazines, a box of Kleenex tissues, a package of cheese-sandwich crackers, and three empty Aqua Vitae water bottles. A twine necklace hung from the rearview mirror, a metal cross pendant facing the driver.

The biker peered deeper into the motor home, but a makeshift curtain was draped across the back of the seats, attached to the ceiling with hooks.

Diego backed off the doorstep and frowned. He didn't want to do anything illegal—not again—but he didn't have many options. He was alone and never carried his cell phone with him. If there was a chance Hazel was inside this truck, he was the only one that could help. There was no way he could walk away.

"Is anyone there?" Diego called out. He gave it a minute and then approached the thin door on the far side of the vehicle. It, too, had a blacked-out window. The biker gritted his teeth and knocked.

As he waited, Diego considered whether it was finally time to replace that shotty he'd lost. Something about this primitive home made him feel defenseless. Guns set people on edge, instigated conflict, and made him look guilty. He wanted to avoid that, ideally, but it would have been comforting in his grip.

At least he still had his riding jacket on. Under the left sleeve, strapped to his forearm, was his knife. It wasn't much, but he could defend himself with it.

When no one answered, Diego tried the door. It was locked, of course, as were the cab doors. The biker slid his knife from its sheath and went to jimmy the side door open. It was an old lock, and the metal bent away and snapped open without too much damage. A musty smell wafted from within. Diego covered his nose and climbed aboard.

The tints did a great job keeping the light out. They were too effective. It was nearly pitch-black inside, the only light coming from the open door and a few scratches in the windows. The door closed itself, though, and he had nothing to prop it open with. The biker could see glimpses outside through the torn areas of tint, but it was difficult to make out details within the RV.

That was okay. Diego didn't need details.

"Hazel?"

The emptiness didn't answer. Diego's eyesight adjusted and revealed a space that was very lived in. Garbage and half-used supplies were strewn on every countertop and seat. The carpet on the floor was worn thin. To his right was the curtain to the cab, but Diego didn't touch it for fear it would fall off its haphazard supports. Instead, he had an idea and opened the fridge.

A white light illuminated the room. It lit the living space and brought the squalor to full color. Considering the mess, Diego was surprised to see the kitchen sink and adjoining counter completely wiped down. He opened a few of the cabinets. Glasses, dishes, beef jerky, Lucky Charms. The cereal stood out.

The room darkened as Diego finished with the cabinets —the refrigerator had closed. He opened it again and its bright, white light filled the motor home. There was no milk or juice, just a few jugs of water, some jars of grease, and a plate covered with tinfoil.

Diego opened the small freezer above. It didn't have a working light but there was enough from below. Inside he saw an ice tray and a brown paper wrapper. Diego glanced out the window behind him and made sure he was still alone in the clearing. He was, but that didn't ease the sinking feeling in his stomach. He shut the freezer door and scanned the back of the RV.

A heavy door leading to what Diego presumed was the bedroom was shut. That was the back of the living space, where one of the windows was covered over with wood. The biker quickly moved to the door and noticed it was latched with metal braces looped by a chain. A master lock prevented access.

Diego winced as he tugged at it. It was a combination lock. The whole contraption was an add-on, an additional layer of security bolted over the frame. For that matter, the door itself didn't belong. It was heavy and solid under his hands. As he examined it, the refrigerator door closed and his light went away.

"Is anyone in there?" He pounded on the door. "Are you in there, Hazel? You can talk to me if you are. I'm a friend of Julia. I know your mother."

Still no answer. The biker put his ear against the panel to listen for breathing, shuffling—anything. As with the rest of the clearing, it was dead quiet.

Diego strained to see in the darkness and clawed at the door. It was loose, but locked. It made a lot of noise as it jiggled. Diego didn't attempt to muffle it. He imagined Hazel sleeping on the other side, scared but needing to wake up.

But nobody did wake up. Nobody announced themselves or called for help. He stopped shaking the door when he realized it was futile, but the silence and darkness threatened to drive him crazy. That was it. He needed to get in there somehow.

The biker moved back to the fridge and opened the door all the way. With the room lit, he moved back to the lock and examined it. He didn't know the combination and the chain was too heavy to break, but the metal loop was attached to the frame with normal screws. The biker drew his knife once more and set the tip of the blade to work as a screwdriver.

"If anyone's in there, I'm coming in. I don't mean you any harm."

The knife kept slipping out of the screw, but eventually Diego had twisted it out enough that his fingers could grip it and twist the rest of the way. He put the screw aside and went to work on the next one, but had to open the fridge again to get it started. The third time the door closed on him, he opened it and looked around for anything that could hold it open.

On the seat next to him, under some newspapers and a thick jacket, was a neatly folded child's plaid skirt.

Diego froze. The feeling hit him deep, between his stomach and chest. It was a sickening nausea, but his stomach was empty. Just panic, he knew.

Julia didn't remember the exact clothes Hazel had been wearing when she disappeared. But this meant she could be here. The reason for her failure to answer was obvious. But if the girl was no longer alive, why the need for the lock?

The light disappeared again and Diego took a few heavy breaths. At this point, he considered just breaking the door down. But he was warned to do things by the book. To allow Maxim and the police to do their jobs. To not get into trouble.

Already, Diego knew, it was too late for that.

"Goddamnit!" he heard from outside.

Diego's eyes shot to the window. Red was in the clearing. How'd he get here so fast? Diego peered between a strip of peeling tint.

The old man's metal crutch was speared into the ground, standing on its own beside him. Red was leaning over, working at his bad foot.

"Son of a bitch," he exclaimed. Red turned towards the RV.

Diego recoiled from the window. His back slammed into a storage cabinet, making a muffled sound. He froze.

Calm down, he told himself. Red couldn't see through the windows. Diego took a breath and peeked again.

Red's leg had gotten stuck in a soft patch of ground. The unwieldy leg brace had jutting hinges that must have made for some awkwardness. The old man tugged at his leg a few times and finally drew it free. He stood again to only a slight hunch and resumed his way to the vehicle, leaving the pole in the dirt.

"Shit," whispered Diego.

He glanced at the locked door. He wanted to say something but knew it was no use. If anyone was inside, they wouldn't answer. Speaking only made it likely that Red would overhear.

The outlaw knew he was done here. He could easily overpower the old man, but what would be next? His brawl with Jason Bower had left local law enforcement with little patience. Whether that was the Coconino County Sheriff's Office or the Williams Police Department, neither were his friends. The only thing to do was get Maxim. It was better than spooking Red and forcing his hand.

The biker hopped outside the door and shut it as softly as he could, but the RV rocked under his weight. He was on the far side of the vehicle, blocked by its massive size, and all he needed to do was make a beeline for the trees.

"Who's there?" Red called out.

Diego bolted, his boots skipping over dried grass and landing silently in patches of dirt.

"Damn it, children," cried the old man. "Leave me alone!"

The biker didn't have time to give the statement much thought, but it confused him. It confused the situation.

What children was Red talking about?

As Diego ducked into the foliage, he saw the old man round the corner of his motor home and wave an arm in the air.

"You want me?" he challenged. "Come at me! I'm right here!"

Diego waited in his hunched position, hoping the man wouldn't give his mysterious visitor chase. Red didn't. He grumbled and paced a bit, but he quickly gave up and entered his RV, seeming not to notice the damage where Diego had jimmied it.

That's when Diego realized he left more obvious evidence of his intrusion behind. He'd been careful to close cabinets and put things back where he'd found them, even the skirt, but a single screw rested on the shelf next to the locked door. If Red really was keeping someone hidden in there, he would be sure to notice the tampering. Perhaps not immediately, but it would come to his attention and tip him off.

There was no more time to waste. Diego sprinted around the clearing and back to his bike. The whole time the outlaw in him wondered: was he being a responsible citizen, or was he merely playing it safe because he no longer had a gun?

Chapter 22

Maxim's Audi hit a dip in the dirt road and his head bumped against the door frame. The sports car had a stiff suspension; it wasn't built for this environment. The detective checked the rearview mirror for the twelve-year-old hunched in the tiny back seat.

"You okay, Annabelle?"

The girl mostly ignored him, wide eyes glued to the window, but she afforded him a nod. Her attention was affixed to the land—the trees, the sky, the tracks. Maxim was taking special notice of Annabelle's attention. Her presence here was not ideal, but with another child missing, it was necessary. Annabelle's memory could be the difference between the life or death of Hazel Cunningham.

Although Annabelle was focused outside the car, her hands were fiddling with her key chain. With only a few keys, the bulk of the jingle came from the collection of ornaments. As her hands played with the key chain,

Annabelle absentmindedly blinked an attached green LED flashlight on and off.

Maxim slowed his car and turned to the woman beside him. Olivia Hayes wore a taut smile and sat with her arms and legs crossed. Maxim was grateful that she didn't raise objections to this outing again. She looked his way with a terse warning. He returned a smile to lighten the mood.

Ahead of the car, Diego waved and pulled his motorcycle off the dirt road. Maxim parked behind the biker and watched him remove his helmet and gloves. With the car still running, the detective released a long sigh.

"This is it?" asked Olivia.

Maxim didn't answer. He scanned the road and the track and saw nothing but a mile of trees. His eyes followed Diego as he moved past the car towards a section of thinning trees. Something was there. Not a path, exactly, but a clearing.

"I think so," answered the detective. "Do you remember any of this Annabelle? The tracks?"

She shook her head. "I've never been here before."

Maxim winced. His little test was practically over before it started.

"Okay, this is what we're going to do. I want to check the place out first. Make sure it's safe." Maxim drew his Glock and made sure it was loaded before returning it to its holster. "Both of you should stay here until I get back."

"That's not the deal," said Olivia. "I don't want to be shut out of this. I'm cooperating under the condition that I know everything."

"I'll tell you—"

"I want to see it," she stressed. "Besides, at the house you said it was just an old man living alone." Olivia placed her hand over his. "I'm sure you can protect me. Annabelle, you stay in the car until I make sure it's okay for you to come out. Understood?"

"Yes, Mom."

"Whatever," said the detective, feeling a bit like a kid himself under her glare. He opened the door and got out. He would do it her way.

Diego leaned on a tree, watching the clearing. Maxim and Olivia approached him. Once they got closer, their angle to the clearing widened, and Maxim saw the dead trees and the RV. For a temporary camp, it appeared long used.

"He's a strange old man," said the biker. "He's definitely hiding something. But his mistake was leaving the skirt out. I saw it."

Maxim narrowed his eyes. "Through the windows, right?"

He felt Diego's pause. It gave credence to his suspicions. "Of course," answered the biker.

From here, Maxim could already tell the RV windows had blackout tints. This was why Maxim wanted to check out this lead alone, without Detective Harper. If Diego had done anything to compromise the investigation, Maxim wanted to put distance between any illegal acts and the rightful authorities. Maxim would simply treat this moment as first contact. As far as the courts would be concerned, everything was legit.

The detective glanced back at his TT. The sun shined off the silver paint. Annabelle was inside. She'd slid over to their side of the car and had her hands and face plastered to the window, staring at them. She was definitely curious about this place. For a girl apathetic to the world, that was notable, but he still hadn't seen any recognition.

"Okay. Let's go," he told them. Maxim marched forward and Diego grabbed his shoulder.

"Wait up," he said. "You can't just walk right up. He's home now. He'll see you."

Maxim shot Diego a smirk. "That's the point, isn't it?"

"Shouldn't you take out your gun at least?" asked Olivia.

"No." Maxim crossed his arms and faced them. "Listen up, both of you. We're following procedure here. I have a lead that I need to confirm. Just like everyone else, I need to give this man a chance to cooperate. I don't care what anyone thinks they saw, I need to see it with my own eyes before I jump to conclusions. Now, if you're concerned for your safety, stay here. Otherwise, you can come along, but I don't want anybody interrupting or doing anything to hinder the investigation. Got it?"

Olivia bit her lip, brushed her blonde hair from her face, and silently nodded. Diego simply looked away. The biker never liked being told what to do, but Maxim needed to do it. This was too important. Assuming they both understood, Maxim spun around and continued to the RV.

If it wasn't for the vehicle, this could have been a homeless shanty. A decrepit sofa. A pallet table. Meager possessions were placed haphazardly. Jugs and bottles everywhere. A wheelchair next to a fire pit. Maxim wondered what would make a person want to live like this.

On the way to the RV, they passed a strange pole planted in the ground. It was black, like old iron. Solid, but thin, and as tall as Maxim. There was a crossbar near the top, and the point above that was styled into a decorative fleur-de-lis.

Maxim paused and slid his hands along it. Something was familiar about the pole, as if he'd seen something like it before. Out here, in the middle of nowhere, he wondered what purpose it served. Then again, he could ask the same about any of the other junk.

Not unexpectedly, Maxim heard a door slam. He drew away from the post and checked the RV. He didn't see a door on the left side and figured the old man had seen them and exited from the other side. Maxim unclipped his badge from his belt and held it up in his left hand. His right hand remained free to draw his firearm at a moment's notice. They waited as Red circled the front cab and came into view.

"Sanctuary Marshal's Office," announced Maxim before the old man could greet them.

Immediately, Maxim felt it. Something was off. Red was built like a gorilla, with extended arms and large hands, but he was thin and hunched over. He wore a brace on his right leg and limped toward them, but something told Maxim it was an act. Like the wheelchair.

Red held a long chef's knife in his hand.

"Put the knife down!" ordered Maxim, resting his hand

on his Glock. Red was dumbfounded and didn't move. "Put it down," urged Maxim again. He was still far enough away that the knife wasn't a threat, but he took a step backwards anyway.

Red came to his senses and turned his attention to the large blade. "Oh, this," he said, as if just noticing it. He slowly limped towards the stack of pallets and stabbed the knife into the tabletop. Next to the blade was a dead squirrel, and a fire crackled in the metal barrel. "It's just lunch."

The old man had a head of red hair. So that was where the nickname came from. But Maxim thought the color a little too crimson to be natural, especially for his age. "Do you have ID on you?"

"It's in the RV."

Red left the weapon behind and approached them again. Maxim let his weapon hand relax and put his badge away. The old man studied the three of them for a full minute before speaking. "I thought you were the park ranger," he grumbled. "I'm legal, you know. I paid all my tickets. Only been here a few days."

Maxim stepped ahead of Diego and Olivia to keep the focus on himself. "Since Easter night," he said.

Red's eyes narrowed and his face crumpled as he thought it over. "Yes, that's right. Who did you say you were again?"

"Detective Maxim Dwyer. I received a tip that you were in the area of Quiet Pines during a window in which a crime occurred. I was hoping to ask you a few questions."

"Of course." Red shot Diego a curious look. "What type

of crime?"

"Will you allow me to search the premises?"

Red gnashed his teeth for a moment. "I thought you said you were a Sanctuary detective?"

"This is an unincorporated area, but you can still allow me to search."

"Why would I?"

"Because you're a concerned citizen."

"You still haven't told me what I have to be concerned about."

Maxim frowned. He might as well get on with it before letting Red decide to become combative. He pulled his phone from his jacket and scrolled through pictures from the case. Brown hair, fair skin, and a crooked smile with dimples greeted him.

"Have you seen this girl?" he asked.

Red squinted at the small screen. "I can't say that I have." He pulled back and considered the other visitors. "She is cute, though. She's not the one that got lost, is she?"

"How did you know about that?" asked Diego.

"I was up in town earlier today," he said. "Everyone was talking about it. That's why you're here, am I right? This girl disappeared from the campgrounds and you're looking for her." The old man stood up straighter, showing off his tall form. He leered at Olivia strangely, and Maxim regretted allowing her here.

"Do you know anything about her whereabouts?"

"Why would I?" he asked, without taking his eyes off Olivia.

"Then let me search your RV. Prove that you're not involved."

Red scoffed. "This is ridiculous! Why do I need to prove anything? It's innocent until proven guilty, isn't it? Besides, everybody at the local campsites knows me. I'm a regular at all of 'em. Why would I steal a child?"

The old man turned to go but Maxim put his hand to his chest to stop him. The detective felt strength beneath the sagging skin. "Don't leave just yet," said Maxim. "You might object to my searching your vehicle, but this is public property. I can look around the outside as much as I want. And I'm gonna need you to stand right here while I do."

Red's lips jutted out. "I'm tired."

"You can sit down," countered Maxim. He picked up the wheelchair and set it beside the man. Red grumbled but accepted the offer. He carefully lowered himself into the seat, leaving his braced leg straight.

Olivia helped him sit. "What happened to your leg?"

The old man stared into the distance, but he couldn't maintain that for long with such a beautiful woman so close. "An accident," he said. "When I was younger."

"Why'd you attempt to stay at the campsite Sunday night?" asked Maxim.

"To dispose of my shit," said Red. "I can't just leave it on the floor now, can I?"

Maxim nodded as he circled the clearing. "Who's the wheelchair for?"

"No one. Me. Some days my leg gives out is all. I'm not a cripple."

"Does anyone else live with you?"

"Does it look like it?"

Maxim peeked into the RV windows. The interior was dark and he couldn't see anything through the scratches in the tint, but as far as he was concerned, that was a judgment call.

"Do you have any children's clothes in your motor home?"

Red coughed up some spittle and wiped his mouth. "How'd you know about that?"

"Can you just answer the question?"

"I had a son. A long time ago. He died when he was five." Red stared into the distance again. "I don't like to talk about it."

The detective circled into Red's view and leaned close. "Why would you have a plaid skirt in there?"

"It's not a skirt. It's a kilt. From the old country. I'm a Scot."

Maxim frowned and walked past the old man again. He turned and made sure Diego saw his displeasure. The biker hissed and stormed to the other side of the RV.

"Don't go in there," warned Maxim.

"I'm just looking around the outside, like you said."

The detective closed his eyes and rubbed his temples. So much for catching the old man red-handed.

Chapter 23

Red handed the driver's license to Maxim and returned to his wheelchair again. The detective had gone with him to retrieve it, hoping to get a better look at the living space. Unfortunately, the ID was in the glove compartment in the cab. Either the old man had nothing to hide, or his skeletons were hidden in the rear.

It was a Texas license, which matched his plates. Like his insurance, it was up to date. "You're from the Lone Star State?"

Red shot out his lip. "As far as Uncle Sam is concerned. Government's nicer there. The land is nicer here."

Maxim studied the ID. Lachlan Munro. "So the 'old country' then, as you put it?"

"And proud of it. Had to move here when things got hard." Red eyed Maxim quizzically. "Still not sure I made the right decision."

Maxim snapped a photo of the ID before handing it

back. Then he did the same with the plate on the back of the RV. He texted the picture to Gutierrez at the station and asked him to run it. If the old man had any outstanding warrants then the issue of consent to search became moot.

"What is this place?" asked Olivia. The prim woman had joined him at the back of the vehicle. She stared with disgust at the dilapidated sofa that rested against the bumper.

Maxim shook his head. He didn't know what to tell the woman. He'd stressed the importance of coming out here but was unsure how to proceed. He wasn't sure about Red. The man wasn't normal, that much he knew. The detective had no doubts the Scotsman had been on the wrong side of the law once or twice. People didn't disconnect like this without a reason. But without a clear link to Hazel, without an open warrant, they had nothing on him. In truth, Maxim wasn't sure the old man deserved his suspicion.

"Why, hello child!" said Red suddenly.

Maxim and Olivia exchanged a confused glance and then rounded the corner of the motor home. Red leaned forward in his seat, patting Annabelle on the head.

Her mother screamed.

Maxim ran to them. "Get away from her!" he yelled, scooping the preteen in his hands. He placed her a safe distance away and shot Red a warning stare.

"She came to me," he said. "I was sitting right here the whole time."

"It doesn't matter. I don't want you to touch her."

Diego rounded the RV from the other side to check on the commotion. His disappointment was obvious. There was nothing to see.

"I told you to stay in the car," chided Olivia.

"You were taking too long," replied Annabelle. "What's the problem? Isn't this the point?"

Olivia almost responded but Maxim didn't want that. "It's okay," he blurted out. Olivia glared at him but he nodded it off. The girl was right. The entire reason Annabelle was out here was to see if she recognized anything. It did no good to discipline her now.

"This is Lachlan," announced Maxim.

"Nobody calls me that," protested the man.

Maxim ignored him and addressed the girl. "Have you two met?"

The Scot made a funny face and Annabelle laughed. "He's an old man," she said, as if the insinuation was ridiculous.

"So you haven't seen him before? Or his motor home? Take a look at it."

Red spun around in the wheelchair and eyed his own RV. "Well anybody might've seen me drive—"

"I never saw it," she said.

Red nodded. "That's right. And what's this about anyway? Anybody that says I did anything is a liar."

"What about Red, Annabelle? Have you seen him around anywhere?"

The girl rolled her eyes. "No," she answered. "I wasn't taken and molested by an old man."

Olivia was shocked. "Annabelle!"

"So that's what this is about!" Red rested back in the

wheelchair and shook his head as he watched the tree line. "Well, this is awkward."

Maxim again turned to Diego. He didn't know what to say. He'd gotten his hopes up again, but Red was looking like more of a dead end than Jason Bower.

The old hermit leaned forward when no one spoke. "What *did* happen to you, child?"

Annabelle's light blue eyes fluttered under his gaze. "Nothing."

"Now, child," admonished Red with a smile. "Lying is a game for adults. Look at these men. They're much better at it than you."

"It's not like that," insisted Olivia. "We just want answers. We don't mean you any harm."

"See what I mean?" said Red, still focused on the girl. "They can't help themselves."

Annabelle pouted but stepped closer. Maxim's instinct was to put a stop to their bantering—but he was curious about it. Red was tight-lipped but enjoyed an audience. If it took a twelve-year-old to get him talking, so be it.

Maxim's phone buzzed in his pocket but he ignored it.

"You're too young and innocent to be going that way anyway," said Red. "Your mother may be misguided but she's concerned for you."

Olivia stepped forward but Maxim grabbed her arm and gently pulled her back. He gave her a knowing glance and she understood.

Red continued. "Why won't you tell her what happened?"

Annabelle's gaze fell to her feet. For the first time, Maxim noticed she wasn't wearing shoes or socks. He scanned the clearing and didn't see them. The girl must have taken them off in the car.

"No one cares," answered Annabelle.

"Child!" Red pressed against his chair and pushed himself to his feet. Maxim took a step closer but let the conversation play out. "That's not true. Your mommy and daddy are out here right now, aren't they?"

Maxim and Olivia traded an embarrassed glance.

"He's not my dad."

Red shuffled past the girl. "Oh. Well, sometimes adults need some company."

Olivia glanced at Maxim, but his face flushed and he couldn't look back. "It's not like that," he told Red.

The old man nodded and leaned his hunched form against the black pole. It appeared that Red used it for support. The hermit let out a long sigh as if the short distance had worn him out.

"All I mean, child, is that nobody would be here if they didn't care."

"There's another girl missing," said Annabelle. "That's who they care about. That's who they're looking for. Nobody cares about what I want."

Red shook his head sadly. It was a pitiful thing to see such a decrepit man saddened by a kid. Maxim couldn't get a read on him. Everything he did surprised the detective, but he wasn't sure any of it was genuine.

"So tell us," said Red. "What do you want?"

Annabelle shrugged. "To live outside. Like you."

"Annabelle Hayes," intoned her mother. "I've warned you about speaking like that."

"It's what I want!" the girl cried. She wasn't a teenager yet but already had the knack for making every conversation dramatic. As easily as she turned it on, it went away, and she again faced the old man.

"What about this?" he asked, pulling the black pole from the ground. "Do you want to hold this?"

Maxim took another step closer. The pole wasn't sharp, but it was large and heavy. It was unwieldy but it could still be used as a weapon in the right hands. But Red only stood still, presenting it in front of her.

"Go ahead," he said. "Try it."

The little girl stared at it, unsure what to do. Red put his weight on the staff and the flat bottom pushed into the dirt. He crouched before her.

"Grab onto it."

Annabelle shook her head. It was a hesitant gesture at first, but her eyes grew wild and she almost collapsed backward.

Olivia ran up to grab her daughter. "Leave her alone!" She tried to hug her but Annabelle pushed away. Maxim forgot about them and kept watching the old man. Red's eager eyes bored into the girl.

The old man struggled to rise and held onto the pole for dear life. His head rose to Maxim's height, then towered above as he stood straighter.

"Poor girl," said Red casually. Maxim nodded and

watched the mother and daughter argue. The detective didn't have kids but knew Annabelle was troubled. It wasn't just an identity issue, or a space issue. Her problems were deeply rooted. "She's not the first, and she won't be the last."

"What did you say?" demanded Diego from the outskirts, suddenly in the old man's face. Red's expression took on an amused ire.

"You know," he said, studying the biker, "I thought it was the kids who were messing around on my property. Now I know better."

"What the hell are you talking about?"

Red stepped away from his crutch and postured in front of the biker. "You know what you did."

Diego welcomed the challenge. He shoved the old man with both hands. Somehow, the feeble man held strong. "What did you mean about her not being the last?"

Red coughed up another loogie and spit it at Diego. The biker barely got out of the way. Without thinking, he socked Red with a roundhouse that splayed the old man to the floor.

"Diego!" Maxim moved between them and shoved the biker away. Red was an elderly man. No matter how strong he was, assaulting him was a bad idea. "I want you two to stop this," he commanded, his voice leaving no margin for protest.

Diego exhaled heavily but stood his ground. Red didn't accept Maxim's offer for help and stayed on the ground, muttering to himself. Maxim's phone buzzed again and he used the downtime to pull it from his jacket. Gutierrez had texted him twice. The first message indicated that Lachlan Munro had no outstanding warrants. The second told him that a full background check came up clean.

At least on paper, Red was not a criminal.

Maxim slipped his phone back into his jacket as Red regained his feet. "Number one, we're going to keep this civil. The next person that throws a punch is spending the night in jail. That's a promise. Number two, I don't know who messed with your property, but I don't want anyone accusing anyone else of anything unless they have proof and want to file a police report. That means I'd need to get a Coconino deputy out here. I'd rather not go through all that. It's easier to keep this a simple conversation. We clear on that?"

Red nodded. The detective faced the biker, who just shrugged. "Are we clear, Diego?"

The man grimaced and zipped up his riding jacket. "Yeah."

"Good."

"I want everyone off my property," said Red.

"Kaibab National Forest is public land."

"I have a right to be left alone."

Maxim scoffed. "Let me tell you how this works, Mr. Munro. When the police conduct investigations, civilians have the duty to cooperate. I don't give a shit what you think of the government—you're gonna tell me what you know."

Red huffed indignantly. "Fine. Anything to get you

crazies off my property. But I already told you, I've never seen that girl or the one in the photograph in my life. I don't know why you don't believe me."

Diego almost said something but Maxim's stare silenced him. "I do believe you," said the detective.

"Okay then," said Red, somewhat vindicated. "Then I don't know how I can help you."

Maxim paused a moment. "You said you thought kids were messing around with your stuff. What kids?"

Red sighed and shook his head.

"Do you know their names?" asked Maxim.

"They don't have names," he said. "Or maybe they do. How should I know?"

Maxim produced his phone again and scrolled to the pictures of Annabelle's friends—Bryan, Grady, Allison, and BT. "What about these children? Have any of these messed with your property?"

Red chuckled. "You don't get it, Detective. You don't have photographs of the wee ones. They don't have fancy clothes and rich parents. They're removed from society, like me."

Diego tensed, but Maxim didn't want to interrupt his flow with Red. "Who are they? Runaways?"

Red's eyes flashed for a moment, but Maxim couldn't tell if it was anger or amusement. "Some, I suppose," he finally answered. "They're all lost. That's for sure."

"And they steal from you?"

"They bother me. They steal things. Or move things. Or break things."

"Why haven't you come to the police?"

Red laughed.

Maxim tried another question. "Why don't you park somewhere else?"

"I do," insisted Red. "I move around all the time. They always follow me and cause all sorts of trouble. Wandering, dancing, singing in the middle of the night. A man can't get a moment's rest."

Finally Maxim met Diego's eyes and understood what the biker was excited about. Jason Bower had said the same thing. He'd been at the campsite the same night Red passed through, and he was unnerved by a child crying in the woods. Were these reports related?

Red leaned onto his crutch, gripping the top crossbar tightly. "Best to live close to the tracks. The tracks are safe. They're old metal. A pipeline to the industrialized world."

A crack formed in Diego's serious expression. "What are you going on about, old man?"

Maxim narrowed his eyes. "Safe from who?"

The hermit shrugged. "Whoever you're looking for. They don't like iron." Red tapped the black pole as he said that.

Maxim laughed and shook his head, realizing how crazy this was beginning to sound. "Yeah, well, what about lead?" The detective pulled back his jacket and patted the butt of his Glock.

Red glanced at the firearm but didn't answer.

The biker took this more seriously. He scratched his wild hair. "What do the kids have to do with all this?"

"Everything," said Red. "The wee ones grab the children. Scurry off with them."

"What?"

"These woods aren't safe. Especially for little ones."

Diego's face burned. "You son of a—"

"Keep it civil!" barked Maxim. He stepped forward and Diego threw his hands up in surrender. They were finally getting somewhere, even if the ramblings were as crazy as Jason Bower's. Maxim paced around the two.

"Kids," he said. "You're blaming the abductions on kids? How could you know that?"

Red shrugged. "I'm no fancy detective with a badge. I may not have the same burden of proof you do, but I know it. In my gut, I know the wee ones are out there." He lowered his voice to a harsh whisper. "I can see them on the edge of my vision when I'm almost asleep. They play tricks with the lights. I hear them chattering when the wind quiets to a breeze. They're out there, Detective, and you either believe me or you don't."

"This is bullshit," exclaimed Diego as he stormed a short distance away. He continued speaking with his back to the other men. "You're telling us you don't know where Hazel is?"

Maxim studied the biker. He half agreed with him, but he could also tell Diego was too attached to the case. Or the family, at least. He had good instincts for an outlaw, but he was too emotional and jumped to conclusions. Jason and Lachlan were skillful discoveries—they just weren't guilty of kidnapping Hazel Cunningham.

"Mr. Munro," said Maxim, collecting his thoughts. "How can you expect us to believe you?"

The old man didn't answer immediately. His wild eyes were amused by their distrust. "It's not what you believe that matters."

Diego scowled and turned away. Just then, Olivia screamed at the top of her lungs.

Maxim reached for his gun. He and Diego rushed around the RV and saw Olivia struggling in the woods. She was past the tree line, where the brush quickly thickened. Diego rushed forward and Maxim waited, scanning the clearing and trying to ascertain what was happening.

Finally Olivia stood and moved toward them, into the clearing, dragging Annabelle by the arm and the neck. Diego stopped and watched the woman march past him.

"She tried to run off into the woods," said Olivia to Maxim. The tone of her voice was especially harsh. "We need to go. Right now."

Maxim watched Annabelle silently cooperate, a subdued expression on her face. The detective realized the grip on his firearm had turned his knuckles white. He eased his hand off the weapon and looked at Red, dumbfounded.

The old man grinned.

Chapter 24

Diego twisted his boot in the dirt.

"I'm telling you, that old man is full of shit."

Maxim rubbed his temples. "It's not him," he said. "She —"

The detective turned to check his car. Olivia and Annabelle were tucked inside with the doors closed. The girl strobed the green LED on her key chain flashlight. Maxim lowered his voice. "She doesn't know him. She would have said something."

Diego wasn't so sure. He didn't know Annabelle. He hadn't been around for her interviews. All the biker knew was she'd been back two days already and hadn't helped the investigation in the slightest.

"Maybe she's traumatized," he offered. "Or I don't know... scared."

"Then she would be terrified of this place," returned Maxim. "She'd be catatonic just seeing his face. I'm telling you, Diego. I read people for a living. She's never seen him before."

Diego pouted. There was a connection he was missing here. "Is it possible she somehow forgot?"

The detective shook his head. He was taking the biker seriously. "I don't think so."

"Well, this guy's bad news," asserted Diego. "You saw how he watched the girl. Olivia too."

Maxim nodded slightly and checked the car again.

"What about the kids?" asked Diego. "Red mentioned kids. Jason said the same thing. They were both at Quiet Pines Sunday night. Do you think that's a coincidence?"

"I don't know. Some of Annabelle's friends are wannabe runaways. They're barely teenagers and they're drinking. Maybe their antics are more sophisticated than I assumed."

Diego sighed over Maxim's words. "You showed Red those pictures. He said those weren't the kids."

"He also said he didn't get a good look at them."

"Listen to yourself. You don't really think a few kids are responsible for the kidnapping. I saw the news reports. Annabelle went out there herself. Hazel isn't like that. She's in real trouble."

"You don't even know her."

The tentative smile in Hazel's school picture flashed in Diego's mind. At first he'd thought the expression hid something, but he now realized the girl had just been nervous and wore her heart on her sleeve. "I've spent enough time with Julia to know the difference."

The detective shook his head again and put a concerned

hand on Diego's shoulder. "And that's the problem here. You're too involved in this. You need to take a step back, man."

Diego spun away from his friend. "Don't treat me like that, bro. What about you and Olivia? Are you worried about asking them the hard questions?"

"It's not like that," said Maxim.

"Well, there's something going on in these woods, and that little girl in there knows what it is. She should be talking to us. Saying something that could help."

The detective's expression darkened. He crossed his arms and avoided eye contact.

"Maxim, you need to consider that she's not telling you the truth."

"She's a kid."

"A runaway! Stealing money and splurging on wine coolers! Running out—"

Maxim threw his hand up to silence the biker. Diego realized he was being a little loud and hushed to a whisper.

"Running out into the woods in the middle of the night isn't something a good kid does."

"You ran from the Commissioned Corps, didn't you?"

Diego knew his glare could melt ice. "That was different. What Annabelle just did out here, taking her shoes off and racing into the woods? That's messed up stuff. She knows something." Diego implored Maxim to hear him with the tone of his voice. "I'm not saying she's responsible for Hazel's abduction, but she knows something. She might know where she is, or who took her. She might know something about this asshole," said Diego, pointing towards the RV. "You need to reach her, man, or get someone who can."

The detective was silent for a moment. Something Diego had said got through. "I'll talk to them again, but I can try her therapist as well. I've been meaning to get to it. But don't get your hopes up. They're like lawyers. Everything they know is privileged." Maxim took a couple of steps to his car. "I'm telling you, Diego, Annabelle is not acting malevolently. She's a confused girl who doesn't know what to make of things. Now let's get out of here."

Diego noticed Olivia exiting the car. She hadn't interrupted them, but her impatient stare was hot enough for Maxim to feel. The detective was itching to leave.

"Go ahead," said Diego.

"No way. Not without you. You nearly went to jail after stalking a man yesterday and you followed that up with a B and E over here. I'm not gonna leave you alone with Red."

Diego scoffed. "I called you, didn't I? I'm not gonna bother him. But it wouldn't hurt to keep an eye on things. What else am I gonna do?"

"Literally anything else would be healthier. Pick up an extra shift or something."

Diego shook his head. He still needed to talk to Harry Pendle.

Maxim must have read his face. "Jesus. What did you do?"

"Like you said. I'm invested in this."

The detective frowned. He was about to say something,

then noticed Olivia tapping on the roof of his Audi. He was conflicted. "Look, Diego. Just don't do anything stupid with the old man. You're lucky he doesn't want to press charges for the assault back there. I promise I won't drop it. I'll look into him some more and call you back later. That's gotta be good enough." Maxim let that sink in before walking to the car. Olivia Hayes appeared annoyed and relieved at the same time. Maxim said something to her and she smiled before they sat inside.

As the car started, Diego shuffled over to his bike and put his riding gloves on. He watched them talking inside, but he knew Maxim was really just waiting to see the biker ride out. Diego straddled the Triumph and fiddled with his helmet, stalling as long as he could. Olivia grew angrier with every delay. The smile outside the car had been a mask for Diego's benefit. Now, apparently outside his notice, her gloves had come off.

The TT slipped into gear and pulled out, driving away along the tracks. Maxim was patient, but nobody wanted to sit through an earful any longer than they had to. The biker didn't envy him the car ride.

Diego de la Torre closed his eyes and pulled in a long, deep breath. The nearby pines consumed his senses. As the sound of the coupe faded, Diego felt at peace. But there was also a sharp edge somewhere, inside his heart. Harry Pendle, Julia, Hazel—everything felt stuck in limbo while his search was still open.

He couldn't rest. Not now. Maybe not ever again.

The biker opened his eyes and hopped off his

motorcycle. Something was out here. He could smell it. And it didn't matter how many lying children or dirty old men or bossy police officers got in his face. Diego was going to dig to the bottom of this with his own two hands.

157

Chapter 25

Olivia gazed at the road ahead. Her bangs hid her eyes, but her mood was communicated through body language. Her arms crossed over her chest. Her cheeks drew in. She exhaled heavily, as if working herself up to something. She resembled a spring coiled to its smallest form, a stance of stillness betrayed by its intent to strike.

In the back seat, Annabelle had stopped complaining. She'd attempted to run off again, this time in plain sight of her mother. Just as the night Maxim had found her, she'd taken off her shoes. Her actions were growing more erratic. Desperate.

Maxim drove the TT silently and considered the evidence. Annabelle was traumatized by her experience, but she was running from something else. Something at home. By all accounts, she had chosen to disappear. The detective had been sympathetic with her lack of cooperation, but Diego thought it was an act. A rebellious daughter who'd acted out and continued to do so.

That aspect of Annabelle's situation was enough to inspire doubt that her disappearance was linked to Hazel Cunningham's. The eight-year-old girl surely had no designs to leave. She wasn't a runaway. One minute she was with her mother, the next she was gone.

But the same thing just happened to Annabelle—had it not?

So maybe the pieces did fit together somehow. Maxim's initial belief had been that Annabelle knew something that could assist in Hazel's recovery. Considering all the angles, he still believed this to be true. It had to be.

So the next question was: why wasn't she telling? The likely obstacles the detective came up with were fear, trauma, or malice.

Annabelle wasn't that nefarious. Anti-authority was one thing, willingly withholding information that could save Hazel was another. She wouldn't ignore a missing little girl. She wouldn't impede Julia from finding her daughter. On top of that, Annabelle Hayes was only twelve. She couldn't have lied about not knowing Red convincingly enough to fool Maxim. No way.

Olivia Hayes huffed noticeably. She was done with her silent tantrum and now wanted attention. Maxim knew it was a trap, but he went in anyway.

"It was vital to rule out Red from our consideration," chanced Maxim.

Olivia snapped back at him. "I told you her therapist said she wasn't ready. My daughter almost died in the woods.

She still has notions of living out there. It's unhealthy. No more field trips."

"Annabelle is one of the lucky ones," reminded Maxim.

"No. Don't you give me that line. This entire experience has troubled her. She's a victim here and she needs to heal."

Annabelle sucked her teeth from the back seat. "I'm sitting right here, guys. You don't have to talk about me like I'm not."

Olivia spun around. "What was that back there, young lady? What were you thinking? You want to get lost again?" The girl didn't answer. She focused her attention on the jiggling key chain in her hands. This just worked Olivia up more. "This isn't a game, Annabelle Hayes. You could have seriously hurt yourself. Who knows what's out there at night."

Maxim saw Annabelle roll her eyes in the rearview mirror.

"Relax, Mom. I would've found my friends."

"That's another thing! If you think you're seeing Bryan again, you have another thing coming. I'm calling his parents. And you won't be going over to Grady's either. This is all stopping right now."

"Good," cried the girl. "I hate them all anyway."

"Then why do you see them?"

"Like you care. You don't even notice me half the time."

"Don't say that." Olivia faced the road and jutted her chin forward. "I love you dearly. I'll stay with you twenty-four hours a day if I need to until you feel better. Whatever it takes."

Annabelle scoffed. "Yeah. Until Mark or Danny wants to take you into Flagstaff again."

Olivia had a tan complexion, but she turned red at that remark. "Annabelle!"

Maxim exited the highway and drove north to Sanctuary. He hadn't interrupted them yet because watching this play out gave him a better idea of their relationship. He was finally getting a feel for what was going on back home. But the argument was devolving into an embarrassing family spat. Besides, Maxim had to keep his eyes on the prize: Hazel Cunningham.

"Annabelle," he said, locking eyes with her in the mirror, "I know you're upset about a lot of things. I get that. But your mother cares for you a lot. Even I care about you. I'm here because I want to help you."

The keys in her hand stopped jingling. "People say that. They always say they care. People always say nice things and ask about your day and say you're precious to them, but that's not the truth. That's just how people talk. Nobody wants to know how I really feel."

"That's not true, honey!" Olivia softened her voice. "Please let me help you. Please tell me why you're doing this to me."

Annabelle almost spat out a quick rejoinder but caught herself. Maxim saw her glance out the window and think over her words. Her shift in mood surprised him. "Sometimes I feel like this is all a dream," she said, "and when I dream, that's what's real. Sometimes I feel like I'm not really me. Not anymore, you know? Like I used to be something else but that part of me got lost."

Olivia shook her hands hysterically. "Don't speak like that, Annabelle!"

"You see?" cried the girl. "You see? You don't wanna hear what I wanna say."

Maxim thought it best to cut in before Olivia exploded again. Besides, they were almost at the house and he hadn't gotten anywhere. "We need you to understand this isn't all about you right this second. There's an eight-year-old girl out there that was taken from her mother. I haven't mentioned this to you yet, but these things usually don't end well. Hazel Cunningham could be starving as we speak. She could be getting hurt or tortured right now. Or worse. She could be an outlet for his sexual—"

Maxim stopped himself when he realized he was speaking to a kid, but Annabelle got the message. Her expression darkened with a knowing look.

"Don't talk like that around her," cautioned Olivia.

Annabelle turned away as he continued.

"I'm sorry. But it's important that you understand: every second counts. I know you didn't ask for a little girl's life to depend on you, but it does. That's the hand life dealt you today."

"Wait a minute," said the girl's mother. "What are you saying?"

Maxim ignored the question and traded glances between the road and the daughter. Annabelle didn't return his gaze.

Maxim sighed. "Annabelle, I need you to be honest with me. Have you ever seen Red before?"

Olivia's voice sharpened. "What are you implying? She already answered you. She's never been there before."

"Annabelle," stressed the detective. "I need to know the truth. About what you did with Bryan and Grady and BT and Allison." The girl lifted her head. "Is what Red said about being harassed true?"

"Detective!" screeched Olivia. "That's enough! My daughter isn't lying! She's not a criminal, and she has nothing to do with that other missing girl!"

"I didn't say that," said Maxim.

"You did, pretty much."

"Well, I'm sorry. It wasn't my intention. But there's a link here, Olivia. Can't you see that? Annabelle and Hazel and Jason Bower and Lachlan Munro."

"Who's Jason Bower?"

Maxim shook his head and sighed. "It's not important. I'm just trying to get answers. I'm just trying to understand this."

No one said anything for a few minutes. As the detective rolled into the nice part of Sanctuary, tensions began to relax, but he knew he was quickly losing his window. There was too much to do today, and as important as Annabelle might have been to the case, he couldn't afford to babysit her while she got her head right.

The detective attempted to ease the mood in the car. "I'm sorry, Annabelle. I'm just asking the questions I need to ask. Because—"

"It's your job," she finished.

Maxim smiled at her. "Yes."

Annabelle didn't warm at the sentiment. "So this is just a paycheck to you. You're trying to help because it's what you're paid to do."

The detective tried to be understanding at the accusation, even though the statement couldn't have been further from the truth. "This isn't just a job, Annabelle. Not to me. It's a calling. I wasn't making overtime when I was in Sycamore in the middle of the night. When I found you."

"When you were looking for the other girl."

"Her name's Hazel. And yes, I was looking for her. But just because I care about Hazel doesn't mean I don't also care about you." Maxim stared at the girl again. No friendly smile. No harsh glare. Just the solid countenance of a man firm in his convictions. "The reason I'm so good at this is *because* I care."

His words at least gave the girl pause. Annabelle avoided eye contact once again. "A year from now, you won't even remember me."

"That's what you believe, Annabelle. Not what I do."

He pulled into the driveway and put the car in park. Olivia opened the door and flipped the seat forward as if she were attempting an escape. Annabelle was reluctant to exit. Her mother prodded her and she stuck a leg out, but she waited on something.

"It doesn't matter if you're telling the truth or not," she finally said. "You can't help me."

Maxim helplessly watched Annabelle slide out and make her way to the house. Unexpectedly, Olivia leaned in for a final word.

"I know you mean well, Maxim. I can only imagine what that other mother must be going through. But my priority has to be my own daughter." The detective raised his eyebrows only because he was surprised this speech hadn't come sooner. "The Cunningham girl is not your case. Annabelle is. You already got to the bottom of what happened with my daughter, and I'm grateful for that. If one of those boys committed a crime and you mean to do something about that, then do it. Otherwise, this is now a family matter. My Annabelle needs rest and relaxation. She doesn't need the guilt of a raped or dead girl on her conscience. Not now."

Maxim opened his mouth to respond but stopped himself. She was right. He shouldn't have gone there with the girl. Part of him wanted to apologize, but another part thought he'd already apologized enough.

"I don't begrudge you your position, Olivia. And I thank you for the assistance you've already provided. Believe it or not, it was a big help."

Olivia nodded hesitantly. "I'm glad you see things that way."

"How about, next time, I speak to Annabelle with her therapist present? He can ensure we don't talk about anything upsetting."

Olivia tightened her lips into a disappointed expression. "You're doing it again, Detective."

She shut the door on him, then marched to the front door where her impatient daughter was waiting.

Maxim rolled down the window. "Olivia."

She spun around and stood in the driveway, waiting for his apology.

"I'm gonna need the name of her therapist."

She flinched, shocked that he was pursuing the matter. Her lips tightened. She didn't want to cooperate. She probably intended to tell him to go to hell.

"I'm a police detective, Olivia. I'm going to find out anyway. You might as well tell me."

After a quick glance to Annabelle, the woman moved to the car and lowered her voice. "Dr. Collins is an intelligent man who can help my daughter. I don't want you intimidating him."

Maxim shook his head softly. "I won't. That's not my intention." He suddenly felt awkward under her glare.

"Yeah? Well sometimes that's not so obvious."

Chapter 26

Diego watched Red from behind tree cover. He was interested in what the old man would do after the visit from police. Now that he thought he was alone, maybe he would tip his hand.

Unfortunately, his vigil was more tedious than when he'd been outside the post office, or Jason's house. Somehow, having the target in sight but being unable to act made it unbearable. Perhaps the biker's cramped pose, crouched in the brush and constantly in danger of being seen, contributed to the torture.

Diego thought he was on to something when Red stoked the fire in the barrel. This was the time to burn evidence. Instead, the tedium continued as Red fixed up a meal. What was worse: the preparations, while mundane, were disgusting. The old man beheaded and skinned a squirrel with a large chef's knife, stuck it to a spit, and set it to char. Diego didn't consider himself a picky eater, but he was from the city. Rodents did not constitute meals. The biker's stomach turned when the grilled aroma wafted to his position.

Eventually, thankfully, the meal ended. Red sat in his wheelchair a while longer, unrattled, before retiring to the hidden confines of the motor home. Diego waited to see if any other action would be taken, but the clearing remained quiet.

After he was confident the show was over, Diego snuck along the tree line, circling the RV. As he quietly moved through the brush, his heavy boot struck something solid. He dropped to his knee to examine a small copper cylinder. The metal was smooth and hollow, with an enclosed loop at one end. He hefted the weight in his hands and wondered what it was.

The biker shrugged and continued along the tree line, keeping his eyes on the ground. Soon enough, he smiled as he found another item. This time, it was a nondescript clay saucer. Its red surface wasn't polished but it didn't appear to be old, like something from a gift shop somewhere. He left it on the ground and continued searching, intrigued by the mystery.

Diego wasn't a clumsy person, but he realized he was focusing too much on the forest floor when his head banged into something. A crisp bell sound rang out. The biker backed up and saw another copper cylinder, this time hanging from a small branch above.

Immediately, the biker blanketed a gloved hand around the metal to silence it. He lifted the loose copper tube and held it alongside the other. The new one was almost twice as large, and seeing them side-by-side, Diego immediately figured out what they were: individual pieces of a wind chime. That was why the sound had been so crystalline.

Diego frowned and checked the RV. He was pretty sure the noise hadn't been loud enough to alert the old man, but that really just depended on how much he was listening. At any rate, no one stirred from within. After a few minutes, Diego figured he was safe.

His gloved fingers ran through his hair as he studied the wind chimes. They could have constituted a poor man's decor, except they weren't visible from the clearing. Just like Diego, the trinkets were hidden within the tree line. Likewise, the chimes were useless individually; without the ability to clack into each other, they couldn't make noise.

If they served a purpose, it was beyond Diego.

Now he made sure to scan the branches as well as the brush. On the north side of the clearing, he saw another piece of the wind chime. But there was something even more interesting.

In the thick trunk of a ponderosa pine, someone had etched a symbol into the bark. A circle, eight or nine inches in diameter, was emblazoned with a horizontal and vertical line right through the middle. It resembled crude crosshairs.

Now Diego was perplexed. The wind chimes were oddities since they were ultimately useless, but in a strange way he could chalk them up to an old man's eccentricities. The clay saucer was probably garbage, some lost piece of crap from the dollar store that was easily forgotten. But this symbol wasn't a random quirk. It meant something.

The biker considered what he'd learned so far. Assuming everybody was telling at least a portion of the truth, teenagers were harassing solitary hikers and hermits. Red had complained about kids stealing his stuff. These trinkets, then, could be a way of staking his territory. Of warning them off. Or they could be objects stolen by the kids and left behind when deemed useless.

The biker turned back to the motor home. The door was shut. The old man was inside. Apparently, he was staying there.

Scanning his surroundings, nothing enlightened Diego. He was getting distracted by junk.

The biker took a breath. Even though he couldn't see through the blackened windows of the RV, he decided to chance it. Since the rear right window was covered in plywood, Diego approached from that angle. It was the vehicle's blind spot. He closed the distance quickly so Red wouldn't see him, then leaned against the tire where he was hidden from anyone inside.

He could already hear Maxim chiding him later. What was he doing? What was his plan?

Diego bared his teeth. He didn't exactly have one. But that never stopped him before.

He slid along the RV until he reached the door and pressed his ear to it. There it was. The sound of Red, snoring. The old bastard was already asleep.

Diego's shoulders sagged. The thought of Red inside, helpless, made him realize what he was doing. He couldn't exactly attack the man. Confront him, maybe. But even then, to what purpose? As far as Red was concerned, the police had left him alone. Perhaps it was better for him to believe that everyone had moved on.

Before he could convince himself to break the door down, Diego rushed back to the trees. He ran deeper into cover and found a wide trunk to put his back against.

This wasn't copping out, he told himself. He just needed to be sure.

Diego slid to his haunches and let the adrenaline work through his system. A combination of indecision and helplessness took root in his thoughts. He began to feel outgunned. The world was against him. How shitty was that when all he wanted to do was find a little girl?

Something darted into his vision in the distance and Diego jerked up. He froze when he saw the source of noise and movement: a large elk stood not twenty feet from him. It was majestic at this distance, beautiful in its natural habitat, but it was also enormous. The bull must have been over eight-hundred pounds. Thick antlers exploded from its head and almost doubled the animal's height. The Arizona elk towered over the outlaw, even at a distance.

The two studied each other, motionless, for a long minute. Then, for no apparent reason, the elk bolted away. The thick brush engulfed it in seconds. Remnants of a small herd followed.

Diego couldn't look away from the empty space. The spot seemed special, somehow. Not just pristine, but hallowed. It was as if, all at once, Diego understood why

Annabelle yearned for the forest, why Red chose to live out here. There was a heartwarming pull to Sycamore. A draw to disconnect from society. To rediscover his primal urges.

And then he saw it. Another etching in the bark where the elk had been.

Diego slithered to it. It was the same symbol: a circle with a cross. This one was a bit smaller. It was below eye level, only a few feet off the ground, but it was unmistakably human.

For a reason he couldn't explain, Diego de la Torre ventured deeper into the woods.

He started north, close to ground already covered by the search parties. They were on the south side of the Interstate, and this area between the tracks and the highway was a crossing ground between Quiet Pines and Williams. If Hazel Cunningham had attempted to get home, she would have come this way.

Red's clearing was nestled above train tracks, but it wasn't long until Diego hit a set of double tracks. These, Diego knew, didn't head into Williams. They wound northwest into the desert to whatever existed in the openness of Coconino County. The biker avoided the tracks and tried to stay in wild ground, but he continued creeping to civilization. Route 66, Interstate 40, trailers, and access roads.

This wasn't right. If Hazel had been here, she would've been found.

Of course, the rescue effort had followed the same logic. Most of the search parties covered the wild ground north of the Interstate, closer to Sanctuary, nearer to where Annabelle had been. But this was a state park. There was plenty of nature to go around. With that in mind, Diego made an about-face and headed south. Past the RV. Past the latitude line of Williams. Finally, the woods took over.

Kaibab National Forest was one of several that dominated Arizona. The public parks converged in Sycamore, an area romanticized by the locals. West of Flagstaff, Sycamore was mostly forest but, like the national parks, included stretches of desert, mesa, and alpine tundra. The varied landscapes and wildlife were the attraction, the reason for the concentration of campgrounds in the area.

But there was a more sinister tinge to the woods than could be read about in any encyclopedia. Sycamore meant something to the locals. If not uncharted, it was unquantified, and its denizens knew to look over their shoulders.

Hazel Cunningham was only eight and never learned that sense.

As Diego pressed deeper into the growth, the darkness drew over him like a shade. The canopy was thick and only allowed stray fingers of sunlight to touch the earth. The environment quickly felt foreign, and Diego patted his left forearm. Beneath the black leather jacket was the solid comfort of his silver knife.

He wandered this way for some time, carried only by determination. Eventually that grit paid off. In the dim confines, he saw a flashlight wave. It wasn't a strong light, more of a point than a beam, but it was definitely unnatural.

As with the etching, this was powered by human hands, even if he couldn't see more than the bulb.

The bloom paused for a moment before rolling in a wide circle. It bounced up and down strangely. The biker ducked behind a tree as he watched, but for the life of him he couldn't make out what was going on. He decided to sneak closer.

The source of the light moved away from him and he followed. As Diego spied on the elusive dance, he realized Red was right. Someone was in this forest. And although Annabelle Hayes was found further north—past the Interstate and adjacent to Sanctuary—this was close enough to where Hazel had disappeared to be suspicious. Halfway between Williams and Quiet Pines, the police had searched this area as well, but nothing had come up.

Until now.

Diego was careful not to be seen. It was what he did best, at least until his efforts crumbled around him. But now he knew: if someone was sneaking around out here, they might be headed to Hazel's location.

For a brief moment, Diego considered the possibility that Red was innocent. But he remembered the locked room in the back of the motor home. He didn't believe the convenient story about his dead son's kilt. The skirt was too new to be a memory, even if it never belonged to Hazel.

Diego followed the glow for another hour. He was tired. Hungry. He realized he hadn't eaten all day. Watching Red cook the squirrel had suppressed his appetite, but it was now raging back with urgency. Diego pressed his stomach to appease the growl and blinked a little longer than he should have.

He walked into a branch and tripped. His foot was too heavy to catch himself. He landed in the dirt with a thud that knocked the air from his lungs.

The outlaw coughed and covered his mouth, doing his best to quiet his racket. Picking himself up to all fours, he forced heavy breaths into his lungs and searched for the light. It was there but moving farther. He was losing it.

As he pressed on, Diego wondered if they were heading north or south. He tried to place the sun, which was past its peak, but that was now impossible. The darkness consumed the world. Diego found it strange that he could see anything at all. And maybe he couldn't. Not that well. All except for a single fiery beacon frolicking away from him.

Something was wrong, thought Diego. He was disoriented. Maybe he'd hit his head. He paused and blinked, running his hands over his face and hair. Feeling too constrained, he slipped off his riding gloves and dropped them to the ground. His bare fingers massaged his closed eyelids. It barely helped.

Diego trudged forward again, wondering why his boots felt so heavy. They slowed him down. He should take them off.

That was stupid, wasn't it? He couldn't wander out here without his boots. But they were heavy, and he was tired.

Up ahead, the light hopped further away.

Diego bent to a knee. He unzipped his leather jacket the rest of the way and noticed a bulge in the pocket. Inside, he felt something cold and solid. When he checked his hand, it was the copper wind chime.

He grunted. Why had he kept this?

Diego chucked the wind chime to the floor and reached for his boot. The metal crashed into a stone and let out a sharp chirp before the ground silenced it. Diego panicked and hugged the ground, cursing himself for making more noise.

He made himself lie still. He needed to make sure he wasn't seen. Hazel depended on him. After some time, he meant to check on the flashlight in the distance, but the ground was too comfortable. He was already prone. Hidden. It couldn't hurt to wait just a little longer.

Chapter 27

Maxim was glad to be alone again. It wasn't just the awkward conversation with Olivia, it was the baggage. He wasn't accustomed to considering the social ramifications of his work. Even back when he was married, he was like this. Now that he thought about it, that may have contributed to why his wife left. But Maxim had never set false expectations. As a detective, he needed to be solitary so he could be agile.

For him, the price wasn't too high.

As he hit traffic on the Interstate, he cursed and watched more time slip away. He had a lot to get done today and it was already the afternoon.

Sycamore was an intersection of districts: cities, national parks, counties. It took some juggling to get a handle on it all. On the plus side, everything was pretty close.

Maxim finally exited back at Williams and pulled into the Williams Ranger District. It was the local office of the US

Forest Service. Diego's lead hadn't produced anything solid, and it was possible Maxim was wasting his time here, but something urged the detective to give things another look.

After announcing his arrival at the reception desk, a well-muscled man in his late twenties shook his hand.

"I'm Ranger Dan Briggs."

The man was solid, with a strong jaw and a crew cut of short blond hair. More surprising than his appearance was his gear. Besides the expected green pants and tan ranger shirt, he wore a brown vest stuffed with equipment: a radio, GPS, handcuffs, and a badge. With that also came the pistol strapped to his belt.

"Detective Maxim Dwyer. They outfit forest rangers with all this nowadays?"

"I'm law enforcement, Detective. Follow me." Briggs led him to his office, his broad shoulders barely squeezing through the doorway.

Maxim knew the national parks had law enforcement, but he hadn't dealt with them much. He was only going on five years as a detective, but even with his nine years of uniformed experience, Sanctuary investigations usually stayed within Sanctuary. The pros and cons of incorporation, he figured. Most of his outside contact had been with the Coconino County Sheriff's Office, who likely dealt with the Forest Service on a daily basis. Detective Harper had no doubt spearheaded the forest searches with the rangers.

"Is this about the missing kid?" asked Briggs, taking a seat behind his desk. "You didn't say over the phone."

Maxim was impressed the man had his own office. He nodded and sat opposite.

"Hazel Cunningham. It's only tangentially related. Maybe."

"Okay. What do you got?"

"Well, I've been doing exploratory work for Detective Harper."

"He's an asshole."

Maxim was taken aback by the forward comment, but he couldn't exactly disagree. "I don't know him a whole lot." Briggs nodded and let Maxim continue. "Anyway, in the course of my investigation, several names have come up. Locals going camping or living in the woods."

The ranger smiled. "Squatters, you mean?" Maxim wasn't sure but he nodded. Briggs leaned back. "There're all types of places to live out here. Lots of water tanks spread out from the frontier days. Lots of little huts and personal properties. Most sites are completely abandoned. But that hasn't stopped the squatters. They're becoming a real problem out here. Sometimes they hide in one location for months, damaging the woods and harming the wildlife. They create sanitation problems and are wildfire risks."

Maxim thought about Red's fire pit and the clearing away of trees.

"What's worse, every summer brings a new influx. The weather's too damn nice out here in the high country."

Maxim knew the term referred to the foot of the mountains. The Flagstaff area and Sycamore was rife with high country. "What about the ones with their own motor homes?"

Ranger Briggs chuckled. "The vast majority of squatters live in RVs or trailers these days. They usually live a few miles from town so they can resupply and take advantage of public services. Maybe even find work. They're not really roughing it like in old times, but it's still pretty hardcore. These days, most people panic when their Wi-Fi connection drops."

Maxim smiled. The ranger seemed fairly open and knowledgeable. He decided to put it all out there.

"There's a spot a few miles east of town, along the train tracks. There's a small clearing where the trees are all cut down and burnt."

"You're talking about Red. Is that old fool back?"

The detective was taken off guard. "You know him?"

"Oh yeah. He's one of the regulars. He likes that spot. It's called Echo Canyon."

"Really? It's not much of a canyon."

"No, it's not. I don't know where the name came from. Has Red broken the law? He's usually very careful."

"Well, isn't squatting illegal?"

"Squatting is. Camping isn't. Citizens are allowed to camp in national parks for up to fourteen days at a time before they need to pick up and move. Some of these guys find a remote spot and hide out as long as they can, but the smart ones constantly hop around like clockwork."

"That makes it legal?"

Briggs nodded. "Not only that, you have three national forests in this area: Kaibab, Coconino, and Prescott. And that's not counting Tonto and Apache-Sit closer to Phoenix."

"So you're saying Lachlan Munro has a lot of options, including infrequent stays at paid campgrounds."

"Yeah. He's a bit batty. You know, he has a thing for trains, but that's nothing considering how truly wacky some of these hermits are. They're the wild homeless, with the full array of mental problems that go along with the label. Red's usually pretty civil around us. You think he's tied up with the missing girl?"

"I don't know," said Maxim, which was the truth. "I'm just vetting him. Getting a feel for his routine, if that's okay. I noticed he has Texas plates."

"Nah, he lives here for the most part. These guys just need a permanent address, you know, for Uncle Sam."

Maxim thought it interesting that Lachlan had used the same expression. "So no matter what's on paper, his practical neighborhood is Sycamore?"

The ranger smirked. "I don't like that name. It's completely unfounded. All the land tracts out here have proper names."

"What else would you call the area?"

"Well, if you're speaking about a municipality or county, you already have a name. Or you can refer to the name of the national park. Or," said the ranger, putting his hand up to interrupt Maxim's protest, "since I know what you're going to say, you can refer to the local area as the Sycamore Canyon Wilderness."

"Okay, Briggs. I'll bite. What's that?"

"It's a federally protected wildlife area governed by the US Forest Service. Most maps don't bother listing them because people care more about the names of parks and counties. The Sycamore Canyon Wilderness overlaps three national parks. It also runs over Coconino and Yavapai counties, as well as a number of smaller municipalities."

"Huh," said Maxim. "And here I thought Sycamore was a purely colloquial term. So you have a problem with what then? People shortening the official name?"

"It's not just that, Detective. If someone talks to me about the Sycamore Canyon Wilderness, then I know they're referring to an area of land—trees, animals, you get the picture. But when the locals start hooting and hollering about Sycamore, they're really talking about something else. They're talking about vampires and werewolves and ghosts. They think these woods are haunted."

Maxim chuckled. "You'd be surprised."

"Don't tell me you believe that stuff?"

For the first time, Maxim lied. "Not really, but you find yourself alone in the woods a lot, don't you? You're telling me you've never seen or heard anything strange?"

Briggs leaned forward and considered the question with a strange expression. He probably wondered if Maxim was pulling his chain. "There's lots of strange activity in the wilderness every day. As a detective, I'm sure you've seen your fair share." The ranger studied Maxim for a second before laughing and leaning back. "Just last week I arrested a man covered in a gallon of his own urine who tried to assert dominance over a black bear. He's lucky he wasn't mauled."

Fair enough, thought Maxim. The secrets of Sycamore were not openly taken seriously, even to longtime residents. Maxim himself used to be one of those residents, before he knew better. But then he remembered Jason Bower's words. "What about stories of kids living out there? Singing songs, crying, stealing stuff."

That made the ranger laugh. "I don't know about kids, but Red's complained about harassment before. He said they were chasing away his food."

"He's a hunter?"

Briggs shook his head emphatically. "Not of protected game. Not that I'm aware of. The coot eats squirrels and other varmints."

Maxim forced away a grimace. "Anything come out of his complaints?"

"Nothing was there in the first place and that's how it stayed. Red disconnected from society. He's not a taxpayer. We don't spend a lot of time investigating his whims. Don't get me wrong. If he's in trouble, we'll help, but he's where he is because he wants to be left alone. He expects it."

It was a good enough answer. The old man didn't have concrete evidence. He rambled about a lot of things. Even Maxim didn't take him too seriously. This right here was just due diligence.

The detective rubbed the growth on his neck and sighed. Briggs had given him a lot of background, but he wasn't sure how much it advanced his investigation. "Do you have any theories, Ranger?"

"Come again?"

"Any theories on where Hazel might be, lost or hiding."

Dan Briggs flexed his jaw twice as he mulled it over. "These woods get extremely dense at night. Several train tracks intersect with various roads and highways. The lights and shadows can get dazzling. The girl might be hiding in one place this whole time and it wouldn't be surprising that we haven't found her yet. That's how much space we're talking about here. I'm about to coordinate with some Coconino deputies to kick off another search. They say it might be the last one. You want to come?"

Maxim winced. He didn't like the ranger's words but, as the days wore on, they were more than likely correct. At some point this operation would transition from rescue to recovery.

Chapter 28

Instead of returning to the station, Maxim continued east on the Interstate another fifteen minutes into Flagstaff. Sanctuary was more or less a satellite of the larger town. Even though his jurisdiction was limited to Sanctuary, his investigations often took him to Flagstaff. Weekly, sometimes even daily, trips were common.

Lachlan Munro was a person of interest, but Maxim couldn't help feeling it was a wild goose chase. He couldn't simply shake down every weirdo he encountered—in the Sycamore wild, that would take all year. In this case especially, he wasn't sure it was the best use of his time. Investigating Hazel's disappearance wasn't a problem for him, but his official responsibility was Annabelle Hayes. He couldn't forget about her. Besides, he still thought he could help them both at the same time.

Maxim parked on the street outside a three-story building in Old Town. He saw the name on a sign by the elevator and went to the second floor. In the office, an older woman greeted him at the reception desk.

"Is Bertrand Collins in?" he asked.

The woman gave him a pointed look. "Dr. Collins?" she corrected, stressing the title. "Yes he is. Do you have an appointment?"

Maxim shook his head and showed his badge. "I'm the police." He expected a lecture but she buzzed her boss over the intercom and he strolled out.

"Yes?"

Bertrand Collins was a diminutive man. His salt-and-pepper hair receded over his temples, and his wire-frame glasses gave him a cold demeanor. He wore a flat-colored sweater over a collared shirt. Slim, tidy, and exacting were Maxim's first impressions.

"Hello, Dr. Collins. My name's Maxim Dwyer. I'm with the Sanctuary Marshal's Office."

"Of course," he said. "You were the one who rescued Annabelle." He shook Maxim's hand then guided him into his office.

Maxim's initial impressions of the man were reinforced by the room. He was welcomed into a sunlit corner office with glass windows from ceiling to floor. The furniture was modern and stylish. A tufted leather chaise with skinny metal legs. An all-glass coffee table piled with architecture picture books. A single white chair with a black cushion sat opposite a fabric couch. The man's desk was shoved against the far wall, out of the way. From the books to the papers to the statuettes, everything was meticulously spaced out and ordered.

"I must apologize," said Bertrand Collins. "I need to keep this brief. I have an appointment in twenty-five minutes and I still need to prepare." The man sat in the small white chair and gestured at the sofa across from him.

Maxim wandered to the desk instead, studying the office. "You know, I tried calling you beforehand but couldn't get through."

"No?" He cleared his throat. "Martha didn't mention anything—"

"I called your cell phone. I looked it up and thought it would be better to deal with you directly."

Recognition flashed across Bertrand's face. "Ah, I understand. I have a strict no-cell-phone policy during my sessions. My patients are required to turn their phones off. I do too. It helps ground our conversations and give them immediacy."

Maxim nodded absently. He wasn't really concerned about Bertrand not answering his phone. He was just chatting. Getting a feel for the man. Looking around. He examined the framed certificates and diplomas on the wall. "You're a doctor?"

Bertrand nodded. "I am, fully licensed. Psychotherapy is only a portion of my workload. I perform research for several mental health facilities in the area. But I suppose you are here regarding my sessions with Annabelle and Olivia."

Maxim turned to the man. "You provide therapy for Olivia as well?"

He smiled. "I have in the past. Gulliver and Olivia both,

during the separation. But I misspoke. My regular appointments are with Annabelle only."

Maxim moved to the sofa and took a seat. He wondered if Annabelle chose the chaise or the couch when she was here. "Well, you're right," he started. "Annabelle's the reason for my visit."

Dr. Collins nodded. "I hesitate to inform you of the law, as I'm sure you're well aware, but I'm not able to divulge specifics that were related to me in confidence."

"That's fine, Doctor. I'm not here to psychoanalyze her. But confidentiality doesn't apply when an individual's in danger." Maxim noticed Bertrand was about to object and beat him to it. "That doesn't mean I'm asking you to dish the dirt. But you have to understand that Annabelle may have information that could help find another missing girl."

"Ah." Dr. Collins adjusted the thin glasses on his nose as he weighed the request. "Of course, I don't know anything about that, but I can certainly do my best to assist you. Why don't you tell me exactly what you need?"

Maxim sighed and considered how best to vocalize his problems. "I don't feel like I'm effectively getting through to Annabelle. I'm not sure if she thinks what happened to her is a game, or even if she knows anything that can help. But she's not..."

"Forthcoming," finished the doctor. "Yes. I'm sure you've noticed she throws up walls at the slightest signs of discomfort." Maxim nodded. The psychologist's voice was even and soothing, instructive and understanding at the same time. "Generally speaking, it is common for children to suffer from feelings of abandonment after a divorce. Disconnecting from others is a defense mechanism, especially in high-stress situations. Dealing with strangers, for example."

"Or being lost in the woods?"

Dr. Collins shrugged.

"The thing is, Doctor, I feel like she wants to talk to me. Or to someone, at least."

Bertrand clenched his jaw as he attempted to retain the confidence of his client. Maxim let the conversation linger on that statement until the psychologist felt compelled to say something.

"I recommend patience above all else, Detective. Annabelle needs a normalized environment."

"There's no time for... normalizing."

Bertrand Collins nodded that he understood. He put a hand to his chin and mulled it over. "I'm not sure what else there is to do. If it helps, at Olivia's insistence, I did chat with Annabelle yesterday. Quite the right call, if you ask me, after what happened. Our talk helped her process the experience."

"Did she tell you she ran away from home with her BFFs?"

The man raised his eyebrows. "Best Friends Forever. Very amusing, Detective. Yes, I can answer this line of questioning since it falls outside my therapy with Annabelle. Running away is often a plea for attention. Her friends, as you call them, are a bad element she clings to in order to stand out. The dark eyeliner and anti-establishment rhetoric come with the territory. Do you have kids, Detective?"

The question took Maxim off guard. He shook his head silently.

"I see. In any case, it's quite normal for preteens and teenagers to become rebellious and stray from home. She's testing her boundaries." Maxim knew he didn't look convinced and the doctor cleared his throat to try again. "In my professional opinion, her defiant behavior is nothing more than a method of acting out. A plea for attention. I'm much more concerned with her ongoing depression and disassociation." He leaned forward. "Between us, of course."

Maxim wasn't sure he would dismiss running away as an empty threat after the girl had been missing for three days. The open question was whether that was her intention or not, whether she was alone or with someone else, forced into it or not. It was reassuring, at least, that the doctor acknowledged there were deeper issues than the ones on the surface.

Now that they were sharing, Maxim got back on topic. "So did Annabelle tell you where she went?"

"She did."

"And?"

"And Annabelle revealed to me what happened in confidence. Even her mother doesn't know."

Maxim leaned forward. "Dr. Collins, there's another little girl lost in the woods as we speak. If anything from Annabelle's experience can point me in a direction, I'm gonna need to know."

Bertrand Collins hesitated and shook his head.

"Detective..."

"*Doctor*," intoned Maxim. "You said it yourself. Annabelle needs time to normalize. To heal. Either I can keep going at her or I can get what I need from you. Once I find Hazel Cunningham, I can give Annabelle all the time she needs."

The psychologist considered the request and sighed. "For the sake of my patient, I would help you if I could. Unfortunately, Annabelle claims the entire episode was a prank. I'm only revealing this to you in hopes that you stop focusing on Annabelle's weekend and instead look for the missing child in some other manner." Bertrand waited expectantly and Maxim nodded for him to continue. "They all camped just outside Sanctuary. At one point she ventured off on her own, purposefully. It's my estimation that she doesn't truly enjoy the companionship of those friends. As I've mentioned, she uses them to act out. They may do the same with her. Sometimes I wish I could get sessions with them as well."

Maxim exhaled sharply. He doubted the other families could afford the doctor. Besides, the psychoanalytical details of the family were not a big help to him. He was interested in tracking down facts. Tangible links of a chain that led to Hazel or where Annabelle had been.

"But where was she, Doctor? Where did she run off to?"

Bertrand's deflated expression revealed the answer before he spoke. "I don't know that, Detective. She camped outside Sanctuary. That's all I know. She never mentioned seeing anybody else besides the aforementioned friends, and I believe her. But if it's important to the investigation, I'll ask her directly when I see her next. I'm unfamiliar with Sanctuary and the surrounding area, unfortunately, but if there are any pertinent details gleaned, I will get them to you."

Maxim fell back into his seat. It was clear the girl was careful even with her therapist. Either she would eventually confide in Maxim, or no one would ever know exactly what happened to her.

"Here's the thing," offered the detective, changing tack. "Annabelle's mother is kind of shutting down my access to her."

Bertrand chuckled, then waved it off when he noticed Maxim's annoyance. He removed his glasses and wiped them. "I'm sorry, Detective. I don't mean to make light of your situation. It's just that I can picture Olivia doing as much. She can be very..." Bertrand trailed off and put the tip of his glasses to his mouth, a smile on his lips.

Maxim finished the doctor's sentence now. "Forward."

Bertrand Collins jerked his head back and returned his glasses to his head. "Yes, Detective."

It was a strange moment of wistfulness. Maxim wondered if there had been anything between Olivia and the psychologist. As their marriage counselor, that must have been one hell of an ethical dilemma. Then again, perhaps Bertrand was simply a professional who fantasized about Olivia. Maxim remembered in exquisite detail what her body looked like under her bathrobe. He couldn't blame the doctor for the same attraction.

"Unfortunately," continued Bertrand, "Olivia is the best person to make that call. For the record, I agree with the decision. We have to also consider Annabelle's physical state. Her physician is requesting bed rest and the week off school. In order to heal, Annabelle requires the space and normalcy of home life. You are the opposite of that, Detective."

Maxim shifted uncomfortably. The conversation was going in circles. When he didn't say anything, Dr. Collins glanced at his watch and straightened his sweater.

"I'm out of time."

They stood. Maxim had no problem getting out of there. He wasn't getting any psychological epiphanies anyway. He thanked the doctor, who walked him to the door.

"I know you don't want to hear it, Detective," said Bertrand, his face painted with resignation, "but the last thing Annabelle needs right now is to be subjected to an interrogation about something she had no involvement in. I won't presume to suggest how you should continue your investigation, but there's nothing Annabelle knows about that other missing child."

Maxim grunted dismissively. That sounded exactly like investigative advice to him, and he didn't like it. After a moment's hesitation, he decided to end the conversation with a gruff nod and returned to the elevator in silence.

Chapter 29

The old brick office was empty, but the buzzing of the fluorescent lights overhead and his well-worn desk chair were enough company for Maxim. This was where he was most comfortable. Everything was so familiar, sometimes even more so than his home.

His desktop PC was the one piece of technology that intruded on his carefully arranged sanctuary. The station had finally gotten the budget for new computers. The sleeker monitors were nice but the operating system frustrated him. It was designed with mobile users in mind, which had its perks, but when Maxim sat down at a workstation he wanted to be a power user. When he was in the groove of an investigation, the last thing he needed was to be confused about the mechanics of what he was doing.

Luckily, the detective was finally getting the hang of it. It had taken several weeks and, at thirty-four years old, Maxim feared he was approaching the hump in his life. The turning point. From here on out, technology might begin to distance itself from him, a slow trickle that wasn't immediately noticeable. Instead of untapped excitement every time a new program or app arrived on the scene, Maxim might grumble, or reminisce about the good old days. It would take extra effort simply to keep up until, one day, he would give up completely.

Jeez. Is that what the rest of his life was going to be about?

Maxim printed some pictures related to the case. He didn't need hard copies but they helped him focus. Introspection was unwelcome now. His life would happen, one way or another—it was the rest of Hazel Cunningham's life that he needed to worry about.

Maxim collected the three color photos from the printer and sat back down. He placed the portrait of Annabelle Hayes on his desk. Next to it, Hazel joined her. Besides a four-year age difference, the girls seemed set apart by personality. Both smiled, but their expressions couldn't have been more different. Hazel's lips stretched into dimples, her eyes pinched tight. There was mirth and wonder in her face, a nervous unease in her pose. It was innocence, untainted. Annabelle, on the other hand, was sly. Her smile was controlled, self-confident. Like her mother's. Her expression placid. She didn't appear upset but she wasn't engaged. Something was absent.

Disconnected.

That led to the final picture Maxim placed between them. Lachlan Munro. Red. The old man's photo was stoic and business-like. It was the latest on file from the Texas DMV. Red's was a face that didn't reveal much except for its physical characteristics. The man in the picture was younger, a snapshot from eight years earlier. He was skinnier. His hair shorter and styled, but it looked odd. When Maxim had met Red in person, his hair was a bright red sheen that reflected the sunlight. In this photograph, a dull burnt-orange barely stood out from the gray.

So the man dyed his hair. It was a small concession to vanity. But considering the character it came from, a hermit who ejected himself from society, it was a strange detail.

Maxim stared at the three frozen faces, searching for any connection. The ties were barely circumstantial but the triangle of photographs felt right together.

Like family.

Olivia Hayes lived a comfortable life now, although that hadn't always been the case. There was a time she resided with her truck-driving husband in Bellemont. It was a good bet that family had never been happy. The pair had often fought. So when Olivia ran into money, the split was inevitable.

It was hard to say whether Annabelle was better off before or afterward.

Julia Cunningham was also a single mother, but her family had been struck by a different tragedy. She'd married her high school sweetheart due to an early pregnancy. Her husband died two years later serving in Afghanistan. Julia, while devastated, was accustomed to going it alone, and although their family had a sadder story, so far Hazel was reported to have been doing great.

The family of Lachlan Munro was a mystery. He claimed to be an immigrant from Scotland, for which Maxim had failed to dig up proof. Red's lifestyle hadn't left much of a paper trail. There were no records at all of his early life, and no signs of family.

Red was a sixty-eight-year-old man. If his story of having a son who was killed was true, Maxim could find no record of it. But that would have been many years ago in another country. Those files likely weren't digitized yet, but maybe they could be tracked down. That was assuming, of course, that Red's identity wasn't fictional.

Maxim went back to the computer. Sometimes people got lost in the system, but it was exceedingly difficult for vehicles to do so. Red's old RV was purchased from a used lot in Texas twelve years ago. As Dan Briggs had mentioned, the Texas registration was one of convenience. A popular RV club based in Livingston handled all the legal back end he needed. The state had no income tax and no personal property tax. The RV club was listed as Red's permanent address on record, and they offered mail forwarding to all their members. Currently he was receiving in a Williams post office box, which was how Diego had tracked him down.

Two years after buying the motor home, and a decade ago, Red was in Arizona. A Grand Canyon National Park ranger had written an overstay citation for the old man. He'd broken the rules and stayed in one park longer than fourteen days, a far cry from his diligent routine today. That probably meant he'd been new at the life. Since then he'd barely relocated, not fifty miles south, and lived in relative obscurity.

But there were traces of Red on the move. Texas required an annual vehicle inspection. Every October the old man returned to his home state to have the RV checked. On top of that, he'd received a parking citation in Galveston and a traffic citation in Wichita, Kansas. The tickets came years apart but both were in November, forcing Maxim to conclude that Red's annual trip to Texas afforded some additional sightseeing.

None of this, of course, was any cause for suspicion, and Maxim began to fear the worst. Not just that he was wasting his own time, but that he was wasting what little Hazel had left.

Chapter 30

When his senses returned, everything was at peace.

Diego was cold and wet. He scanned the darkness and knew it was blacker than before. It was already past sunset.

The biker jerked to a sitting position. He turned—panicked for the slightest of moments—but he was alone. The serenity was not an illusion.

The woods looked different now. It wasn't just a play of the low light; he was in a different physical location than he last remembered. Not that he could recall much. He'd been alone. Searching the forest. He was following... someone.

Hunger pangs tore at his side and commanded his attention. His stomach wasn't just reminding him to eat, it was scolding him. His survival instincts took over.

Diego checked himself over. He wasn't wounded. There was no clear reason he'd passed out. It had to still be the same day.

This was one of those occasions when he wished he

carried his phone with him. Checking the date would have gone a long way towards settling his nerves, but he liked the transient feel of life without the clock. Without being tied down. Frankly, the best use for his phone right now would have been as a flashlight.

Instead, Diego searched his pockets. The wet leather pulled at his skin. Strangely, the copper wind chime tube was missing. It wasn't in his jacket or pants, meaning he must have dropped it. Diego wiggled on the floor and pulled the plastic lighter from his pocket. Good thing he'd started smoking again.

The flame illuminated enough to get a better look. Diego was wet from head to toe, but the dirt next to him was dry. He pulled off his steel-toe boots and wrung his socks out. It didn't help warm him up much.

He stood up. Spikes of pain surged through his legs. They were sore from walking already. That was too soon, he thought. A gym workout would take a day for the large muscles in the leg to burn. Maybe he *had* been sleeping longer than he thought.

He clicked the lighter on again. A few yards away, the shine of silver caught his notice. A knife was stabbed into the dirt. Diego felt at the sheath on his wrist and was amazed to find the blade missing. That was his knife in the ground.

He went to recover it and noticed it had been used to scratch a symbol into the earth. A circle, two feet in diameter, with two intersecting lines traced through it. The knife was plunged directly into the center of the cross.

The biker hesitantly plucked up the blade. It was his prized silver hunting knife, undamaged. He wiped it off and returned it to his wrist. Someone had known about it—or found it—and drawn this symbol in the dirt. It could only have been Red.

The implications of the situation dawned on him. Diego had been searched while unconscious. The knife had been procured to deliver a message, but much worse could have been done with the weapon. Diego's life could have been taken.

Whoever it was—Red or someone else—they had decided to spare him.

Chapter 31

It took Diego more than an hour to find his Scrambler. Luckily, he stumbled onto the tracks and followed them back to Red's place. He walked the bike in the quiet of the night until he was far enough away to rev it up and get out of there.

His little apartment in Sanctuary was a welcome sight. Diego's legs almost gave out as he dismounted. He shuffled to his door, thankful he didn't live on the second floor. At this point, the concrete steps would've made a more inviting bed than obstacle.

Because of his weakened state, Diego didn't notice the person inside the parked car he passed, or that the driver exited and followed him. It could've been a costly mistake in different circumstances.

"Diego?" The biker spun around and almost tripped backwards. Julia's voice was hesitant. "I've been calling you all day. Where've you been?"

The biker backed up and relaxed against his apartment door. "I didn't see you. Why are you here?" He tensed. "Do you have any news?"

An expression of sorrow overtook the mother's face. She almost broke out into a cry. "No. I was hoping you did."

Diego released a heavy breath from the depths of his soul. He wasn't sure what to say. He'd promised this woman his best yet couldn't even account for the majority of his day. He knew he was on to something with Jason and Red, but he couldn't make sense of it. Not yet. Nor could he wrap his head around why he'd passed out in the forest.

And after all that, Diego now needed to face Julia and tell her he'd failed to find her daughter. Of his many problems, that was the worst.

Diego put his arms around her. He supported her weight just as she supported his. It was comfortable there, in the silence, and he thought that at least there were some good things in this world.

"Come on inside," he said, turning the key in the door. He tried removing his jacket but it was too difficult to stretch his arms back. He gave up.

"Why are you all wet?" Julia asked.

He groaned. It was the best response he could come up with.

"Look at you," said Julia. "You're exhausted. You need to rest. When was the last time you ate anything?"

Diego shrugged. His mind was clouded, half from the elements and half from noticing just how beautiful Julia was. He didn't have any brainpower left to remember when he'd eaten.

Julia escorted him to the couch. She pulled his jacket off and sat him down. As she removed his boots, he noticed his cell phone on the cushion beside him. The notification light blinked. He'd probably gotten several messages from her today. The poor woman had been desperate for any word from him.

"Just rest there. Let me see if you have anything in the kitchen."

Diego inhaled deeply. He was so relaxed that he didn't bother telling Julia she'd find an empty refrigerator.

"What do you eat?" she asked.

"Anything but squirrel."

"What?"

Diego shook his head at the bad joke. "There's some stuff in the cabinet."

He heard a few doors open and close, then she entered the living room holding a can of food. "You can't be serious. SpaghettiOs?"

"Ooh, yeah, that," he answered. He ignored her glower, and something about his pained face must have caused her to give in.

"Oh, all right. Be right up in two and a half minutes." Julia found a bowl and the can opener and put the food in the microwave. "You know, you live like a kid." As she waited, she whistled a singsong melody. It was unfamiliar but catchy.

Diego smiled and shut his eyes. If he'd known Julia was going to cook for him, he would've bought a porterhouse or something. But it was nice enough to be able to kick his feet up on the table and wait. In the meantime, he listened as Julia whistled. It was a sad tune that sounded old, like a long lost nursery rhyme. He imagined being a kid, lying on a blanket in the grass, basking in the sun. It wasn't a memory, but a vision. Just a sense instilled in him by the melody. It made him think of family.

Julia surprised him when she put the bowl down and sat beside him. His eyes flicked open.

"Okay, eat up now."

The man leaned forward and did as he was told. "What was that?" he asked after a few bites.

"What?"

"That song."

"Oh. I didn't even realize I—" Julia suddenly quieted. The peace abandoned her face and she took a moment before answering. "It's just something I sing to Hazel when I cook for her. She likes to help out..."

Her words trailed as their destination became meaningless. Julia fought off a tear. Diego put his arm around her.

"I'm sorry. I didn't mean to mention..."

"It's okay. It's not like I can forget her. But sometimes, like when I first wake up, or when I'm not paying attention, I almost forget, just for a second, that she's missing. And then, when I realize, it's like my entire body wants to seize up."

Diego tightened his grip. "It's nice to remember," he said. "The song. It's lovely. I promise you that you'll be whistling it to her again."

Her glassy eyes bobbed between different points on his face. Her lips jerked but froze. Almost a smile, he thought. When her gaze avoided his, Diego put his hand to her chin and lifted her head. Their faces were inches away.

"I promise," he repeated. His voice was confident and smooth, and he meant every word of it. And although he really wanted it, what happened next was not his intention. Diego de la Torre leaned in for a kiss.

"Don't do that!" Julia shot to her feet and threw her fists to her sides. "Don't do that. You can't say that. You can't keep telling me that." She brushed away his reaching arms and left the room, slamming the bathroom door behind her. She ran the faucet but Diego could hear the sobbing anyway.

What an idiot he was. He didn't know why he'd done that. Making moves on the mother while the daughter was missing—it was disgraceful. And his words, they were supposed to be reassuring, but what if they were a lie?

Diego took another bite of canned pasta and his face twisted in disgust. He studied the spoon with the sticky red sauce on it before dumping it into his unfinished bowl. He needed to get his shit together. And not just for himself.

Diego snatched up his phone to call Maxim for an update. The notification light blinked again. He decided to check his voicemail first. He deleted a message from Julia and a hang up, but the third message was from Maxim making good on his promise to call.

"Listen, Diego, it's Maxim. Things... I don't want you to

get your hopes up. It's been a slow day."

The biker rolled his eyes.

"I'm only calling because I told you I would, but there's not much to say. The therapist wasn't much help. He said more than he should've but he doesn't know anything. I don't think Annabelle trusts him."

"Big surprise," said Diego to the recording. "What about Red?"

"I'm gonna take another stab at her. I know I can get through. I just need to figure out what it'll take to convince her."

Diego repeated, "What about Red?"

Maxim breathed into the phone. "I saw something in her face today. In the car, when I dropped her off. I think she finally believed me. That I want to help."

Diego snorted loudly as if the voicemail could respond to him. "What about Red?"

Maxim cleared his throat. "As for Munro..."

Diego smiled.

"We still don't have a whole lot on him."

Diego cursed.

"I think we've been derailed here," continued the detective. "We're trying to force pieces together that don't fit, and it's not getting us anywhere. Tomorrow morning, I'm going to restart the investigation from the bottom up. Don't worry. That sounds worse than it is, but it's a common procedural technique when we hit dead ends. It might not feel like it, but we know a lot more than we did two days ago. Looking at all the evidence and clues with a fresh start might trigger..."

Maxim kept talking, but Diego tuned him out. He heard the false assurance in the detective's voice. The man wasn't hopeful anymore, not on the inside. Diego also heard Julia, still crying in the bathroom. She still clung to hope, but it was tearing her apart. And if it turned out that she was only holding onto air, she'd float away with it.

The outlaw tightened his grip on the phone. He'd done what he was supposed to do. He'd turned to his friend. The police. He'd held back. And it hadn't gotten him anywhere.

When the message ended, Diego deleted it without a second thought. He would now need to do this his way. The hard way. Opening up old wounds would be uncomfortable, but Diego couldn't think about himself anymore. When the law no longer worked, it needed to be cast aside.

Diego was about to hang up his phone when another message started. It was Harry Pendle, his boss at the tow yard.

"Hey look, Diego," he started meekly. "I'm sorry about that missing girl and everything. You've got a nice heart, but... you're irresponsible as fuck, man. You're just not a reliable person. I think it would be best if we just parted ways, okay? Just... just don't bother coming back to work. Sorry."

Diego hung up. Maybe Harry was the smart one here.

Chapter 32

Diego swallowed hard as he stared at the woman through the chain-link. Kayda Garnett crouched beside several schoolchildren in the playground. The Yavapai reservation elementary school did not appear well funded, but if they had anything aplenty, it was dreary desert space. Some of the kids climbed the faded jungle gym equipment and others played in the sand, but the other half attended their mentor on the flat swath of concrete. Bars of colored chalk scattered the walkway as boys and girls alike drew images.

Kayda was pretty, with a tan that belonged in the sunshine. She was naturally affable and worked well with the children. It was good to see her face again. Diego remembered a time when she was receptive to his charms, but the extent of that relationship was a single flirty conversation.

Diego didn't have regrets. He didn't know if anything had been there, anyway. But he did feel the burden of

Kayda's ire. What Diego had done was necessary but unforgivable in her eyes.

Diego's boot scrubbed the sidewalk. He knew he couldn't afford to stall any longer. He hadn't spoken to Kayda in almost a year, a part of his self-imposed exile. He knew he had to break the oath for the sake of Hazel Cunningham.

Finally willing the boot to take a step, the biker moved to the entrance. He didn't know what he expected, but it wasn't Hotah Shaw leaning against the gate at the opening. More faces from the past. More enemies for the present.

"I had my money on you turning tail after a quick look."

The man flexed his strong arms across his chest. His wild hair covered most of his face, but not enough to miss the glint of hatred in his eyes. Hotah was one of the reservation's top enforcers, and Kayda's personal bodyguard. Diego had dealt with men like him before, but Hotah was dangerous because he was precise. In the outlaw world, he was a survivor, and the only one of the old regime to remain standing. Just the fact he was still alive was a testament to his abilities.

Diego squared his body to the side, keeping his knife arm away from the man. "Believe me," he said, "if it were up to me, I wouldn't even ask for that much."

Diego had agreed with him and been respectful—that didn't leave a lot of room for objection. Still, Hotah found a way.

"No Seventh Sons allowed on the reservation."

The biker shook his head. He was still friends with the

motorcycle club, but he'd left their ranks. "You know I cut all ties with them."

Hotah shrugged. "Kayda's an important woman now. She's busy volunteering with the kids."

Diego glanced her way, disappointed that she hadn't noticed him yet. She was holding a little girl's hand, tracing out a symbol in red chalk. Those glyphs. They were the reason he was here.

"I only need a few minutes."

"I can't help you."

"It's not your help I need."

Hotah stood up straight off the fence and broadened his body into an obstacle. "You can't get past me without my help."

Diego snorted. "So you're a glorified bouncer now?"

"Don't start, little man."

"You should know me better than that, Hotah. Last time you got on my bad side, things didn't go so well for you."

The man's face soured. "Don't mix things up. You fucked with my crew—with a lot of help—but you never laid a finger on me." Hotah clenched his fists in anticipation. "I see you, readying for that knife up your sleeve. You think you're fast enough to get it?"

"That's not why I'm here."

"Well, you can't kill Kayda's brother again, so why are you here?"

The words cut deep. Diego's reply dried up in his mouth. It was true; he'd dealt her brother a lethal blow. He'd slashed the wolf's throat with the very same silver knife strapped to his arm. But Diego had been strung up at the time, at the mercy of Hotah's old crew. The biker had tried to help Kayda, even after her brother turned on her, but the guilt of dealing that kind of blow to her family couldn't be shaken.

Diego eyed the woman again. This time with a different kid, her back to them. She didn't need this. His intrusion into her life. And he didn't need to get into a beef with this cocksure muscle head. Diego had crossed the line with the authorities two days ago. This situation was more risky because the tribal police were in Kayda's pocket. He knew it was dangerous to be here, even without his motorcycle club affiliation.

Diego retreated from Hotah and headed down the sidewalk, back to his bike. He shook his head as he stomached the insult of being turned away. He needed to stop finding himself backed into corners. Information didn't always need to be obtained through violent means. He could start thinking like Maxim, a real investigator. This fly-by-night thing was clearly not working out for him.

Diego started his Triumph and felt the power rumble beneath him. Something about the sensation sparked his mood.

Being the reasonable one wasn't in Diego's repertoire.

He revved the motorcycle loudly a few times. Everyone in the yard, including Kayda, finally noticed him. But that didn't mean he had their attention yet.

Diego bore full-speed toward the playground entrance. Hotah, who'd already laughed him off, spun around. Diego expected the man to swing, but when his tire jumped over the curb, Hotah was still in shock. His superb reflexes saved him from harm as he leapt away from the bike.

Diego sped past him and headed to Kayda. She stood as she began to understand the situation. She waited calmly as he swerved on the cement, giving a wide berth to the children.

But that precaution hadn't taken him near enough to the woman, and Hotah was faster than he looked. When Diego dismounted the Scrambler, the Yavapai enforcer tackled him.

The two men rolled on the concrete. Diego's thick riding gear protected him from scrapes, but he was more concerned about the overbearing strength of the man now on top of him.

"Not with the children!" shouted Kayda with authority.

Hotah—on one knee with an arm above his head to strike—stopped cold. Diego panted beneath the man, relaxing the arms he'd raised in defense.

"A well-trained dog, I see."

"Don't push it," said the woman he had come to see.

Diego shot her a slanted smile. She was right. He raised his hands in surrender.

Hotah glared at him but took to his feet and stepped back. Diego sat up and rested his arms on his knees. The children who weren't frightened were giggling. Diego winked at an especially precocious girl and gave her a nod for his performance.

Kayda wasn't as easily amused. "Okay kids, go play with

the others." Some of them objected but Kayda's face was firm, and the children all ran to the playground equipment. "You too, Hotah."

The man raised a single eyebrow.

"I'll be fine," she said.

Hotah cracked his knuckles and took up position at the gate entrance once again. Diego couldn't help but smirk as he ended up alone with Kayda. As he stood, he dusted off his leather pants and noticed the chalk drawings once again. Intersecting lines of brown and red dominated the artwork, all simplistic symbols that resembled cave drawings.

"Indoctrinating them young?" asked the biker, finally turning to Kayda.

The woman was younger than him, probably just twenty-two, but she had changed dramatically from when she'd first returned home last year. She was still slightly heavyset but stood with a more authoritative posture that matched her new personality. Gone was the lost little girl he'd once met. Kayda Garnett still possessed her worldly manner, but she'd taken to her half Yavapai side. She'd become more tan from long days in the Arizona sun. Feathers dangled from her right ear and long brown hair, and a string of tattoos, each with a signature style, banded her left forearm.

"I'll admit I'm surprised to see you here," she started. "I thought Kelan would do in spirit what he couldn't do in life."

"What's that?"

"Keep you away."

Diego dropped his gaze to the walkway. The mention of her brother was expected. He had to confront what he'd done to her if he wanted to get past it. But a simple apology was too trite.

"He was going to kill me, Kayda."

She nodded grimly. "I still haven't decided whether you deserved it."

"He tried to kill you too." The woman didn't respond, and he didn't give her a chance to. "Speaking of which, you look good for someone who took a bullet."

"Don't change the subject. The Seventh Sons have a lot to answer for."

"They're not that bad. They just want to operate unimpeded."

"It's their operations that concern me. The wolves of Sycamore are dangerous. They don't even have the guile to wear the clothing of the sheep they prey on."

Diego shrugged and rested a cigarette on his lips. New day, new pack. "It's nothing your clan isn't guilty of."

Kayda had been polite so far, but her face finally betrayed scorn. "That was the old way. The way of the wolf. The crow rules here now." The woman pointed to a chalk symbol at his feet. Diego realized he was standing on the symbol. He jumped backwards as if it were capable of biting him. The red circle surrounded a T with two vertical crossbars. The top one was larger and had a small triangle rising from the center.

"I may not have been around Prescott lately," said Diego, "but I've heard the stories. They call you the moonwitch."

Kayda smiled. "It's a customary title."

"Is it? That's what you're teaching these children? Customs?" Diego peered at the symbol. "That's a moon, isn't it? Or a sun because it's red."

"Your first instinct was correct. The color of the chalk represents the medium of the glyph, not the meaning."

"The medium?"

She nodded. "In this case, blood."

Diego shook his head. "You've got a hell of a way with children."

Kayda crossed her arms, annoyance marring her patience. "Blood represents strength. Vitality. It flows through every living thing and connects us all. The Yavapai know the importance of instilling a sense of place in the younger generations. A sense that there is more meaning to the world than which iPhone model they have."

Diego relented. He wasn't a fan of technology himself. He'd decided to stay in Sanctuary because of the freedom of the road. An office job glued to a monitor would never be for him, even if that meant driving a tow rig or operating a forklift. Or who knew what now.

Diego checked the yard and saw Hotah giving him the evil eye from afar. The biker raised the lighter to his cigarette and let the silence speak for itself. Still, he thought it best to change the subject more forcefully.

"What about that double-T thing with the triangle? What's that?"

Kayda Garnett put her hands on her hips. "I've already

told you."

Diego cocked his head, thinking back on their conversation. He didn't have a head for this kind of metaphysical stuff, but he was pretty sure they hadn't discussed the glyph yet. After a moment, he searched her face for the answer.

She shook her head. "You make a worse student than these nine-year-olds." Kayda crouched and pointed to the T. "This is a crow, the one who sees all. These lines are his great wings, and this tip his beak."

Cave scribbles. Diego could see it now, but it was crude. "And the blood? Why scrawl a crow and a moon in blood?"

The woman chuckled and looked away for the first time. It seemed she did have some secrets. "You didn't come here to speak of glyphs," said Kayda. "Yet you are commanded by a purpose. Out with it."

The biker raised an eyebrow. "That's where you're wrong." He leaned down to pick up a piece of chalk. The thought of blood didn't sit well with him so he chose brown. In a small empty space, he also drew a circle. Except within it he scratched out a cross.

"The lines are sloppy," said Kayda.

"That's how I saw them."

"What's going on, Diego?"

He sighed. "You know I wouldn't have come to you if I wasn't desperate. There's a man in the woods. He's linked to a missing girl somehow. I found several of these symbols scratched into the bark of the trees around his camp, and some deeper in the forest."

Kayda's eyes narrowed. "What kind of man?"

"Not an Indian, if that's what you mean. He said he was Scottish, born overseas, but now he just lives in the woods. But I'm getting the feeling he's not the important one. You see, I've been hearing rumors of children in the forests of Sycamore. Red—that's the man's name—says the kids have been hounding him. Stealing stuff. You should see the poor geezer. He carries around a metal pole everywhere he goes. Says he has a bum leg but walks fine. I think the crutch is a weapon. And the symbols, I think he's sort of marking his territory or something."

"A warning," interrupted Kayda. "If he lives among the trees, he could be steeling himself against a foe within." The woman stared at the symbol and frowned. "You should have drawn it in green."

"It was in bark. Wood's brown."

"But nature is green. Blood is power, nature is life." Kayda paused and studied Diego. "And death."

"Death," repeated the biker, lingering on the word for some time. "What are you saying these kids are?"

Kayda took time to measure her response. The very fact that she considered holding back convinced Diego he was in the right place. Those without knowledge couldn't keep secrets, after all.

"My people speak of this land as a home for the dead."

Diego grunted. "Sycamore has lots of stories."

"And you are well familiar with some."

"What, wolves? Disease? That's science. But you're talking about ghosts. I don't buy that."

"Science is simply the explanation," she said. "It's what makes the supernatural natural. It behooves the scholar to admit there are things in the world that are ill understood. I know the northern locals have fanciful imaginations. My people here are no different. But truth can sometimes be learned from fable. You of all people should know that, Diego de la Torre."

He snorted. "But ghosts?"

"Believe it or not, the spirits are very active here."

Diego turned his back on the woman and watched the kids playing. He also wanted to keep an eye on Hotah without being too obvious. Kayda was acting friendly so far —he just wasn't sure how long he could count on that goodwill.

"You get all that," said Diego, pointing to the glyph he drew, "from these crosshairs?"

"Emphasis on *cross*. There's a lot of power in that old symbol. Whether you believe or not, history has proven that many do. What better way to ward off vampires or demons?"

Diego rolled his eyes. "You were just selling me science. Now you're straying into religion."

"They are just points of view."

"Sure, but don't tell me you believe Sycamore is crawling with creatures of the night".

"I haven't yet encountered any," she answered. "Besides the Seventh Sons."

The concession was aggravating. "And Hotah."

"And my dead brothers," she finished. "But why limit

ourselves to the world we already know? The point is that lots of people over time have put faith in that symbol. It's a Celtic cross, a Christian cross, but ancient usage was different. Prehistoric cultures viewed the wheel cross as a representation of the sun. The Middle Ages saw this symbol adorned on many monuments, and the Victorians relegated it to gravestones. Many meanings. What's important is what the one who drew it believes."

Diego thought he understood. "So the glyph alone has no power?"

"I didn't go that far. But without context, power can be invisible. Intent can be misunderstood. Watch this." The woman crouched and picked up a red piece of chalk. She traced familiar lines on the sidewalk. "What do you see?"

"A swastika."

"Yes, but what does it evoke?"

"Nazis. White supremacists. Racism and evil."

The witch nodded. "Naturally. Except the gammadion cross is a symbol of well-being. Its significance ranges anywhere from holy symbol to good luck charm. Even so, modern usage has a habit of erasing old meanings. Something once sacred is now printed on Hot Topic T-shirts."

The biker scratched his goatee. "So symbols are reused and abused. They rarely mean today what they once did."

"Unfortunately," conceded Kayda. "And in this case, it's hard to understand everything from just your glyph." The woman frowned as a thought came to her. "You said this man in the woods carries a metal pole. It's widely believed that spirits and fairies don't like metal of the earth."

"You're talking about fairy tales."

"I'm talking about belief. Historically, iron guards against the fay. It's a life-giving metal. A vital component to our blood. It threatens them. If that's what the old man believes, it would explain his penchant for the metal."

"It's just metal."

"Funny words from a man armed with silver. But it's not just any metal. *Old* metal. Iron. Steel. Of the earth. Ask yourself what this man knows that we do not."

Diego thought of Red's weapon, spiked in the dirt while he was safely home but in his hands when trekking to the city. Over the tracks, he realized. Red always stuck to the old metal of the tracks.

"Protection," he said, and was pleased to see Kayda nod. He recalled the iron leg brace Red wore without seeming to need the support. How did that protect him? Then Diego studied his own boots, with buckles and toes of steel. He remembered his heavy legs in the forest, wanting to continue but needing to stop. He'd considered taking his boots off completely. Maybe the steel had protected him.

"That settles it, then. I need a gun."

"Lead won't help you."

"Let me worry about that part. It's dangerous out there. This is what I do." He began to walk away, then stopped and turned halfway to her. "There's a light. Someone. Or something. It knew I was following."

Kayda moved square to him again. "Don't fall for the glamour. The only light you need for guidance comes from the moon. The crow knows this."

"It's too dark," said Diego. "The trees cover the sun and moon. Besides, what if the moon's not out?"

"It's always out, even when in shadow. I thought you were the outsider most likely to know this, given your history with wolves."

"Fine," he said, dismissing the mystical moonwitch stuff. As Kayda had said, facts were filtered through perspectives. Some truth likely hid behind the stories. "What about the girl, then? How do I track her down?"

Kayda Garnett released Diego and turned away. She used the silence to consider her answer, but it also highlighted the futility of his mission. "That depends," answered the woman, "on whether or not she wants to be found."

Diego pictured Hazel with a crooked smile. A sweet and unassuming girl. He was positive she'd want to be back with her mother. Kayda's esoteric response couldn't have applied to her. But then he recalled Annabelle Hayes dashing into the forest, making a break from civilization.

"And what if she doesn't?"

Chapter 33

Olivia Hayes turned her nose up at Maxim. She threw him a hard look and spun around, her eyebrow raised just enough to let Maxim know his visit wasn't entirely unwelcome.

"You sure you won't have a glass of wine?" she asked for the second time, swirling a sparkling white in her hand. "I appreciate that you're taking an interest in me and my daughter, but you'd be more supportive if you eased up a little."

Maxim sighed and followed the woman into the living room. He relaxed into a cream leather couch and decided to play this differently. "Do you have something heavy and red?"

Olivia smiled and seductively rubbed the back of her neck. "Now you're just trying to be difficult. Let me see what I can open."

Maxim shrugged as the woman went to the kitchen. He didn't feel bad about making her open a bottle just for him

—she was the one who had pressed the issue—but the last glass of white he'd drunk was in memory of his late wife. If Maxim had anything to say about it, he'd never touch the stuff again.

After a minute in isolation, the detective rose. The house was large but not the type to get lost in. It couldn't hurt to look around. After lapping the room twice, he wandered into the hall.

Where the living room was prim and sterile, the den he entered was used and messy. The living room was a place to impress guests, but now Maxim found the real heart of the home, the part that was lived in. In place of a posed family picture on the mantel and a large impressionist painting, the den was strewn with personal items. A small blanket on the recliner next to a book. A set of fur slippers. Two magazines on the end table. The flat screen plugged into a cable box. But something struck Maxim as odd. The paperback was a trashy romance novel. The magazines were about home fashion. No video game systems or anything more modern like tablets were around. To the detective, it was clear this was Olivia's space. If he had to guess, Annabelle preferred her room.

On his way past, Maxim peeked into the kitchen but didn't see Olivia. He continued through and glanced up the wooden staircase. It was strange. Where was the girl?

Olivia appeared behind him and seemed to read his thoughts. "Annabelle's been in a pouty mood since yesterday."

Maxim accepted the glass of red. "Is that when it

started?" he asked.

"What do you mean by that?"

The detective shook his head. "Just trying to get into her headspace. That's all." Maxim tasted the red. He wasn't cultured enough to identify what he was drinking, but it tasted okay and had a bite.

Olivia beckoned him back to the sofa. When she sat, she tapped on the cushion beside her. Maxim chose the couch across from her. She smirked.

"You're a tough man to figure out, Detective."

Maxim sipped his wine. "Yeah? How so?"

Olivia leaned back and stretched her arm out in a sultry fashion. "It's obvious you're attracted to me."

Another gulp of red. After a moment, Maxim cocked his head. "Well, I don't see what's so hard to figure about that. I'm sure you're used to it. You're a very pretty woman. And single, from what I can tell."

"I'm not the only one without a ring on my finger," she said. Maxim's thumb instinctively moved to the spot above his knuckle, now barren of the silver band. "Are you going to tell me you've stayed distant because you're a professional?"

"Something like that, Ms. Hayes."

Olivia laughed. Maxim hadn't called her that in a while. It felt forced and artificial, and they both knew it. They drank in silence, but something told Maxim that while he thought the moment was awkward, the woman entirely enjoyed it.

Mercifully, she broke the silence.

"I hope I don't offend you by saying this, but you strike me as the type of police detective that gets emotionally invested in his cases."

"If you mean I care about the victims, I plead guilty. I want to get Annabelle all the help she needs. The same goes for anyone else."

Olivia swirled her glass of bubbly and frowned. "I don't want you visiting her anymore."

"Hazel—"

"I don't want to hear about other people's children. I can only do what's best for mine. If that means grounding her until she shows progress with Bertrand, then that's what I'll do."

Maxim nodded in disappointment. After yesterday's car ride, he hadn't expected anything more. But his suspicions acted up again.

"You're on a first name basis with the psychologist?"

"Dr. Collins?" she asked, moving back to formalities. "He's the family therapist. He said you two spoke briefly."

"He mentioned me?"

Olivia seemed bored with the questions. "In passing."

The detective wondered what words they shared about him but didn't bother asking. He asked a question he already knew the answer to instead. "So he has sessions with you as well as her?"

"He counseled me and my husband before we went through with the divorce. He also helped Annabelle get through it."

"If you ask me, she's never gotten through it."

Olivia sipped her wine. "Dr. Collins says there are residual issues. She was getting better until this recent episode."

Maxim nodded even though the doctor had conveyed a different impression to him. "Is your daughter at his office now?"

"No," said Olivia. "She's upstairs. But she's seeing him soon. Of course, you already know that. Don't play coy with me."

Maxim didn't take her meaning. Olivia saw the puzzlement on his face.

"Isn't that why you're asking? So you can interview my daughter under his eye?"

He shook his head. "I didn't know they had a session today. He said he just saw her Tuesday."

"He's here every Thursday morning. Tuesday was just an emergency. After getting Annabelle back on Monday, I couldn't wait."

Maxim couldn't blame Olivia. Annabelle barely said a word the first day she was back. But something else Olivia had said stood out to the detective.

"Wait. Do you mean the doctor comes here?"

Olivia didn't understand the question. "His weekly session."

"No, I mean Bertrand Collins comes to the house?"

"Yes. He holds a morning session in her room. She's safer under this roof. Besides, she's more comfortable there. She doesn't like going to his office."

Maxim glanced towards the staircase to make sure

Annabelle wasn't around. "Isn't it odd for a practicing psychologist with an office to pay house visits?"

"He's..." started Olivia, trailing off for a moment, "familiar with the house."

He knew it. Maxim shook his head and put his empty wine glass on the table. "Familiar, huh?"

The woman shrugged and stood up. "I'll get you another glass."

"Hold on a second."

Olivia turned around sharply. "Detective, I know what you're going to ask, and the answer is none of your business. All you need to know is that anything is long over and our relationship is strictly professional now." She cut out of the room before Maxim could respond.

So there was the wildcard Maxim was searching for. Annabelle's parents were divorced, and Olivia had a relationship with their marriage counselor. Even though it was over, it must have been hard for the girl to confide in the man who was with her mother. Had Dr. Collins ever been a father figure in the picture? Had he been abusive? Maxim realized he didn't know enough about the man yet.

The detective glanced at the staircase again, wondering if it was too late to cancel the second glass of red. Something shimmered on the smooth wooden surface of the steps. It wasn't just a fresh coat of polish. There was movement. A thin ribbon of water snaked across several steps, dribbling onto the next, stretching halfway down the staircase.

Maxim stood up as Olivia reentered the room.

"What is that?" he asked. He moved toward the stairs.

Olivia huffed. "I told you I don't want you talking to her
—"

"The water, Olivia. Why's there water running down the
steps?" Maxim took the first step and scanned what he could
see of the second story. He thought he heard water running.

"The bathroom!" she chimed. Olivia rushed past him.
She was quick. Maxim hadn't even noticed her putting the
wine glasses down.

He followed her up. A few yards down the hall was a
closed door with a bar of light seeping beneath. Water
flowed from the crack and across the wood floor. Olivia
frantically jiggled the handle.

"Annabelle? Annabelle, open the door!"

Maxim marched forward and sternly brushed the woman
aside. He lifted his foot and planted it under the handle.
The cream white door frame splintered and the bathroom
opened up to them. A fresh wave of water escaped into the
hallway, soaking their shoes. The bathtub and sink faucets
ran at full power, both basins overflowing. Annabelle Hayes
stood in the middle of the bathroom wearing pajamas. She
stared at her submerged bare feet.

"What are you doing?" cried Olivia, barging past the
stunned detective and shutting off both faucets. Olivia
grabbed her daughter by the shoulders and attempted to
shake her from her reverie. "Annabelle!" She dragged the
girl away, into her bedroom.

Maxim flipped the sink and bathtub levers to drain the
basins, but they didn't give easily. Something jammed the
plugs. Maxim stuck his hand in the tub drain and pulled at

the cloth clogging it. He yanked out a black sock and a bubble announced the blockage cleared. He did the same with the sink and took the wet articles to Annabelle's room.

The girl was covered in a bathrobe. Her mother fussed at her hair with tears in her eyes. "Why won't you tell me what's wrong?" she asked.

It surprised Maxim how neat the room was. No punk-rock posters or teen idols adorned the walls. No slew of stuffed animals or clothes on the floor. Also strange was the Ouija board laid out on the bed, which had been stripped down to the mattress.

"Where are the bedsheets?" he wondered aloud.

Annabelle spun around and dropped her jaw in shock. "Get out of my room!" she yelled, clutching her arms tightly around her robe.

Maxim suddenly realized the girl was old enough to deserve privacy. He'd been examining the contents of her room while she was half naked. He hurried outside and glanced up and down the hall, then down at his wet shoes. He kicked at the water and threw the wet socks to the ground.

It was only then that he realized: one of the socks was not a sock at all. It was a black, nondescript pair of girl's underwear.

Chapter 34

Quick in, quick out. That's what Diego swore as he approached the outlaw motorcycle clubhouse. Off a dirt road in the middle of Sycamore, it wasn't an easy place to find unless you had a legitimate reason to be there.

The MC used to be Diego's pack. He'd rolled with them for a year before everything went to hell. The biker had realized there was a difference between real outlaws and him. The guys in this cabin? They were killers, eager to fight the necessary turf wars to stay in control of the Interstate and their drug business.

Diego de la Torre had the skill set for the job, but he also had a conscience.

The front door opened before Diego could knock.

"The golden boy returns home!" mocked Gaston from the doorway. He was a stout man, imposing, with a muscle shirt and head of spiked hair. He flexed his bicep as he held the door open.

"Not today," muttered Diego.

"You're riding without gloves these days?"

"I... lost mine in the forest. It's a long story. I can explain inside."

"Sorry," said Gaston quickly. "Only club members allowed in here."

Diego grimaced. The president was still sore that Diego had chosen a different path. But they were friends, ultimately, with a lot behind them. Both bikers were just blustering, and Diego waited it out with a bored expression.

Gaston measured him. "You've been avoiding us."

"Just trying to get my head straight."

The MC president nodded. "You're not bringing your buddy Maxim out here again, are you? He's always asking favors without giving any in return."

Diego shook his head. "I've about had it with the cops. But I do need a favor myself."

Gaston scoffed but didn't appear disappointed. He knew Diego was here for a reason. "It figures. Let's talk business." The big man went inside and collapsed on a couch. Diego followed but remained on his feet. He noticed West Wind silently watching them, leaning against a pool table with his arms crossed. Diego nodded at the Apache, who returned the gesture with a straight face.

"Kind of empty in here," said Diego.

Gaston shrugged. "Our guys have a bit of a break. After calling them in the last two days, I figured they earned it."

Diego agreed. As promised, Maxim had mobilized much of Sanctuary to search for Hazel. The bikers weren't residents but they'd sort of adopted the town. Most of the MC had spent long days in the forest with the other volunteers. If anybody knew the woods, it was them, but they had still turned up empty.

"She's still lost, Gaston. And worse, if we don't do anything about it, it'll happen again."

"I hope you're not asking for more manpower. We tried, man."

"It's not that. There's something in the woods. Lights. Children. Kayda said—"

"You visited the Yavapai?" Gaston stood up suddenly and Diego realized his mistake. "I've declared them off limits. Nobody goes down to Chino Valley without my say so."

Diego gritted his teeth. "I'm not yours to command, Gaston."

"Just the same, I can't have you cavorting with her. She's our sworn enemy."

"*Your* enemy."

He chuckled derisively. "Do I need to remind you what you did to *her* brother with *that* knife?" West Wind snickered in the background.

Diego didn't answer. He only regretted his actions for Kayda's sake. Kelan had deserved what he got. Diego had done what needed doing.

Gaston brushed it off and laughed again. "You were always such a pain in the ass, Diego." He returned to his seat and relaxed. "Hell, I couldn't even control you when you were a one-percenter."

"Still is one," cut in West Wind, his first real words of the encounter. "If you ask me."

The president shook his head and turned back to Diego. "Can you believe this guy? The hardest man in my group has a soft spot for you."

Diego shrugged. "I'm likable that way."

"Ain't that right. How did our little witch receive you?"

Diego bobbed his head back and forth as if it were on a scale. "Still trying to figure that out. But she understood I was looking for a girl. She likes kids. She didn't give me any trouble."

Gaston turned to the Apache. "Her own little army," he announced. "The reservation's gonna be a different place in fifteen years." West shrugged.

"I need a gun," said Diego, getting to the heart of the matter.

Gaston feigned surprise.

"And money's a little tight."

Now the president really was surprised. He laughed and West shook his head and disappeared into the back. "So that's your business," concluded Gaston. His face grew serious. "Except it's not really business if you can't pay."

"It's just a shotgun."

"Mmm hmm. I remember your shotguns. You have expensive taste. Who is it you need to shoot?"

Diego hesitated. "I don't know who it is. Or what it is. There's something in Sycamore."

Gaston snorted. "Look, Diego. The scariest thing in the woods is us. Especially if someone's taking children. If that was happening around these parts, I'd know about it. And I'd eat them alive."

Diego knew the wolf meant that literally.

He thought about what Kayda had said, about not limiting knowledge to what was already known. The MC thought they were the toughest customers on the block. The only thing going. But more was out there. Diego couldn't prove it, and he wasn't even sure how much he believed, but there was something in the forest that needed shooting.

The biker was a trained hunter. It didn't much matter what the prey was, as long as it deserved it.

West Wind returned to the room and placed a heavy piece of metal in Diego's hands. It was a brand new Benelli M4 autoloader shotgun. The monotone weapon had metal the color of smoke—a far cry from the bright silver of Diego's old one—but everything else was identical.

"Just like the one you lost," said the Apache. "We ordered it the very next day. By the time we got it, you were gone, but I held on to it. I knew you'd come asking one day. Guys like us can't lay brick for a living."

"The last one was towing cars, actually."

"Whatever," chuckled West. "I figured you earned it."

The MC president grumbled at the kind gesture but West ignored him.

Diego shook the man's hand in thanks. Gaston just shook his head.

"See, Diego? Everyone likes you. Even I like you. And that's your problem."

The biker hefted the shotgun, testing the familiar weight. "How's that a problem?"

"Because you're too eager to help people, man. You put yourself out there too much. It's gonna catch up to you one day."

Diego winked at his friend. "Yeah, well, not today. And I owe you guys one."

"There you go again," said Gaston. "And you're damn right."

The biker hurried to the door. All he needed now was a pair of new riding gloves and plenty of buckshot, and he'd be good to go.

Chapter 35

Maxim leaned his back against the Spanish-style door, arms crossed. It was a relaxed posture with an intimidating function. The man approaching on the walkway recognized his path was blocked pending another conversation.

"Hello again, Detective," said Bertrand Collins.

Maxim remained against the door. "You didn't mention your sessions were held in the Hayes residence."

The psychologist stopped on the porch with a blank look on his face. "I didn't think it was germane to—"

"You let me make that call."

"Certainly, Detective. What is it you wish to know?"

Maxim moved into Bertrand's personal space. "I need to know what's really wrong with Annabelle!" he barked.

The man widened his eyes and frowned, startled but ultimately unimpressed with the theatrics. "We've had this discussion before. Her mental state is off limits. Your badge doesn't give you the right to break confidentiality."

"Yeah, well, while you were sitting on your high horse up in Flagstaff, Annabelle had another one of her episodes. Kind of calls your therapy skills into question. Don't you think?"

"What are you talking about?"

"Annabelle's zoning out. Not acting all there. What kind of meds have you prescribed her?"

He shook his head firmly. "I'm not a physician. I don't prescribe medicine to any of my patients. Cognitive Behavior Therapy is problem focused. I attempt to correct unhelpful thoughts and stimuli, not dull an active mind. Is Annabelle all right?"

Maxim was annoyed at his mistake. He should have realized Bertrand wasn't that kind of doctor. "She's fine. But she was standing in the bathroom as the tub and sink overflowed, oblivious to what was happening. She made a real mess."

Worry faded from the psychologist's face. "Yes. This is post traumatic stress symptomatology. It's unclear if she's oriented to time and place."

"What does that mean?"

The doctor sighed impatiently. "It means she's dissociative, Detective. She does not respond to the present as you or I would, which is why questioning her is counter-productive."

The door behind Maxim opened. It was Olivia.

"Maxim! What are you still doing here?"

He shifted his gaze between Olivia and Bertrand. "The good doctor here was just gonna sit in while I speak with your daughter."

Bertrand pinched his glasses to his nose. "Olivia, I didn't —"

She flew off the handle. "I said no, Bertrand! I won't have her subjected to it anymore."

The doctor tried again. "Olivia, I agreed to no such thing. The detective is simply pushing his weight around without concern for Annabelle. I'm sorry, Detective, but Annabelle eschews social interaction, especially with strangers. I can't allow it."

Maxim put a heavy hand on Bertrand's chest. "Oh, so what are you? Her father?"

Olivia let out a panicked exclamation and the doctor grew nervous at the implication. "I... I don't step on Gulliver's toes, but to some extent he's removed himself from the situation. Of course, it's not my place to act as more than counselor."

Maxim narrowed his eyes and pressed the man into the wall. "Too late for that, don't you think?"

Olivia regained her composure. "Detective, Dr. Collins is here to see my daughter. I don't want you interfering."

"You're not gonna let him see her like this, are you?" he asked indignantly.

"That's ridiculous," countered Bertrand. "Annabelle needs me now more than any other time. If she's close to an episode—"

"Close?" interrupted Maxim. "Cancel the appointment, Olivia."

She stared at him, angry at his insistence. The doctor

stood tall and pushed his weight against Maxim's hand.

"I did nothing unethical, Detective. My relationship with Olivia is long over. Perhaps these residual feelings of anger are due to your interest in her."

Maxim growled and shoved the man back into the wall. "Give us a second, Olivia," he said gruffly.

She didn't move for a long moment. "But—"

"Just one more second," he repeated without looking her way. "Then you can have him." He could practically hear Olivia's pout, but she closed the door and left them alone.

Bertrand swallowed nervously. "What do you want, Detective?"

Maxim wished he knew. "Are you still seeing Olivia?"

A satisfied smile played on Bertrand's lips. "Are you asking as a detective?"

He gritted his teeth. "Of course."

"I am not, professionally or otherwise," he answered. "I'm here for Annabelle. The divorce was hard on her. Even beforehand, the troubled marriage had taken its toll. Annabelle feels emotionally abandoned. She acts out and will continue to do so for attention. Until she feels properly secure."

"What if she's not acting out? What if she really wants to run away?"

"That's ridiculous."

"If it was just a stunt, a cry for help, then why'd she bother covering for herself the entire weekend? It kind of defeats the point of attention if neither parent misses her, doesn't it?"

Dr. Collins face was turning red. Maxim wasn't holding him that tightly, so he knew the man was angry. "Will you allow me to attend to my patient or not?"

Maxim sneered. He didn't know what it was about the doctor that set him off. Or about Olivia. He understood being overprotective of Annabelle, especially after what she'd been through, but nobody seemed concerned with finding out what she knew.

The detective released Bertrand and backed off. The man exhaled slowly, relieved. "Thank you, Detective." He squeezed by Maxim's shoulder and opened the front door.

"Have you ever asked her?" posited Maxim.

Bertrand turned around, eyeing the detective carefully, afraid of another confrontation. "Asked her?"

"Have you ever just asked her?" he repeated. "What it is *she* wants?"

The psychologist frowned at the ensuing awkward silence, then shut the door. Maxim chewed his lip and stared at the solid wood, wondering why no one else was asking the same thing.

Chapter 36

Diego tightened his grip on the handle of his Benelli M4. It made him feel alive, invigorated, like he was seeing an old friend again. One who didn't judge him or hate him. More than that. The shotgun was a part of him. A missing piece, reunited. It had slipped into the holster on his bike as though it was there yesterday, and it fit his hand as if he'd never lost it.

It suited him. Finally, Diego felt like an outlaw again.

Red and Kayda believed the weapon wouldn't be enough. They preferred pikes and glyphs, perhaps. For Diego's part, he figured nothing short of werewolves were a good match for a pocketful of 12-gauge buckshot. But even if it didn't kill them, it could put them down.

The biker strode confidently through the forest. While grit had always been in his arsenal, now he packed that alongside the knowledge that he might be seeking something supernatural. And again, that was a good fit for the man. Once he'd been a hunter of wolves, sanctioned by the US government. Diego was good at it, but he hated being an assassin.

Law. Crime. Those were distinctions that Maxim needed to concern himself with. To Diego, what mattered was the pursuit. The purpose. Were his actions right or wrong? Hunting was fine with the man. As long as the prey deserved it.

In this case, a little girl, an *innocent* girl, was the victim. God help anyone who stood in Diego's way. And whether his foe was superstition or not, he needed to give Hazel that chance.

The biker wasn't sure what the Celtic cross glyphs meant, but they were linked to Red. Hazel, too, was linked to him somehow. Diego had been on to something before when he discovered the symbols. When he woke up next to one scrawled in the dirt. The wild forest south of Williams was only lightly explored thus far, and that gave him all the hope he needed to still believe he could rescue the girl.

After two hours, Diego was confident he still had his bearings. Although it was midday, the dense canopy of the forest bathed him in near-constant shadow. The sun was weak today, trapped behind a dense fog, but still useful. Beams of light stretched through the foliage and served as his compass, but now they straightened into vertical pillars.

Diego stopped for a breath. It was unusually humid now and he was sweating like crazy. His small water bottle was just about empty, but he knew hydration wasn't something best rationed. Get the fluid into the body early and often, so it would be ready to perform without any hang-ups. When he gulped the last of it, he crushed the plastic container into a ball and put the cap back on, then slipped the trash into his pocket.

The sun was directly overhead. Diego considered sitting until the sunbeams leaned westward so he wouldn't get lost, but the memory of waking up in the dirt discouraged him. That wouldn't happen now. He was calm, well-hydrated, and had a decent night of sleep. But still, he couldn't bring himself to risk sitting down.

Before he made a decision, he saw it again: a flash of light swaying in the distance. It lolled up, down, and around. It seemed to disappear when it moved behind tree trunks, leaving little ambient light, only to suddenly burst on again in a different place, a bit farther than where it should have been. The glow had an unnatural, disjointed motion. There was no doubt it was the same thing he'd seen the night before.

"Don't follow the lights," muttered Diego under his breath. He wondered if Kayda knew the reasons behind her advice. Was it just obfuscation? A trick to make her seem more knowledgeable? More powerful? He licked his lips into a slow snarl, agonizing over every moment he stood still. "Easier said than done."

The light danced in what Diego was sure was a taunt. He flexed his jaw.

The distance between him and the bulb was what—a hundred yards? With his heavy boots and leathers, and while avoiding obstacles, he could do that in twenty-five seconds. That meant, if he went all out, he'd be able to answer one nagging question in half a minute.

On top of that, he was sure he could play this smart. If he were to chase the light, he swore not to get involved in a protracted hunt. He'd simply change his position from here to there, without any danger of getting turned around. Just to test whoever was out there.

It sure was tempting.

Diego noticed his cheek twitch under the strain. He was often accused of being spontaneous. Of acting before his brain analyzed the situation. Sometimes, the label "reckless idiot" was floated around. On the other hand, no one had ever called Diego de la Torre a pussy.

With a deflated sigh, he grabbed his Benelli by the barrel and took a single step towards the forest glow.

A loud caw jolted the serenity. Two. Four. Diego turned, and a mad chorus of chirps assaulted his ears. A murder of crows hopped and chattered and flapped wildly in the dirt, a single beam of light shining on them from above. The chaotic grouping meshed into a flat circle on the ground, then a sphere as they jumped and nipped at each other, always moving, blending as one. It reminded Diego of a painting he'd seen once. Had it represented hell?

The biker had never been good with imagery.

Diego glanced at the spinning light again. Still lackadaisical. Still within reach. Then he considered the crows. They were from Kayda's flock, were they not?

The cawing reached a fevered pitch and two of the crows flew into the air. Diego became consumed with the feeling that he would miss something and rushed forward. Against the cacophony, he didn't even make a sound, yet before he reached them, the tangle of birds launched skyward. The biker covered his face as several wings whisked around him, and he looked up.

In a break of the canopy, Diego saw the scattering forms of the flock set against the blinding sun. A single feather brushed his face, and he covered his eyes and turned away.

His pupils burned. The whole forest was darker now. When he searched the trees, he couldn't see the dancing glow anymore.

"I thought the light of the moon was supposed to guide me," he said offhandedly.

But the biker couldn't ignore what had just happened. He shut his eyes and wondered if it was truly possible to sense the moon without seeing it. Diego concentrated. Whatever was supposed to happen, he didn't feel anything. Whatever it took, Diego didn't have it in him. Then he heard an awful chirp at his feet.

On the ground next to him, where the band of birds had jostled, was a wounded crow lying on its side. It blinked at him twice, then died.

Diego slowly drew a breath in and out.

Somewhere in the bushes, a child giggled.

The biker spun and fell backwards.

"Who's there?"

He rolled in the dirt and pulled his 12-gauge close. Green eyes shimmered in the brush, then vanished. A rustling sound sped behind him. Diego rotated, trying to locate the source.

"Wait," he shouted. "I can help you!"

"Buh buh bah," came a voice to the other side of him. It sounded like a baby's. Unformed.

He caught a blur of movement behind a tree. Diego backed away, on his knees. A twig snapped to his left, and someone sobbed to his right. Trying to ascertain the threat was dizzying.

And then his eyes locked with those of another, peeking from behind a sycamore. A little boy with bright green eyes stared back at him. Bright locks of gold fell over his ears. He did nothing but watch. Diego followed the child's lead.

Neither moved for what seemed an eternity.

Slowly but abruptly, the area brightened. At first, Diego didn't take his eyes off the face peeking from behind the tree. He figured it was just the fog finally giving way. But then his back began to burn, and something told Diego he was going to die.

The biker rolled onto his back and thrust the shotgun up. A piercing white light, stronger even than the sun, loomed over him. The intensity threatened to drive him senseless. To shut him down. But Diego squeezed the trigger of the semi-auto three times until the swimming stopped.

Besides the ringing in his ears, the woods were quiet.

Diego's eyelids were clamped shut as if frozen. He strained to open them but his body resisted, unwilling to risk exposure. Diego chanced taking his left hand off his weapon to rub his eyes and shield them as they opened.

It wasn't dark, but he lay only in the veiled light of the sun. Everything was still. Leaves didn't rustle, branches didn't sway—even the feathers lay motionless on the dirt. It was as if the breeze had abandoned the world completely. As Diego scanned his surroundings while on his back, he came face to face with the dead crow. He jumped to his knees.

He didn't know why, but he was exhausted. As before, his body needed to rest, even though he hadn't done anything intensive. Diego stuck the barrel of the shotgun into the ground and propped himself up with it.

The light was gone. The children were gone. Somehow, it had already been a long day, and it was only noon.

"Why don't you come out and talk to me?" yelled Diego, deciding it best to remain crouched.

In the distance, Diego heard someone whistling a song. He couldn't make it out, but it reminded him of the melody Julia whistled to her daughter.

Diego drew in a deep breath and whistled back. It was a short tune, repetitive, and catchy. Within moments, the whistler replied with the same song.

Diego turned to face the sound and whistled again. The mimicked tune came back to him, this time to his side, but closer. The biker faced the new position. He was getting somewhere. He took in another breath and whistled softly, beckoning the other person forward.

"How did you do that with the bird?" asked a child beside him.

Instead of moving frenetically, Diego remained crouched and slowly pivoted on the grip of his M4. Before him, not more than ten feet away, was the same small child, maybe eight, maybe ten. He was still pale with blond hair, but his eyes were now a light blue. Faded almost. The boy wore neither shirt nor shoes, but around his waist was the same red kilt the biker had seen in Red's RV.

"Where'd you get that?" asked Diego. The child's brows wrinkled as if he didn't understand. The biker ignored the tension in his muscles. The last thing he wanted was to come off too intimidating to the child. "The, uh, birds..." stuttered Diego, glancing down at the dead crow.

The boy giggled. "Yeah. That was funny."

Diego scanned the trees for others but didn't find anything. "Who are you? Where are your parents?"

The boy's expression soured. "They're very far away, but it's not bad here. Call the birds back."

"Do you know a little girl named Hazel Cunningham? Have you seen her out here?"

"You're old. Old people ask too many questions."

"It's important," stressed Diego.

The boy beheld him, pondering. His face eased into a passive mask. He wasn't upset or scared or sad—he was simply bored. He turned his back to the biker and stepped deeper into the brush.

"You can't come with us," he said with detachment, "if that's what you're thinking."

"Don't leave!" ordered Diego, taking to his feet.

The child, as if on a spring, launched away from him.

Diego barreled ahead in pursuit. The boy was faster than him, more adept at sidestepping the trunks of errant trees, but the biker would be damned if he'd let anything take the boy from him at this point. He charged forward and used his size to ignore the smaller obstacles, barging through the brush and smaller branches. His long stride was an advantage as he leaped over patches of foliage. Even though he was big city through and through, he liked to think he did an admirable job of keeping up.

But his fatigue still lingered. The little boy drew ahead. Diego lost sight of the child here and there. He scrambled to keep him in view, and did for a time, but ultimately the boy triumphed. Diego surged over a small hill and, although the trees didn't provide much cover ahead, his quarry was nowhere to be found.

The biker continued sprinting, stubbornness seeking the impossible, but eventually logic prevailed. As he reached a huge overturned tree, Diego slowed and coughed, suddenly acutely aware of his smoking habit. He slung the Benelli over his shoulder and rotated in a circle, taking in a three-hundred-and-sixty degree view of the terrain. Beside him, a large pine had uprooted and collapsed fairly recently. Clusters of fresh dirt had been ripped from the ground and hugged a heavy tangle of roots that stretched into the air.

No place to hide here, though, nor anywhere in the distance. Had he overshot the boy?

Diego whistled the tune as loudly as he could muster, but only silence answered. "Hazel!" he screamed. Again, no lights, no sounds. No children. Diego continued spinning around, absorbing the environment, searching for something, anything, that would allow him to continue his pursuit.

His boot rapped against something solid. An ivory object protruded from a section of upturned earth. Diego crouched to examine it and immediately went white. It was a bone. He dropped his Benelli and dug at the loose soil with his fingers. More bones. Piles of them, neatly stacked, of all sizes. Fingers. Legs. There was probably a complete skeleton here, and they were unmistakably human. Diego fought back his emotions as he clawed the ground frantically. He thought he could uncover something to reveal this all as a joke. A fabrication of someone's sick devising. When Diego uncovered the skull, his worst fears were realized. This was a child's skeleton.

The biker fell backwards and rested on the ground. Dirty hands supported his head. He fought to stay in control, to rationalize his discovery away.

And then it came to him. Because the shallow grave had been unearthed by the upturned tree, it was difficult to gauge how long the child had been buried. But there was no flesh here. Not a sliver of meat or fat clung to the bones. Not even a trace of cartilage. Decay couldn't act so quickly, and wild animals didn't scavenge so completely. These bones were perfect in their purity, polished bare, set in a stack, and not a drop of blood in sight.

Diego's eyes watered at the sickening sight. This wasn't just tragic. It was unholy. Evil. But they couldn't be Hazel's bones. The biker guessed they'd been in the ground for a long time.

Before he realized he should stop messing with the

evidence, a splash of red caught his eye. Under a patch of loose dirt was a cloth, its bright red and blue lines instantly familiar. This was the plaid kilt, newly placed over naked bones.

The boy hadn't stolen the kilt from Red—he'd returned it to the corpse it belonged to.

Chapter 37

The overcast sky finally came through with its threat and rained hard over Sycamore. Maxim and Diego stood under the concrete roof of the outdoor train station and could do nothing as the visibility diminished. Finally, a white SUV with sheriff's office badging pulled into the parking lot.

"You can come along," said Maxim to Diego as they waited, "but I want you to hold back. This is a police matter."

The cocky outlaw smiled. "And the police would be nowhere without my help. Besides," he said, hefting his Benelli over his shoulder, "you might need the firepower."

"I don't," said the detective, suddenly stern. "You remember why you haven't carried a gun since last year, don't you?"

The memory was wet like blood on Diego's fingers. He didn't answer the rhetorical question.

"You allowed your firearm to be taken from your person.

As a result of that mishap, a good man was shot and killed with it."

"Those were isolated incidents—"

"We confiscated that weapon and it'll be tied up in the legal system for years, and although it's your legal right, I'm disappointed you've replaced it."

Diego lowered the shotgun to his side and turned away from the detective. Maxim could tell his words burned. Diego meant well, but it was only a matter of time before his amateur antics got him hurt.

"Besides," said Maxim, giving the biker a conciliatory smile, "I thought Kayda told you bullets wouldn't be effective out there."

The biker ground his jaw and remained silent.

The Coconino County SUV parked beside them. Maxim traded another glance with the biker before barging through the rain and into the back of the vehicle. He shut the door and wicked the water from his short hair. A deputy was driving and another sat in the back with him. Detective David Harper bent around from the passenger seat to consult with Maxim.

"So what do we have?"

Maxim shrugged. "Just what I mentioned on the phone. We believe Red is still at Echo Canyon but backed off at your request."

David peered through his window at the biker, who'd stayed under the cover of the platform. "You're still working with a civilian, I see."

"I called the sheriff's office, didn't I? I can't help it if he contacted me first. You said I could assist on the case and we're all here, so let's get moving."

David Harper faced Maxim again. "Shouldn't he lead us to the crime scene first?"

Maxim hissed. "I thought I asked you to bring two teams so we could do that in parallel. We have enough reasonable doubt to pick up and interview a drifter before he moves on. Let's not waste any time."

The Coconino detective thought about it for a second and acquiesced. He pointed a thumb at the driver. "This is Deputy Garza. You met her at the campgrounds. Next to you is Renteria."

Maxim nodded at both of them.

David Harper faced forward again and slid his window down halfway. He beckoned Diego with a jerk of his head. The biker fitted on his gold helmet and jumped into the rain.

"I don't need a ride," he told Detective Harper. The biker pointed to his Triumph Scrambler next to the train platform. "I'll be right behind you."

"No you won't," declared David. "I have another unit inbound. You're to wait here and ride with them to the crime scene you discovered."

"Not until after we deal with—"

The biker's words were cut off as Detective Harper looked away and shut his power window.

Maxim leaned forward. "I told him he could come."

"I'm sure you did," he answered, "but we do things differently than in Sanctuary." David lifted his hand and pointed down the tracks. "Let's move."

Garza lurched the vehicle forward and exited the lot before joining the access road along the tracks. Maxim grimaced as he watched Diego's form disappear in the rear window. Eventually, the access road turned off and Garza navigated over the dirt path that led to Echo Canyon.

Between bumps, Harper clocked Maxim in the rear view mirror. "You've previously interviewed the suspect. Is that right?"

"Yes. He was just an old man complaining about kids looting his property."

"The government's property, you mean."

Maxim clenched his jaw. "I was speaking about his possessions. I should've arrested him when I had the chance, but we didn't have anything on him. But a boy's kilt that was seen in his possession has now been paired with a dead body."

"Was seen by *you*?" asked Harper.

"Yes," Maxim lied. He needed to keep the investigative procedure legitimate from start to end. He only hoped it wouldn't bite him in the ass.

Garza cocked her head. "What's an old hermit doing with child's clothes?"

Maxim nodded. "He said it belonged to his dead son, except there's no record of him having a son. Really, there aren't enough records to confirm or deny much. I haven't gotten anywhere with Scotland. So we don't know if it's the same kilt or how it got there, but it's a link."

Harper was still unconvinced. "What if the children stole

it?"

"Maybe they did, but why? And they matched it to a child's skeleton. It could be a ruse, but if it gets us in that RV then it's worth it. We're either chasing our tails or Hazel's in there. We need to be sure."

Detective Harper had no rejoinder. Already they had allowed Red too much leeway. If Hazel Cunningham was under their noses all this time and something happened to her as a result of the delay, both departments would feel the heat. But Maxim left the politics for the marshal, and whatever he thought of David, he didn't believe the man would disregard the life of a child.

As Garza parked the vehicle just before the entrance to the clearing, Maxim knew that within minutes they would have Red in custody and get a look inside his motor home. He just hoped the other detective was taking this seriously. At least, he noted, they were all wearing their bulletproof vests.

Chapter 38

"I want to go in soft," yelled Detective Harper over the rain. It was still difficult to hear the words. The four officers marched towards the path to the clearing named Echo Canyon. "This is my initial visit, so we treat him as a witness first. Keep your gun holstered and stay at my back as a show of force."

Maxim scowled. Detective Harper had to do things his way. As the investigative lead, it was his right—Maxim just hated the idea of starting over. Still, what did it hurt? Red was no threat to them. Four men against a senior weren't even odds.

Before they moved into the woods, Maxim took one last look down the tracks. If Diego had followed them, the poor visibility prevented a confirmation. He wasn't sure if the outlaw not being present made him more or less nervous. It was what it was, he figured, and continued ahead.

Maxim tensed as the RV came into view. Red's makeshift

furniture was still scattered about. Dark smoke rose from the metal barrel—signs that a fire had gone out with the rain. For Red, it was just another day.

As they approached, the deputies maneuvered carefully around the dead trees. It was a disquieting scene. Creepy. As if only death was allowed to reside here. Maxim again examined the strange metal pole spiked into the ground. Black iron, if Diego was to be believed. For protection.

David Harper put up his hand as the large window on the side of the RV slid open. Red stood above the four of them, sneering. He appeared paler than before. His red hair was grayer, but it could just have been the lack of lighting.

"What do you want?" he demanded as coarsely as he appeared.

"I'm Detective Harper with the Coconino County Sheriff's Office. We need to ask you a few questions."

"I won't come out," answered Red. "It's raining. I'm an old man, you know."

Maxim shielded his eyes from the water to get a better look at him. First and foremost, they needed to make sure he wasn't a threat.

David Harper nodded. "I noticed both those things," he said with a pleased smile. "How about we talk inside?"

"No. You don't have the right. Come back later." The old man suddenly shut the window, its blackout tint concealing him.

Maxim stepped to Harper's side. "We need to go in hot," he urged. "If the girl's in there, we can't give him time with her."

Harper shook his head and said something, but Maxim couldn't hear through the rain.

"What?" he yelled.

Harper spoke more forcefully. "I said we're not SWAT. This isn't a hostage situation. Not yet. We just need to isolate him in a one-on-one scenario to neutralize him. We can do that with conversation."

Even though they spoke loudly, Maxim knew it was impossible for Red to hear them in the rainstorm. "Conversation? He's a danger right this second." Maxim turned to the deputies. "We need to stay clear of the windows. We can't see inside but he can peek out. If he has a weapon, we're sitting ducks."

Deputy Renteria took several steps away from the RV.

David didn't argue with the logic. "You two back away and take flanking positions. Garza, you do the same on the other side while you watch my back." The detective waved his hand to make his point clear, and Garza followed him around the back of the RV. Renteria backed away some more and put his hand to his holster. Maxim nodded to him before approaching the front cab.

The front windows weren't tinted and Maxim could clearly see inside when he hopped onto the step. The cab was empty, as before, littered with water bottles. The curtain to the living space was drawn closed. They still didn't have eyes on Red.

The vehicle vibrated and Maxim realized Harper was knocking. The beating of the rain against the RV drowned out everything else. Maxim quickly jumped back to the mud and circled to the far side. David stood by the side door. Garza was at his back, moving away to form a perimeter as Renteria had.

"Mr. Munro," announced Harper calmly. "Could you please open the door? This is a minor matter that can be handled quickly. I don't even need to come inside." The man leaned forward and strained to listen for a reply. As far as Maxim could tell, there was no answer. Harper banged loudly on the door again.

Maxim cursed. The storm was making it more difficult to effect an arrest than he'd imagined. It gave the outdoors an unexpected oppressive quality. Besides the noise, visibility was drastically falling. The Echo Canyon clearing was fairly small before the forest took over; Garza had backed up to the edge of the space and Maxim could barely see her.

Harper reached for the door and pulled the handle. Surprisingly, it fell open.

"Mr. Munro?"

Nothing about this was good. Red was going to resist. Maxim could feel it. The detective wondered if the old man would simply attempt to drive away, but so far the cab was empty. Then Maxim wondered, if the side door was open, maybe the cab was unlocked too. Harper hadn't given the order to go in yet, and probably wouldn't, but what if Maxim just peeked in?

Maxim Dwyer stepped closer to the cab door and reached for the handle.

Movement in the trees caught his eye. Behind Garza. It was—

"Watch out!" Maxim yelled.

Red wasn't in the RV at all. Somehow, he had snuck outside. He must have used the rain and their temporary indecision to his advantage. As soon as the window had shut, he escaped unnoticed and set up an ambush. Now, he emerged from the tree cover and, with two enclosed hands, clunked Garza on the back of the head. She immediately dropped to the ground.

Maxim brushed his jacket aside and closed his hand around the grip of his Glock 22. As the weapon came out, Red charged back to his motor home with incredible speed.

Detective Harper was caught off guard. He released the door and turned to see the large man lumbering his way.

Maxim pointed his gun but Red was already too close. The wrinkled man with the leg brace was surprisingly agile. The distance to his target covered, Red slammed Harper between his shoulder and the RV. The detective resisted and reached for his belt, but Red pounded his head against the vehicle.

Maxim couldn't get a safe bead on him without putting Harper in the path of his shot.

"Stand down!" commanded Maxim. Red grabbed his now docile victim and used him as a body shield, arm around his neck. Detective Harper was now a hostage.

The detective was semi-conscious, barely able to stand. Maxim wanted to check Garza's status and see where Renteria was, but he couldn't take his eyes off the threat.

"Let him go, Red."

The man gnashed his unusually large teeth, wet with

something more than rain. Since Maxim was at the front end of the vehicle, Red pulled his victim to the back.

It didn't make sense. Red had essentially escaped. There was no reason to come back and attack four armed police officers. Not unless he wanted something in the vehicle. Maxim's aim followed Red but the rain blurred his vision.

"Don't do anything permanent," he warned. "You don't want to mess with a cop. Not in this town."

The old man yanked Harper behind the RV.

Maxim cursed. Garza was still down but there was no time for her. Renteria should have been assisting. He was on the other side of the RV. With the noise, it was possible he didn't even know there was a situation yet. Maxim called out but his voice sounded like an echo against the deluge. Instead, he pointed his Glock straight up in the air and squeezed off two rounds as he ran around the front cab.

Renteria had heard the shots. He stood alert, both hands around his pistol, facing Red. The old man scrunched his gnarled body behind Harper well. The deputy was unwilling to take the shot, and Red slowly advanced on him.

"Back away!" ordered Maxim. The last thing he needed was for another uniform to get too close.

The old man jerked at Maxim's voice. Harper, who must have been pretending to be more dazed than he was, took the momentary advantage to elbow Red in the stomach. Red's arm fell away for a brief moment. Harper spun away from his captor and raised his own weapon.

But Red, like a cat with a toy, pounced on the detective with unnerving grace. Harper fired a shot but the old man banged his hand away. Red smothered Harper's weapon with a massive fist and kneed the detective in his exposed side. Both men still held the pistol, but it was clear who was in control. Harper's arm swung in Maxim's direction. The weapon discharged.

Bullets pierced the cab with hollow clunks. Maxim dove behind the bumper. The shots kept coming and Maxim crawled through the mud to the other side of the RV.

The firing stopped, but another burst took its place. Renteria's weapon. On the ground, Maxim checked under the vehicle to see if he had a clear line of sight to the shootout, but Red's furniture blocked the way. Then Maxim noticed his gun and right hand were submerged in a puddle. He pulled his firearm up, wiped the weapon, and cleared the round.

This was an awful time for a gun jam.

A stifled yell barely rose above the cacophony, but Maxim couldn't tell who it was. He kicked himself up and dashed around the back of the RV this time, vowing to take a quick shot if he had it.

Rounding the corner, he found Detective David Harper lying over a dead log as if he'd been thrown from the melee. Renteria was sprawled close to his original position.

Red was nowhere in sight.

Maxim circled the vehicle to expand his cone of vision. He'd just discovered firsthand how fast Red was, but he couldn't have made it to the tree line. The dead logs didn't seem large enough for the old man to hide behind either. As Maxim scanned the field, he noticed a round object a few yards from the wounded officers.

Maxim grimaced in disgust. Somehow, Renteria's head had been completely severed.

Damn it. Maxim was the only one left to fight. The detective considered running for the county SUV to call for backup but wasn't sure he'd be able to make it.

Still trying to locate Red, Maxim crouched to check the underside of the motor home again. It was clear. Only police officers littered the wasteland of Echo Canyon. Red was gone.

So was the metal pole that had been staked into the ground.

That was it—what Renteria had succumbed to. Red was using his crutch as a close-range weapon. And somehow he was faster than a bullet.

As soon as Maxim realized that, he spun around and saw the old man lunging from the roof of the RV, iron pike in both hands over his head. The detective fell backwards to the ground as the bar crushed the makeshift table beside him. The stack of pallets splintered beneath the overwhelming force.

The Glock released two rounds before the pole was swinging his way again. Maxim rolled away in the mud. The heavy iron should have been cumbersome but Red waved it with ease. It smashed the ground then swung upward and to the side in smooth sweeps. The assault almost caught Maxim but he managed to lunge behind Red's fire pit. The metal barrel clanged loudly as the black iron slammed into it. The blow left a solid dent.

Again, Maxim raised his weapon and fired. The round clearly impacted the center of Red's chest, below the neck. Before Maxim could pull the trigger again, the old man kicked his metal leg forward into the fire pit. The barrel trucked right into Maxim's body and flung him backwards in a shower of embers and ash.

Maxim landed hard. His elbow struck something solid and he dropped his firearm. He kicked the barrel away and scrambled for his weapon. Without it, he knew, he was dead. Watchful for the blow that never came, he recovered his weapon and spun on the ground.

Red was gone again.

"How does he do that?"

The detective lurched to his feet and raised his Glock. Red was coming back for him—he just didn't know from where. Maxim checked his surroundings and saw a blurry figure coming from the tracks. How did Red get over there? Maxim raised his gun.

No. It surprised him when he realized the man was Diego. On second thought, it wasn't surprising the biker had ignored Harper's command. Diego held a shotgun against his shoulder, pointed at the motor home. So that's why Red had backed off.

The large vehicle's engine rumbled. It was a lazy sound, but ominous nonetheless. The headlights flared on and the RV turned towards them—the only direction of escape.

Maxim emptied his magazine into the windshield of the impending vehicle. He couldn't see through the haze, but he figured Red had ducked because the RV still bore down on them. A large blast tore through the top of the windshield and the roof. Diego was firing now too.

Maxim sidestepped the motor home and ran alongside it, meeting up with Diego, who did the same. The ground was rough in the Canyon and the vehicle had to avoid the fallen trees, but it was about to outgain them.

"Give me that!" said Maxim, snatching the Benelli from the biker's hands without asking. As the RV hopped onto the smoother ground near the tracks, Maxim took aim at the vehicle. He didn't have time for careful aim, but he needed to keep his shot wide of the living space. If there was a little girl inside, he didn't want her caught in the crossfire.

As the trigger eased back, the powerful 12-gauge butted Maxim's shoulder back and reminded him of the pain in his elbow. Sparks joined the sound of a tire explosion, and the RV continued barreling wildly towards the train tracks.

Both men chased the vehicle as it pulled further from them. Red attempted to turn it to the side but the steering was shot. The heavy truck rammed into the metal rails and skipped into the air, tumbling down awkwardly on its front end. The momentum of the RV propelled it ahead anyhow.

Right into the trees on the other side of the tracks.

"He crashed!" yelled Maxim, running ahead. He was beat, but the adrenaline would not let him slow. He hopped over the tracks and approached the vehicle from the left side, next to the blown out tire. Maxim raised the shotgun to the window, but the cab was empty. The passenger door on the other side was open.

Diego rushed to the other side of the RV. Maxim crossed

into the tree line, sweeping his weapon over the horizon. When he didn't see anything, he continued around and saw Diego stepping into the motor home.

Damn it. Diego didn't have a weapon. If Red was inside, the biker was in serious danger.

Maxim jumped through the open cab door and climbed past the seats, noting the blood where Red had sat. With the barrel of the 12-gauge, Maxim swept the curtain aside. There wasn't a lot of light, but he already saw that it was only Diego inside.

"Step aside," said Maxim, marching to the back room. "We need to clear the back."

"He's not in there," said Diego, pointing to the padlock on the door. "This is where he keeps her. Don't fire that gun."

Maxim pushed past to see the door was obviously locked from the outside. It would have been impossible for Red to get back there. With a hiss, Maxim leapt out the side door and scanned the area. The rain was starting to slow now, easing up visibility some, but he didn't see Red either way down the tracks. Maxim knew the man had slipped away again. He was hiding in the Sycamore woods.

The detective scowled and stepped back inside the vehicle. He handed his cell phone to Diego. "Call 911. Tell them there are officers down at Echo Canyon."

Maxim moved to the back and studied the locked door. "Back away from the door if anyone is in there."

Diego put his hand on the detective's shoulder. "You can't shoot in there."

"I know," said Maxim as he cleared the rounds from the autoloader. He stuck the tip of the barrel into the loop of the chain and pulled back on the handle like a lever. The rusted metal shattered under the might of the new steel. Without bothering to reload, Maxim opened the door.

It was a small room with a bed. Maxim had known one of the rear windows was broken and patched with plywood, but he now saw the other ones were covered over with wood as well, from the inside. A metal bar stretched over the bed. Several extra-long shackles hung from it. Juice boxes littered the floor and Maxim detected the faint smell of urine.

This was a prison. The only problem was, it was empty.

Act 3 - Whispers from the Dead

Chapter 39

"This is definitely a dump," said Brody, the Coconino medical examiner. Diego watched as the older man pointed out notable features on the bones. "Notice the clean soil. The lack of insects. All that on top of the obvious."

The ME's student was a young crime scene technician named Damian. Diego had, unfortunately, crossed paths with him before. He was bright for his level of experience.

"The fact that the bones are stacked in neat piles?" Damian offered sarcastically.

Brody nodded with a laugh. "Bingo. You're a sharp one."

Diego noted the cold distance with which they regarded the victim. It was strange to think they'd seen so much death as to be numb to it. He wondered if Maxim was like that too.

The three men were surrounded by several others. Some deputies had cordoned off the area and were searching nearby for more remains. Other techs were snapping photos and sectioning off the area of loose soil to be examined piecemeal. It all looked to the biker like menial setup that would take many hours. Like painting a house, most of the job was the prep work.

Brody's laughter stopped. "Unfortunately, this will make our job much more difficult. The surrounding soil will be inconclusive without meat or fat present in the ground. These bones appear to have been boiled." He sighed at the imagined hours ahead. "At least whoever did this saved us that much work. We can get to analyzing these straight away in the lab. In fact, this scene is so clean I think it might be worth getting everything to Flagstaff ASAP."

"Is that all then?" asked the biker, eager to get moving. The police were a burden at this point. Whether they smiled or warned, they slowed him down. Diego would be happy to leave them in the dust.

"Huh?" Brody seemed startled by Diego's presence.

"Is that all you need me for? Can I take off? I have a little girl to find."

The medical examiner scrunched his brow. "You're talking about the one that went missing Monday?"

"Who else?"

"Well," stuttered the man, "no one else. I just assumed this was her."

Diego took the invisible blow admirably, but he stepped backward a few steps as if he'd received a stunner to the head. He pieced together his next question carefully. "How could this be her?"

Brody pulled away from the bones. "Well, keep in mind

I'm not saying this is her. There isn't enough information to even determine the sex of this child. Before puberty, the differences in skeletal structure are quite subtle. But I'd estimate this victim to have been between seven and ten at the time of death. How old is your little girl?"

The biker's legs almost buckled but he held strong. "Eight."

"Exactly. And this soil's all loose. That indicates a fresh grave."

"But the tree could've caused that when it uprooted."

Brody nodded. "That's true. Between that and your digging and that of possible scavengers, it's just another set of inconclusive information. I'm afraid my tank of speculation is empty. We'll know more in a few hours." Diego mulled over the facts quietly, so the ME answered the biker's original question. "As long as the officers have your information, I think you're free to go."

Diego nodded absently. All the police departments in the county had his contact information.

But now he was listless. A few seconds ago, he'd had a mission. He'd assumed these bones weren't Hazel's, that she was still alive somewhere. That was the only reason he didn't want to be slowed down here. Now, if these were the girl's bones, where would he be rushing off to?

How would he tell Julia?

"But..." he started feebly, grasping for anything to keep his mission, and Hazel, alive. "But these bones are old. Look at them."

Brody sighed. His eyes revealed that he knew now. Knew

that Diego was invested in the girl. Knew that he was a liability at the crime scene. But the ME's face softened with the realization.

"I'm very sorry, Diego, but like I said: These bones were boiled. They were cleaned and boiled. They don't appear very old to me—I would expect more yellowing—but I can say with confidence that they could be as little as a few days old."

The outlaw didn't have the heart for any more. He keeled over. The techs and the deputies seemed concerned about him contaminating the scene. He tuned them out. Nothing mattered in that moment.

Chapter 40

Maxim approached the thick-wheeled Range Rover before it parked at the edge of the crime scene. The rain had stopped and everything was soaked, but the black SUV was an exception. Not only was it dry, but next to all the used law enforcement vehicles, it appeared to have just come off the showroom floor.

The spatter of activity around Maxim was to be expected, but the Range Rover was a surprise. He couldn't remember the last time he'd seen it in the field.

"Good morning, Marshal," said Maxim as the door opened.

The short man pulled the jacket of his power suit from the back seat hanger and slipped it on. He scanned the RV while fixing his cuffs. Maxim waited patiently.

"Where's the suspect?" asked Marshal Boyd.

"Coconino has the dogs out. Williams PD's assisting with the perimeter. But if you ask me, we're looking for a man who's more comfortable in these woods than many of the animals. He's old but he's fast, and he's already had the chance to outrun the lockdown."

"So the sheriff's office allowed him to escape?"

Maxim smiled. The blue-eyed marshal was young but no boy. He was already preparing for blame assignment, and even though Maxim had been present during the bust, County had taken the lead.

"The weather played a part. It was a monsoon for an hour out here."

Boyd dismissed the explanation with a quick shake of his head. Then he locked his glare on a motorcycle beside the tracks with a shine that rivaled his Range Rover. "What's he doing here?"

"Nothing, sir. Diego did not participate in the bust, although I did use his shotgun to disable the suspect's vehicle. Right now, Diego's leading Coconino detectives to the bones that started all this." Maxim paused as they approached the RV and turned back to his boss. "Truthfully, we could use the help. Lachlan Munro's dangerous. Took out the entire arrest team."

The marshal straightened his jacket and avoided eye contact. "About that... What are their conditions?"

"Well, I was kinda hoping you could tell me. The last word I got was half an hour ago. Renteria's dead, of course. Beheaded with a metal pole that's still missing. Detective Harper got banged up: a broken rib, some internal bleeding —they say he's in and out of consciousness. Deputy Garza was the luckiest of the bunch. Since she was first, the old man just left her with a bump on the head. Didn't even need stitches."

Boyd nodded. "You okay?"

Maxim sighed and continued leading the marshal to the vehicle. He didn't like to think about how close things had been. "The soggy underwear's gonna give me a rash, but otherwise I can't complain."

"I was beginning to get worried, Detective Dwyer," said the marshal sternly. "It had been almost a year since your last close call." Boyd stepped ahead of Maxim and into the RV. The marshal didn't crack a smile, but that was the closest he got to telling a joke.

Maxim followed him inside. The open window and propped-out door helped light the small space.

"Tell me what we've got," requested Boyd.

The detective didn't bother referring to his notes. "The first thing to understand is that we have two interrelated scenes. One is an unearthed body some ways north. A dead child's bones. I haven't visited the crime scene yet, but the bones show signs of being cleaned. That means we don't know how old they are. County has their technicians looking at it." The marshal didn't respond so Maxim continued. "That scene was superficially linked to Lachlan Munro by a piece of clothing found with the bones. A kilt that was believed to be in Red's possession the day before."

Boyd's face lit up. "So Mr. Munro visited the body, proving he knew its location."

"Pretty much. The kilt is no longer in the RV so it's likely the same one. There may be extenuating factors but it was good enough for reasonable doubt. Because the link was tenuous, Detective Harper didn't want to go in hard. He approached Red peacefully but the old man resisted from the start. He got behind us, somehow."

"So," said the marshal, taking in the interior of the motor home, "we have to assume our initial supposition was correct. Mr. Munro is a murderer. Are there any links to Annabelle Hayes or Hazel Cunningham?"

The detective sighed. "That's the catch. Most of these conclusions are circumstantial. There's no evidence of a link to the girls yet."

The marshal pressed his lips together in concern. "What have you found?"

Maxim jumped into motion and opened the back door. "This room has been used to hold someone against their will. Likely a small child. We're analyzing DNA on the juice boxes and we recovered blood from the shackles. Also, there's this."

The detective walked to the fridge and opened the freezer door. A tinfoil package had been unwrapped to reveal two frozen pieces of steak. "One of the techs said this meat was possibly human."

Boyd pulled away from the appliance. "Cannibalism?"

"Looks that way. Don't ask me how they can know that from an ice cube. It jives with the cleaned and stacked bones, though. Coconino's gonna get this to Flagstaff, but they said keeping it in the freezer for now was the best thing." Marshal Boyd covered his mouth and fled the RV. Maxim closed the freezer and stepped outside after him.

"Disgusting," said Boyd after a dry heave.

The detective nodded and noticed Park Ranger Dan Briggs in the distance. He was approaching.

"Detective Dwyer," said the marshal under his breath, "you're taking over this case. I've consulted the sheriff. With Detective Harper sidelined, you're the one with the most experience. You'll still coordinate with the sheriff's office, and they may resume lead in the long term, but for now you're on point. Do you have an objection to that?"

Maxim stared into the marshal's piercing eyes. "Hell no, sir."

Boyd nodded and stepped away. Maxim could feel the rush sweep through him. In his heart, he'd already committed to the case. Now the might of the sheriff's office was behind him. The responsibility for Hazel Cunningham was on his shoulders. And the target for blame, in case of failure, was painted squarely on his back.

"Detective!" called out the ranger as they met.

Maxim shook the man's extended hand. "Ranger Briggs."

The law enforcement officer crossed his arms over his vest, radio in hand. "I hear you're running a manhunt in there. You know how impossible that is, don't you?"

The detective nodded.

The ranger's radio barked with someone checking in. Briggs spoke a confirmation and lowered the volume. "So Red's a weirdo after all, huh?"

"I don't know what he is, Briggs."

"Well, if it helps at all, that coot's either going to town or to water. He's used to living off the land, but only within the comforts of a recreational vehicle. Without his tools or supplies, he's gonna need to come up for air real quick."

Maxim had already wondered about Red's survival skills. "That might help. Coconino's running the search. Can you coordinate with them?"

Dan Briggs smiled and flexed his forearms. "Copy that. Anything to get that scumbag out of my forest."

As he spun to walk away, Maxim called after him. "It's the people's forest, Briggs. Even if you don't like them calling it Sycamore."

"Actually," rejoined Briggs, turning for a single moment, "I don't think these woods belong to anything we'll ever understand."

As the ranger headed on, Maxim was left wondering if there was any levity in the statement.

Chapter 41

Diego hiked through the brush, lost in his head. The same images kept repeating in his mind. The same moments. Julia's smile. Hazel's class picture. The discovery of the RV. Had Hazel been alive then? The biker should've broken the door down when he first found it.

Second-guessing was a harrying game. It was impossible to know if he could've made a difference. He didn't even know for certain whose bones he left behind in the forest.

Diego desperately wanted to hope. He didn't know if it was more for Hazel's sake or for his. But his grit was an act. He was moving, but he was slowing down, and he had no goal in mind. He started with the long walk back to his bike.

Although Diego made progress through the forest, he felt like he was on a treadmill: sprinting forward, but getting nowhere. The day had started promisingly. Now the sun was nearly set and everything seemed a waste.

As he trekked back, he passed through familiar ground

and was startled to see a woman kneeling on the forest floor. Diego reached for the knife at his wrist before recognizing her.

"Kayda?"

The young woman quickly rose, eyes red, distressed but calm. "You're alive."

She said it matter-of-factly. There was relief in her face, at least, but Diego realized her tears were for another.

"The crow that died. It was yours."

Kayda's eyes fell to the spot in the dirt where she had buried it. It was the same spot where Diego had fallen and been nearly overwhelmed by the light.

"The crow court," explained Kayda. "It's a ritual performed by tight-knit communities. Crows are smarter than many realize. And they have severe penalties for those among them who cross the line."

Diego stepped closer. "What line?"

The Yavapai woman shrugged. "Not belonging to the group. I used to be like that." Kayda studied the mound of fresh dirt with horror. "It must have been brutal."

Diego was still stuck on belonging. His fears about Hazel weighed his mind down. "How does a crow not belong with crows?"

"They were under the control of someone—or something—else."

"What kind of control?"

"There is muddiness here, Diego. It stains the water and makes it black. Sycamore is alive with spirits."

There she went again. This time, however, Diego

entertained the possibility. "The lights. The children."

"They are not children. Not anymore."

After his encounter, Diego could no longer deny that. An involuntary shiver ran up his spine. "They're dangerous. I almost died right beside that crow."

Kayda Garnett circled the loose dirt at her feet. "They know not what they do. They don't consider the consequences. Their minds are not like yours or mine. They survive by staying in the shadows and dazzling intruders with lights and misdirection."

"But they showed me..." said Diego. "One of them led me to the bones."

"The bones of the girl?"

"We don't know that. The bones could be from any child. Until the DNA links them to Hazel, she's still missing." The biker wondered if his words sounded as hollow as they were. Kayda's assumption was normal. Expected. Deep down, Diego feared the same thing. But giving voice to the possibility made it more real.

Her face softened. "Those aren't the only bones in the forest, Diego. That isn't Red's only victim."

She was right. She had to be. If the old man was careful, if he was good, then there was a simple explanation for the girl not being in the RV anymore. If those weren't her bones, they would be in another grave nearby.

The witch continued. "Fay bear fay—the green children must have a father."

The biker furrowed his brow and stepped closer to the woman. "No more oblique references, Kayda. No more riddles. You know something about them. Tell me what you're talking about."

She sighed. "The old man. I understand the glyphs in the trees now. They were warnings. But it wasn't the old man who marked the trees. It was the children. They were warning each other about him."

"Red..." Diego's face darkened. "He's not an ordinary man. He wears a leg brace but runs like lightning. He overpowered a bear of a man. He's limber, strong, and I think he took a few bullets."

"He's not a man at all." Kayda circled the ground once more and, like a cat, sensed something unseen that compelled her to sit. She stared longingly at the dirt.

"But he's not a spirit," said the biker. "He bled all right."

She shrugged. "Not one of them then, but not human. The green children have an aversion to original metals. This man wears them. That rules him out but only widens the mystery."

Diego's skin burned as he thought about Red. Whatever he was, he was a pestilence on this land.

Kayda traced a line in the dirt as she spoke. "He's not from around here, so we may never know what he truly is, but my family tells an old story of a man unhurt by the metal of the invaders, a man not living or dead, but feeding on both worlds. His strength waxed and waned like the moon, only it was powered by blood and death."

Diego crouched beside the Yavapai woman. "He gained strength by killing others? By eating them?"

The moonwitch ignored the question and continued her

folktale. "None of the able hunters who challenged this man returned to their homes. Their souls were condemned to forever wander the in-between, never to see a harvest again. It's a terrible dishonor among my people to not be put to rest. That was the end of many great families."

Diego couldn't get the image of the monstrous child-killer from his head. Of Red's large teeth. "And what about the story? The man unhurt by metal. How does that end?"

Kayda Garnett met his gaze. "With a flood, Diego. When the land drowned, only First Woman remained. All others disappeared, good and evil alike."

Diego returned to his feet, wary of old legends. "So all we need is an act of God." He reached for his pack of cigarettes. "Well, Kayda, I hate to point this out, but the rain already stopped. This is high country. We won't see more than a few puddles."

She shrugged again, still worried about her stupid bird. With a scowl, Diego de la Torre lit his smoke and trudged towards his Scrambler. Whatever sadness the woman was feeling, he had a greater death on his conscience.

Chapter 42

The front porch light was on, standing out on the dark street. It was a small house, an old house, but it was a house. A home. Somewhere to raise family. A place once full of life and laughter.

Now it was quiet. Lonely. The single mother who lived there had nothing but good memories and grief. Hope and sorrow. It was funny how those conflicting emotions could reside beside each other.

The biker took a drag on the cigarette through his open helmet. He hadn't bothered taking it off. He'd been sitting outside Julia's house for two hours, and he hadn't even bothered getting off his bike.

How could he confront her now? What could he possibly say to her?

She was expecting him to say something. The outside light was on because she was waiting for him. Waiting for Hazel. The girl would never come.

Diego didn't know if it was his fault, but he couldn't be the messenger. He wasn't the type to come up empty-handed.

Some things, though, could never be set right.

The futility turned to anger again. Then rage. The outlaw thought about going after Red with everything he had. If Diego's hands were meant to be bloody, he might as well spill the old man's too. He would put him down whether it was legal or not, no matter what the cops could prove. If guns didn't work, Diego would find another way.

Red needed to pay for what he did to Hazel.

And that was the silver lining. His only possible offering to a grieving mother. The head of the man who took away her little girl.

But the man had disappeared. The police were chasing their tails and Diego wasn't gonna find Red all by himself.

Futility. Anger. Hopelessness. Rage. The biker kept going in circles. Kept running in place. Kept dropping the ball.

The front door opened and Julia Cunningham stepped out. She looked right at him. She must have seen him through the window. Diego threw his smoke to the ground and twisted his boot on it. He didn't know what he had to offer the woman. Not now. Not yet.

With a flick of his hand, his dark visor slammed over his face. Diego's Scrambler came to life. The disappointment was plain on Julia's face as he pulled away. She tried to wave him down but he clenched his jaw and sped past along the road.

He only made it to the end of the block before he turned around.

Diego was embarrassed about the display but he swallowed his pride. As he pulled into Julia's driveway, he realized he would've been more ashamed to cut and run on the woman. She deserved better than him, that was sure, but that didn't excuse not offering his best.

"Have you talked to the police?" she asked with urgency. She flung her arms around him before he could even get his helmet off.

That was good. Diego wasn't ready to wear his mask yet. He didn't even know if he should. Julia wanted to hear that Hazel was okay. Diego had offered false promises before. Now he wondered if he was only leading her on, setting her up for a greater fall.

He should confess his failure. He should brace her for the news that Hazel was probably dead.

"No," was all he said.

"Oh my God," said Julia, strangely hyper. She helped him take off the helmet. "You didn't talk to Maxim?"

He eyed her curiously. Julia was energized. Excited almost. "What's going on?"

"He told me he tried to call you but you didn't pick up. He said the bones would be on the news and he didn't want me to worry."

"Julia—"

"It's not Hazel, Diego! The bones are from a little boy. Maxim said the Flagstaff office made the determination and he wanted us to be the first to know."

The biker gasped. He opened his mouth but nothing came out. He didn't know what to say. Julia laughed and hugged him again.

It was strange to feel relief at the news, to prefer one child's death over another, but Diego didn't have the headspace to confront those emotions now. The moment was what mattered.

The biker clasped Julia tightly and buried his face in her shoulder. All the grating unease of the day evaporated and tears welled in his eyes. A dead boy wasn't good news but it stayed the bad news. It wasn't cause for celebration, perhaps, but maybe it was cause for hope.

Chapter 43

"Goodnight, Marshal," said Maxim.

"What'd you call me?"

Maxim unglued his attention from the bright computer monitor. He had to squint to make out the uniformed police officer. "Gutierrez?"

The patrol officer chuckled. "Who else?"

The detective rubbed his face with both hands and leaned back. "I thought you were Boyd leaving for the day. What time is it?"

"The end of B Shift. I'm headed out."

Maxim surveyed the empty office in surprise. The marshal was gone by six most days. If something special came up, he sometimes pushed his dinner late, but Boyd was certainly never around by the end of B Shift. Not only had Maxim not noticed him leave, the detective had skipped the formality of dinner altogether.

He checked the computer to make sure the officer wasn't

playing a trick on him. Nope. The internet agreed. It was 2 a.m. and he was still without a play for the next day.

Not a great start as the new lead detective.

"You have anything tying Munro to those bones?" asked Gutierrez.

Maxim cleared his throat. "Not really, but his motor home is littered with DNA."

"The dogs didn't find more graves?"

The detective shook his head. "I don't think Sycamore lets us find anything it doesn't want us to."

Gutierrez raised an eyebrow. It was odd for Maxim to talk like that, even if they both knew more about the area than most. Maybe the long night was getting to him. He brushed it off and returned to the facts.

"Brody confirmed the remains are recent. Not more than six months old."

The officer leaned against the exit doorway he'd been about to walk through. "So you think this grave is a previous victim, and grandpa could have abducted Hazel next?"

"He had the opportunity," afforded Maxim. "But the blood we found on the shackles didn't match her blood type. We're testing it against the other trace DNA we recovered. I have no doubt we'll get some matches when the lab results come back, but right now there's no tangible link between her and Munro."

"All this can't be a coincidence, though."

Maxim wished it was that easy. "Remember, Annabelle had no knowledge of Lachlan Munro either."

Gutierrez snorted. "Seems like a spoiled brat, if you ask

me. I told you not to trust her."

"It's not that..." said Maxim, trailing off. As a witness, Annabelle Hayes was unreliable. But there was a good reason for that: trauma. Back at Echo Canyon, her face had been desperate. The girl had developed an urge to run. To escape. All Maxim needed to figure out was the trigger. "We're looking at the details and missing the bigger picture," he insisted. "Children missing in the forest. Accounts of strange sightings that don't match the victims. A likely child murderer living off the land. This is wider than we realize."

The young officer pushed away from his perch. "Well, it's nothing a good night's sleep can't fix. It must feel good to have a Coconino task force mobilized at your command. I'm sure you've got big plans for them in the morning. No point staying here until then."

Maxim scowled as Gutierrez headed out. It was good advice. Only he needed said plan first.

The detective brushed the stack of papers aside and minimized the report he'd been typing up. He'd taken on his new responsibility to the case eagerly. Overtime. A skipped meal. He was determined to see Lachlan Munro's crooked smile again and was willing to make whatever sacrifices it required. But assessing the entire investigation was an exercise in the banalities of police work.

The detective rubbed his tired eyes and stood. He hooked his jacket over his shoulder with one hand and retrieved his Glock with his other. He nodded to the officer manning the overnight desk on the way out and headed for his Audi.

It would have been easy to drive home. That didn't mean he had to call it a night. The laptop that rested on the passenger seat beside him attested to that. But something about the monotonous rhythm of the reflectors on Interstate 40 cleared Maxim's mind.

The past few days had seen the detective focused almost exclusively on Annabelle. Not only had the rest of the case been the responsibility of the Sheriff's Office, but the little girl they had in safety was the best chance to recover the little girl that was still missing. Now, with his assuming Detective Harper's role, Maxim had spent the entire day on Hazel Cunningham. And Red. But those were dead ends too.

Coconino had spun its wheels on Hazel already. And Red was, for all intents and purposes, a ghost. If Maxim was going to make any headway in the investigation, he needed to go at it from a fresh angle. Sycamore was enigmatic, and he'd be forever lost in the wilderness if he couldn't see the forest for the trees.

It wasn't long before Maxim realized he was driving right to Echo Canyon.

He took the bumpy road slowly in his roadster. His headlights were the only source of illumination at this hour; their beams cast strange shadows on the tree line. Turning them off when he parked didn't help ease the quiet tension, though. Echo Canyon would forever be a tainted place after what they had discovered.

Maxim clicked on his Maglite and hiked to the clearing.

He illuminated the dead trees as he carefully stepped over them, intent on avoiding another midnight fall or wasted pair of shoes. It hadn't rained since they'd lost Red but the air was still heavy, the ground moist.

Maxim replayed the scene in his head again and again. Tumbling away from the iron pike. Rolling in the mud. The detective realized he still needed to clean his weapon after submerging it in rain.

The clearing felt odd without the RV. The smashed planks of wood and abandoned furniture were just trash without their centerpiece. The overturned barrel that had been kicked into Maxim was no longer here, either. At Maxim's request, the techs had taken it downtown to examine its contents.

He remembered seeing the smoke rise from the fire pit when they'd first approached Red in the rain. Maxim knew Munro had a fire going before it was drenched. He knew the old man liked to cook up squirrels. He also knew evidence could be burned.

Maxim ran the beam of the flashlight over the area where he'd fallen on the ground. He had pushed the barrel away from him and expected Red to strike. Instead, they chased his RV across the tracks.

What they never did was probe Echo Canyon with a fine-tooth comb. Aside from the horrible weather conditions, in the minds of the police the crime scene had moved. It was with the shackles and the blood and the human meat in the freezer. It was inside the motor home, not outside.

Besides wood and coal and animal bones, the techs at Flagstaff hadn't been able to identify the ash in the fire pit. Science might find an answer in another day or two, but as Maxim's Maglite passed over a darkened spot of red glued to the dirt, he knew he wouldn't need to wait.

The strip of red protruded from a flat section of ground. The dirt was so smooth that Maxim knew it was a dried puddle of mud. He grabbed the red ribbon and yanked it loose, tearing a clump of dirt from the ground. The strip of cloth was no longer than two inches.

The dried top layer of soil crumbled away as Maxim rolled the ribbon in his hand. The red was still stained but became brighter, and Maxim noticed two things. First, the tiny piece of cloth was not a flat color but, in fact, plaid. Next, its edges were blackened, not by dirt, but by fire.

The significance of the find immediately dawned on him. This was the plaid kilt Diego had seen in Munro's motor home a day ago. This was evidence the old man had tried to burn. The heavy rain was the only reason this sliver survived the flames.

But more was at work here.

The kilt Diego had found with the boy's bones was complete. It wasn't torn or burnt. That meant there were two separate kilts. Which could mean...

"There have to be other victims," he whispered to himself.

And it made sense. Red had lived off the grid for a long time with a custom-built prison. If he had indeed killed the young boy and eaten his flesh, then it was unlikely to have been the first time. Not when all the incidental details were considered. The prison was old. The bones were too clean. Red was no amateur.

Maxim stomped back to his car. He slammed the door and turned on the AC to fight off the humid air, but he didn't drive away. He opened his laptop and immediately went to work, tethering it to his cell phone and going online.

He forgot about Annabelle Hayes and Hazel Cunningham. He broadened his search parameters for any missing children that didn't lead to arrests, whether the victims were recovered or not. Knowing Lachlan Munro had been mobile, he widened his search area to multiple states. It was a completely new crime profile. The victims that would break the case weren't the two girls, they were the countless dead that a twisted killer had left in his wake. The ones he had already gotten away with. And, after an hour, Maxim narrowed the pool down to some interesting hits, if nothing definitive.

A Flagstaff boy had gone missing two years before. The case was never categorized as a missing person because his body was found the next day in Little Colorado River. There'd been no foul play to suggest the incident was anything less than a tragic accident, but when Maxim dug up the time of death, he was surprised to find the child had been on his own for twelve hours.

A situation a little more similar to Annabelle Hayes was a six-year-old case of a girl who'd disappeared while camping further south near Phoenix. She was located later the same night, lost and disoriented. Unfortunately, Maxim discovered that she had died in a car accident some years later, so that also left him with nothing. Except...

Hadn't someone mentioned another child that had been recovered? A reporter at the mistake of a press conference he'd held. Maxim searched for the *Post* article online and found a transcript. He saw it now. The eleven-year-old autistic girl who'd wandered away during a parade in Williams. That couldn't be a coincidence. She'd found her way back the next day. And by all accounts, she was still alive and living with her family.

It wasn't much of a plan, but at least it was a start.

Maxim's phone chimed. A call at this hour usually meant bad news for someone else. The screen reported the number as Olivia's. Worry set in, and he answered the phone immediately.

"What's going on?"

A long breath occupied the line. Then a giggle. "You don't sound sleepy."

It took Maxim a second to place the voice because it was deeper than usual. "Olivia?"

She sighed. "I know. You didn't expect to hear from me after what happened earlier."

"Sort of," he admitted. "Is everything okay?"

"Sure. Annabelle's doing better, if that's what you mean. Bertrand works wonders with her. You really should stop giving him a hard time. They had a long talk and agreed she was acting silly. But let's not talk about my daughter for once." Olivia paused and Maxim heard a swallowing sound.

"It's been a rough day and I don't want to argue."

Maxim massaged his forehead and realized how tired he was. He briefly considered asking about access to Annabelle, but decided the time wasn't right. After a short silence, he accepted the peace offering. "Sure thing, Olivia. We can talk about something else. What, uh, what are you up to?"

She giggled again. "Oh, you know, just watching late-night TV in the den. Alone." The last word came out almost as a moan.

Immediately, Maxim knew the score. "Enjoying some more wine?"

"Why not?" she asked. "You know, I have a bottle of red waiting for you, if you want it."

"Oh yeah?" He didn't know what to say but had to keep the conversation moving. "What kind is it?"

"A Washington State Syrah. But that's not important, Maxim. Why don't you stop by and try it?"

"Uh..." he stalled. It wasn't an expert maneuver.

"You remember when you first came to my door?" she asked, oblivious to his hesitance. "Well, I just took a shower and have the same bathrobe on. It's so soft against my skin." She sipped more wine and hummed with pleasure. "What about you, Maxim?"

"Me?"

"What are you doing? What are you wearing?"

Maxim closed his laptop and set it on the seat beside him. He noticed something on the floor in front of the passenger seat. "Uh, Olivia. I'm wearing my suit. I'm in the driver's seat of my car."

She snorted. "Are you alone?"

"What? Yes." Maxim leaned forward and grabbed the shiny metal. He retrieved Annabelle's hulking key chain from under the seat.

"What are you doing? Are you still working?"

"Yes, Olivia."

He stared at the key chain, wondering. Annabelle must have accidentally left it behind when she was in his car yesterday.

The sound of a wine glass clanged down on a table. "How long were you going to let me go on like that?"

"Look, Olivia. Relax. It's been a rough day, like you said. A deputy's dead. A detective's injured. Our suspect is on the run. And now I'm in charge of the investigation."

The woman's tone continued to sharpen. "You're on the other girl's case?"

"Yes. Isn't that what you want?" he asked, confused. "To leave Annabelle alone? To let her decompress?"

"Of course." She said it as if she meant the opposite. He didn't know what to do or say. Salvaging the phone call felt impossible at this point.

"Olivia, I still care about how Annabelle's doing, if that's what—"

"Here we go again," she said. "I thought we'd be able to have a single talk without bringing her up." Maxim heard a cork pop and the pouring of more wine.

"Come on," pleaded Maxim. "I can't win." He rubbed his temples and set the girl's key chain on top of his computer. "Olivia, you're absolutely gorgeous, but I'm sorry. I can't sit here flirting on the phone with you when I'm working. And I don't know if it's appropriate to spend... time with you now."

He stopped. What he wanted to say wasn't coming out right. He pictured the woman in the bathrobe and she was hot even when upset. Why didn't he want to go to her house now?

Olivia breathed heavily into the phone. Gone were the tantalizing gasps and giggles.

"Listen, Olivia. It's just that I've been pounding my head against this thing all day now." He sighed and stretched his neck. "I'm exhausted. I'm beat. I'm about five seconds away from passing out."

For a minute the woman didn't respond. Maxim wondered if she had passed out herself. But then she spoke, and her voice softened. "I was just trying..." she offered. "This is just how everything's been lately. Everything's rocky. Nothing's easy."

Maxim could sympathize.

"I like it when you ask about Annabelle," she admitted. "I really do. She's my daughter and I want her to be happy. It's just that, she hasn't been herself lately. As the only responsible parent, I have to make the tough choices. It makes things harder on me. It strains our relationship." She paused thoughtfully. Maxim thought she sat down again. "It feels like it's not her anymore, you know?"

He shook his head but said, "I guess."

"Don't humor me, Maxim."

"I don't know what you want me to say. I thought you

said the session with Dr. Collins helped."

"No," stressed Olivia, "you're not listening. I feel like the girl sleeping in Annabelle's bed isn't her. Like what came back from the forest isn't really my Annabelle."

Maxim's eyes widened slowly as the statement fully dawned on him. Olivia waited for his reply, and he was afraid to give it. Finally, he decided to be direct. "That's crazy, Olivia. I'm sure Dr. Collins would just say you're rationalizing."

She scoffed. "Rationalizing?"

"It's a coping mechanism. Like the glass of wine in your hand."

An awkward silence followed and Maxim wished he could take his last statement back.

Her voice sobered. "You really know how to make a girl feel special." He chuckled accidentally and quickly cut it short, but Olivia followed suit. In a moment, they both laughed.

"I'm sorry," she said. "You must think I'm a wreck. Drunk and booty calling you at three in the morning. How embarrassing."

"No," he said. "Don't worry about it. We're all a little extra stressed out."

She sighed. There was a hint of wistfulness in it, and Maxim wondered what could have been. "You can say that again, Detective."

He smiled, unsure how to follow that.

"Well..." she started.

"Why don't you get some sleep?" he offered.

"Yes. That's what I need."

"That's what we both need. Let's talk tomorrow."

"Okay, Detective. That sounds better. I'll see you."

Maxim felt the moment slipping away. "Rain check?" he asked jokingly, but Olivia had already hung up.

Chapter 44

The last thing Maxim remembered before crashing hard was popping open a single Bass Ale. He woke up on the couch, fully dressed, a half bottle of warm beer on the coffee table.

He had vague recollections of troubled dreams. Now awake, they manifested as an underlying feeling of dread. Sleeping in on his first full day as lead detective didn't help settle his nerves, but what really rattled him were the possibilities of his findings last night. The more he discovered about Lachlan Munro, the more behind he felt. The potential pool of victims was large. He would need to get the sheriff's task force investigating the leads immediately.

Maxim checked his phone and saw the messages had piled up. His routine tasks were cascading over one another —they threatened to occupy him for hours. Instead, Maxim canceled his check-in with the sheriff's office. He wasn't in the mood to deal with it. He didn't have the time. And there was an urgency about the morning. The trepidation of the last four days had caught up with him, somewhere in his dreams. Even now, he couldn't shake it.

Maxim jumped into his car as soon as he could. Like the night before, he would be mobile, work on the laptop and the phone. But one visit needed to be done in person. The detective threw the Audi into drive and headed to Williams once again.

The lead was already cold. He just hoped it wasn't snowed over yet.

On the way, he got an update on Detective Harper's condition. The detective was showing promising signs of recovery. He also got a message from Diego, thanking him for keeping Julia and him up to date. Then Maxim touched base with the lieutenant in charge of Coconino Criminal Investigations. Maxim had emailed his new crime profile in the predawn hours and wanted to make sure the lieutenant knew what he was looking at. He also wanted to request the expanded search parameters that he couldn't kick off from his laptop the night before. He informed the sheriff's office that he was running down the one solid lead he had and would catch up with them later. He also got the expected update that there hadn't been any forensic breakthroughs yet. As was often the case, lab results could be used in court but wouldn't actually come in time to help the victim.

Maxim was in the small city of Williams before he knew it. He drove to a wide-open side of town with nineteen-sixties real estate. The dusty, residential strip must have been full of opportunity long ago. Now, he parked his Audi at the curb of a faded yellow ranch house that was past its prime.

"Louise Radford," he announced, knocking on her door. After a minute with no answer, he called out louder. He heard muffled giggling. Maxim strolled to the side window to peek inside but the curtains were drawn.

The giggle came and went again, and he frowned. He definitely wasn't hearing things, but he was letting his nerves get to him. Maxim stepped off the porch and peeked over the side gate. A small passage led to a cracked concrete patio in the back. The giggling returned, this time louder.

"Louise Radford," repeated the detective, opening the gate and moving in.

The laughter stopped. A woman came around the corner of the house. "Yes?"

Maxim flashed his badge. "I'm Detective Dwyer, from the Sanctuary Marshal's Office. I spoke to your husband an hour ago."

"He's at work," she said. "It's just us now."

"Us?" The detective entered the backyard and saw the girl on the swing set. She was Annabelle's age now, but the pure glee displayed on her face suggested a more innocent mindset. "Ah," said Maxim. "Your daughter, Alice. I was hoping I could speak with both of you."

Louise had a tired face, and it knotted up more at the statement.

"Did your husband mention me?" he asked.

She shook her head. "He was in a hurry. He woke up late."

Maxim smiled. "I know the feeling." He waved at the girl in the distance and shot her a wink.

Louise narrowed her eyes. "You're searching for that missing girl in the woods, right?"

"I'm heading the investigation."

"And how are we involved?"

Maxim patiently went through the same discourse he'd had with the husband. "I've been doing some background on similar cases over the last few years. Your daughter went missing from the east edge of Williams last year and reappeared the next day. Is that right?"

Louise nodded.

"That's over by the train tracks, isn't it?"

"Yes," said the mother. "Alice likes to follow the tracks. We figured she wandered into the woods and got turned around, but eventually found and followed the tracks back."

"You figure?" asked the detective. "You haven't gotten more specific information from your daughter since then?"

Louise exhaled pointedly and led Maxim to her daughter. The concrete backyard was not tiny, but it was dominated by a rectangular sand pit. Like many parks for kids throughout the country, this had some playground equipment: a double swing set, a trampoline, a see-saw. Only it was all for one girl. Alice slowed on her swing as they approached, tennis shoes brushing the sand.

"My daughter is autistic, Detective." He nodded to show he was aware, and she continued. "She doesn't convey stories the way we do. She can't process new experiences well. Her life is about routines. Play time, nap time, lunch time. Unfortunately, she's never been able to tell us where she went that day."

"She didn't say anything telling?" Maxim took a deep breath and considered his misfortune. Just as with Annabelle, the witness was unreliable.

"Some," answered Louise. "She said she visited friends. Why don't you ask her?"

"Uh..." Maxim stammered. He was embarrassed for not doing so. "Hello Alice."

"Hello."

The answer came fast. A canned response more than a true greeting.

Maxim wondered how best to broach the subject. "Do you remember last year, when you were in the forest overnight?"

Louise cut in. "The field trip, Alice. You remember?"

The girl giggled. "Yes."

Maxim lowered himself to his knees. "Do you remember seeing any people there?"

"Yes."

"Do you remember an old man with red hair?"

Alice shook her head with a shy grin. "No. Only boys and girls. Mommy says no talking to men."

Maxim turned to Louise, who shrugged. He could've been offended but supposed he couldn't blame her. It must be difficult to raise an autistic child. A stringent set of rules was likely very necessary.

"How many boys and girls?" he asked.

Alice heaved her shoulders in reply.

"Was it five boys and girls? Ten?"

Alice chewed her lip. "Okay."

Maxim furrowed his brow and Louise cut in.

"You need to be careful about giving her information. If she thinks you're instructing her then she'll go along with whatever you say. I've spoken to her about her friends many times. From what I gathered, it was a handful of them only. All children, some younger than her. Alice doesn't have a lot of friends, and my husband and I figured they were make-believe."

Maxim could feel his face darken. He had a feeling the stories of children were all too real, but none of it made sense. The local children that went missing in recent years could certainly fill the numbers, but how or why would they gather in the forest? Without adults?

"Were any of them hurt, Alice?"

"No."

"What did you do together?"

"Play."

Her mother cut in again.

"What did you play, sweetie?"

Alice smiled and turned to Maxim. "Hopscotch. And skipping. And hide-and-go-seek. And swimming. But swimming's bad. Mommy always says don't play in water. I don't like water. Sand is better." The girl hopped off her swing and landed in the sand. She scooped it with her hands.

Maxim backed away. He now realized the rectangular sandbox built into the concrete was a filled-in swimming pool.

Louise knew what he was thinking. "Alice had an accident when she was very young. We knew she was autistic, and swimming was a good outlet for her energy. She loved it, too. But she had too many accidents. She got caught in the water intake once and my husband had to yank her out. Another time she jumped in while she was tangled in a net. We considered buying a new house but the market was awful and we couldn't afford taking the loss, so we just had it converted to a playground." Louise took careful steps through the grains of sand as if the water were still there. "She likes this better, now. She gets plenty of sun and exercise and it's much safer."

"I like the beach," exclaimed Alice.

Her mother smiled. "I know, sweetie."

"I like the sun. The bad lights don't come out in the sun."

Maxim cocked his head. "The bad lights?"

"Don't let the lights see you," warned the girl, as if her meaning was clear.

Louise shook her head. "I'm sorry, Detective. It's hard to get straight answers out of her sometimes. She likes to play on the train tracks. I let her do it because it makes her happy, but we constantly warn her how dangerous it can be. The bad lights are the train lights. And the cars. I always tell her to watch out for traffic, whether she's on the road or not."

The detective nodded.

"Don't play in the road," parroted Alice. "Don't play in

the water."

Maxim stepped out of the sand and shook some from his shoes. The girl's words made him feel uneasy, no matter how innocent they were meant to be. In some ways, Alice Radford and Annabelle Hayes had similar stories, but their upbringing was necessarily different. Maxim wondered if all the hard rules had played a part in sparing Alice from potential trauma.

Louise followed the detective a few steps away from her daughter. She lowered her voice. "Are you close to finding the girl?"

"Huh?" he asked, broken from his thoughts.

"I can see she's on your mind."

"Oh. I don't know how close we are. She wasn't who I was thinking about. There's another girl, the one we did find closer to Sanctuary."

The mother allowed a small smile across her lips. "How's she doing?"

Maxim weighed his response. "It's tough to say. She's emotional. Acting out. But I can't get past that she has nothing to say about her disappearance either. Tell me, has Alice seemed any different to you since she came back?"

Louise raised an eyebrow. "Different? No, Detective. She's a strong girl. She took it in stride."

"That's not what I mean." Maxim scratched his chin, unsure how to phrase his concern. "Her mother, well, she told me her daughter wasn't the same. Like, it wasn't really her."

Louise's face relaxed into something that saddened him.

"Sometimes it's easier to think that, Detective. My husband and I were in denial about our daughter for a short period. It was a lot to process. Things would've been easier if she wasn't ours. If we could have started over."

The detective didn't know what to say. It sounded like an awful train of thought, the type that would make any parent feel guilt for the rest of their lives.

Louise turned back to her daughter and beamed proudly. "At the end of the day, you need to accept your child for whoever they are. You need to let all the baggage drift away so it's only you and them, and then you'll see how much they mean to you. Then you'll see how much you love them, and how you could never live without them."

Maxim gave the woman a half smile. He didn't have kids. It was hard for him to empathize. But he knew this mother would do anything in her power to protect her child.

He had to admit, he didn't get the same feeling from Olivia.

His phone buzzed and he checked it. Strange. Olivia Hayes was calling, as if she knew she was the subject of conversation. It might have been providence, but Maxim's uneasy feeling returned. And, somehow, he knew something had gone horribly wrong.

Chapter 45

Maxim slalomed between the police cruisers and Fire Rescue vehicles. He didn't slow down until it was too late, and his front left wheel skipped onto the curb. He grumbled and threw his Audi into park, leaping from the car without bothering to shut it off.

The front yard of Olivia's house was not as serene as it normally was. First responders crowded the perfectly manicured lawn. The lush grass, the trimmed hedges, the old-world charm—it was still there, but now it had twisted into an ironic, dark parody of itself. Hitchens, Cole, and Stokes were there, but his fellow officers wore grim masks.

The group centered around the grand fountain next to the walkway. Barney Hitchens saw Maxim approach first. He didn't bother saying anything.

"Out of my way," barked the detective, brushing past a poor EMT who was standing around with his hands in his pockets.

The bubbling water and bright blue paint didn't appear so magical anymore. Not with the soaking wet body of Annabelle Hayes lying on the brick next to it.

Somebody had pulled the girl out of the water, but it was too late. Her skin wasn't as blue as the paint in the fountain, but it was eerily similar. She wore a white fluffy dress that was a little too small for her. It was something a little kid might wear when they played princess. Her bare toenails and fingernails were painted bright red, and she wore no makeup except for matching lipstick. Her eyes were still open, their glassiness and her dress giving the eerie impression of a doll.

"Damn it!" screamed Maxim, flipping away and taking in the scene.

Olivia sat on the porch with a blanket over her shoulders. A paramedic attended to her, holding an oxygen mask to her mouth. She made no noise, as if her tears and voice had long evaporated. Dark lines of eyeliner ran down her cheeks and Maxim recalled the same lines on Annabelle's face when she'd been found. Except Olivia's eyes were red with grief, staring into nothing, unaware of those around her. Annabelle hadn't appeared to be crying.

The water.

Maxim spun around and surveyed the fountain floor. The streams of water from the upper level splashed below and agitated the pool, making it hard to see.

"Why is this still on?" he asked, addressing but not facing the sergeant. "Can someone please shut this fucking fountain off?"

Sergeant Hitchens motioned for Cole to take care of it and stepped closer to Maxim so he could speak in a low voice. "The mother found her, dragged her out, and called it in. By the time we got here—"

Maxim waved Hitchens away. He didn't want to hear it. He didn't want to hear anything except answers. He'd saved this girl. Annabelle had already been safe. This wasn't supposed to happen.

The detective circled the base of the fountain and examined the inside edge. Eventually, the water flow stopped and he got a clearer picture of the floor. Besides a few copper pennies, he didn't see anything out of the ordinary.

At the far end he found an intake filter. Maxim ran his hands into the crevice and scraped the surface. Nothing had been sucked against the grate. It was operating as normal. By the time he returned to his starting position, nothing had come up as suspicious.

Maxim finally faced the body again and thought a long moment. Hitchens had silently followed a few paces behind the detective the entire time. "Who did what with Annabelle?" Maxim asked him.

Hitchens grunted. "Oh, it's okay for me to talk now? You're not gonna snap at me again?"

"I'm not in the mood for this shit, Barney."

"Son, you better slow your roll. We all understand how upset you are, but don't take it out on us."

Maxim gritted his teeth. He almost told the sergeant off

but noticed Cole walking by. Maxim intercepted him instead.

"Cole, tell me who touched Annabelle after Olivia pulled her from the water."

The officer shrugged. "Stokes got here first. Pulled the mother away and initiated CPR. Fire Rescue was next and took over. They pronounced her ten minutes ago. Since then the sergeant ordered everyone away."

Maxim nodded. Hitchens had done the right thing, and it would've been easy enough for him to say as much. The detective looked to the grumbling sergeant and frowned. "Can we please get Olivia inside?"

Hitchens grumbled. "She didn't want—"

"I don't care what she wants. This is a crime scene now. Either she gets on the truck and taken to the clinic or she goes inside."

The two men stared at each other for a moment before the sergeant scowled and stormed away. Maxim kneeled by the dead girl and put his hands to his face.

This was his fault. He'd known something was going on —was going to happen—but he'd been unable to crack Annabelle.

After a minute, he opened his eyes and made sure Olivia was inside. He donned a pair of black nitrile gloves. Then he swallowed hard, lifted Annabelle's dress, and peeked under. He let the cloth fall and nodded. The girl was still wearing underwear.

He took a quick peek in her mouth. Nothing was there, and the emergency responders would've cleared the passage.

He checked for bruising on her arms and along her neck and shoulders. He didn't see any. His gut was that this was a suicide. Annabelle's behavior of late only reinforced that idea.

Maxim couldn't believe it, but he felt a tear come to his eye. He'd seen this kind of thing before, but this one hurt. A shadow crossed over him and he figured Hitchens had come back for round two. The detective spun around, ready to uppercut, and saw a man with wire-rimmed glasses standing over him.

"Dr. Medina," said Maxim.

The part-time Sanctuary medical examiner didn't take his eyes off Annabelle. He wordlessly shook his head.

Maxim drew away, not wanting to expose his emotions. "I'll let you get to it, Doctor." He marched to the porch and inside.

Olivia Hayes was on the couch. The paramedic was packing up the oxygen tank, about to leave, but Maxim was too impatient.

"Give us some privacy," he demanded.

When they were alone, Maxim sat down next to the grief-stricken mother.

"She's not my daughter," murmured Olivia.

A crack lined Maxim's forehead. "What?"

Olivia lifted her head. Her eyes were swollen, but dry. They even betrayed a glimmer of hope. "Annabelle is still alive," she whispered. "Ever since she came back from Sycamore, she wasn't the real Annabelle. That... *thing* outside isn't my daughter."

Maxim lost some steam. He didn't remember what he was going to say. "That's... crazy," was all he could think of. He realized how insensitive it was to say after it came out.

Olivia shook her head firmly. "No. It's not. They want you to think it is. They want to make *you* the crazy one, but it's all just tricks. Shine a light on it and reveal the truth." She scooted closer to him. "That's what I need you for. You can find her, Maxim. I *need* you to find her for me."

Maxim collapsed back into the couch. He'd been angry at Olivia. He remembered that now. He was going to chew her out for letting this happen. It beat blaming himself, anyway. But hearing what came out of her mouth doubled the sick feeling in his stomach. The anger had been good. It focused him. Without it, he felt lost again.

Olivia put a hand on Maxim's chest and he gasped for air.

"This has been so hard," she admitted. Maxim knew it was a hard confession for a woman like her to make. She put her weary face into his shoulder. "I need your help."

Maxim's voice cracked. "I tried."

Olivia swung her leg around and straddled his lap, facing him. He could feel her hot breath on his neck. He could feel his blood stirring.

"What are you doing?"

She grabbed the sides of his head. "I need you to believe me, Maxim."

Olivia smiled, a bit too emphatically. Her face pleaded for him to give, if only an ounce. For him to validate her hope.

"Olivia..."

She leaned in and pressed her cheek to his. In a whisper, lips tickling his ear, she said, "I need *you*, Maxim."

Her toned thighs tightened and she gyrated her hips over his. He could imagine her tanned legs through the thin clothing. A light whimper escaped her lips as she pressed against him.

"Olivia!"

Maxim swept the woman to the side none too delicately and jumped to his feet uncomfortably.

"I can't believe you!" he boomed.

She went limp. Her voice came weakly but she was unashamed. "I can't do this alone."

Maxim became nauseous now. Part of it was directed at himself as the thought of Olivia on top of him still turned him on. But he felt something else. The rage that he fostered against himself, against her. It boiled up again. His neck and ears burned and he couldn't take it anymore.

"Your daughter is lying dead in the front yard, Olivia! This is real! This happened!"

"Dwyer!"

Maxim spun to see Hitchens in the doorway. If the detective had thought the sergeant was angry before, he didn't know how to describe what he was now.

"Why don't you come outside, Detective," said the sergeant. It came out as an order, not a question, even though Hitchens didn't outrank him.

The mother sobbed into a handheld cushion and Maxim's resolve cracked. Every step he took was wrong, each journey only leading farther from the destination. The detective was still upset, but he realized he'd been wrong to release his pent-up anger. Olivia's only child had just been taken from her. He put his hand to his head again, unsure of his next move.

"It's not her who drowned," said Olivia quietly. "My baby wouldn't kill herself. My baby wouldn't run away."

Barney Hitchens swallowed his next words and looked from her to the detective. He didn't know what to say either. Maxim straightened his jacket. He knew he couldn't help anymore and started to leave the room.

"She never liked swimming," said the mother. "Annabelle never played in the fountain or the pool before. She never even liked baths."

The detective stopped. Last he'd seen Annabelle alive, she wasn't exactly taking a bath either. But she'd overflowed the tub and the sink. Her motive hadn't been apparent.

"Do you have a pool?" he asked.

Olivia Hayes nodded, still facing the floor. "A small one, indoors, with the spa. I had to lock the room because I caught her in there with her clothes on. I thought she was going to overflow it like the bathroom."

Maxim almost fell backward. His mind raced. Louise Radford had filled her pool in after her daughter had acted strangely. In the woods, Annabelle had been found wet, with running makeup. It didn't make sense at the time. But it did now, in a strange, compelling way.

Without a word to either of them, Maxim marched out the front door and towards his car. He dialed his friend, the other best hope for Hazel Cunningham, and was relieved to get an answer.

"Diego," he said, "it's the water. They go to the water."

Chapter 46

Diego parked his bike on the sidewalk at the Williams Ranger District building. He left his gold helmet on the seat and unzipped his leather jacket. It was getting hot again.

He entered the building and immediately saw Maxim and a park ranger huddled over the reception counter. They were referencing points on an unfolded paper map.

"Find anything?" he asked them.

"Who's this?" asked the ranger.

Maxim appeared excited to get things started. "Ranger Dan Briggs, Diego de la Torre."

Diego offered his hand at the hasty introduction. Dan clasped it a bit too tightly.

"What department are you with?" he asked.

"He's not," cut in Maxim. "He's a civilian."

The ranger's eyes widened. "You're a private investigator?"

Diego dismissed the question. "Not really."

"Well, who do you work for then?"

"Actually, I'm kind of in between jobs right now."

Maxim rolled his eyes at the news. He was probably afraid Diego would fall back into his outlaw ways. Still, it was those tendencies that had broken this case.

"He's a good tracker," explained Maxim. "Used to do domestic service for the Commissioned Corps. He's been looking for Hazel nonstop since she's gone missing and we could use an extra pair of eyes."

Dan Briggs frowned. "It's just that we can't be liable if you get hurt."

"I can take care of myself," assured the biker.

"Ranger," maintained Maxim, "I understand your concerns. But he's been invaluable. If anything goes south, you could say he's with me."

"Besides," Diego added, "I was here first." He didn't know what Dan's involvement here was, but he wouldn't get cut out of this. The ranger seemed to pick up on that fact and waved the point off.

"Fine then. Just let us handle anything official," said Dan. Diego glared at him. Law enforcement had been a real pain lately. He decided to let it slide and changed the subject.

"So what's this you said about the water?"

Maxim's face lit up. "I expanded my search parameters and isolated a few more incidents of missing children. In some cases the kids returned or were found, just like Annabelle. In others, they disappeared for good, like..." The detective stopped short of saying Hazel, but they both knew what he'd implied.

"She hasn't disappeared for good yet," insisted Diego.

Maxim cleared his throat. "I didn't say that."

"Bullshit you didn't."

"Look," said Maxim firmly. "I know we can still find her, okay?"

The biker huffed. "So that was just a slip of your sensitivity training, huh? Or have you become just another jaded cop like the rest of them?"

"You're wrong," asserted Maxim.

Diego didn't let up. "You know, if you always think the worst will happen, you'll never be able to stop it."

The detective wordlessly stared at the map. Diego noticed something on the man's face that he'd seen before. What was it?

Ranger Briggs butted in. "Hey, asshole, that's some way to talk to your friend after what just happened. He's supposed to be investigating a dead girl but instead he's over here, trying to find one still alive."

The outlaw's tongue caught in his throat. He'd sworn he was about to punch the ranger in the face until he processed what was said. Diego turned to Maxim. "What dead girl?"

Dan answered again. "The one he rescued from the forest at the beginning of the week. He just fished her out of her rich family's fountain. Right in front of mommy."

"Annabelle Hayes?"

Maxim winced at the sound of the girl's name. That's when Diego recognized the expression in his friend's face. Pain. He'd seen it before when Maxim had lost his wife.

Accusing the man of not taking his job seriously had been off base. The proof of that was evident in Maxim's eyes.

"I didn't mean—"

"We don't have time for this," said the detective. "I was only comparing Hazel to the others to build a profile. Some of the kids returned unharmed. Some were never recovered. One boy was found drowned."

Diego caught on. "The same as Annabelle."

"Exactly. Even the kids who got home had strange predilections for water. And it's not only afterward. When I first found Annabelle, her clothes were damp and her makeup was streaked."

The biker weighed the information. "I thought the police searched the lakes and reservoirs already."

"We did," said Maxim. "Several times. And again looking for Red. Briggs said the old man could only hide out near water. But you remember the Paradise Killings a couple years back?"

Diego could never forget. "The bodies were stuffed in barrels and dropped into Paradise Tank."

"Which was in the middle of nowhere. Arizona's rife with water tanks like that. Most of them are little used or abandoned."

The ranger cocked his head. "Many of them aren't even on maps," he added.

"Okay," said Diego. "But like you said. They're all over the place. How do we know which to check?"

Maxim shook his head. "We don't. But look at this." The detective planted his finger on the map. "Because Annabelle was recovered west of Sanctuary, most of our follow-up searches were north of the Interstate. Besides that, the Quiet Pines campgrounds are on the north border of the 40 anyway. Most of us assumed Hazel couldn't have crossed without being noticed or picked up."

Diego chewed his lip and stared at the bumping horizontal line that bisected Sycamore. Interstate 40 was a natural wall, but it hadn't completely prevented the police from looking elsewhere. "I helped with a search party on the south side, but I admit the effort wasn't as exhaustive as the north. That's why I was down there yesterday."

"And those were good instincts," said Maxim. "The more I think about it, it makes sense. The forest is thicker south of Williams. Another girl from town went missing and wandered back along the tracks. Echo Canyon is outside town, south of the Interstate. That's where Red ran off to. If there's a place for Hazel to have slipped through our fingers, it's down there. Especially if she's trying to get back to Williams."

Briggs grunted. "It's been long enough for her to have walked from Quiet Pines to Williams twenty times already."

Diego had figured the same thing before. "Maybe she's lost."

Maxim's suggestion was darker. "Maybe she's trapped."

The three men contemplated the grim possibilities.

"Here's the thing," said Maxim. "I have task force investigators running down leads in other states. I have deputies canvassing the park. Briggs has rangers doing the same. With the new focus around the area of the grave site, something might turn up. But, we're starting all over again. It can take days. Hazel—"

"She doesn't have days," finished Diego.

The ranger checked the national parks map and picked a location south of Williams. "How about this? Dogtown Reservoir?"

The biker shook his head. "We can't just make arbitrary guesses. When I found the bones, I wasn't randomly wandering around. I was—" Diego stopped, aware that Briggs would laugh off anything he said.

"There's something else," inferred Maxim.

"Yes. The symbols in the forest. Celtic crosses carved into the barks of trees." The outlaw drew the glyph over the map with his finger.

"My ass," chimed the ranger. "Inconsiderate vandals are marking their territory in public parks these days. You heard about that graffiti at Joshua Tree?"

"Forget about that. You've seen these symbols?"

"Sure," said Briggs. "Around Echo Canyon, and the grave site, like you said. The markings have been spreading."

"Where?"

"Hold on a minute," said Maxim. "What's the deal with the symbols?"

Diego lowered his voice. "They scratch them in the trees to warn each other about Red. The glyphs are something they leave behind. It shows where they've been."

Maxim rubbed the scruff on his neck. "If we're looking for water *and* Celtic crosses, that has to narrow our search quite a bit."

"Exactly," said the biker, turning to Ranger Briggs. "If you've seen these markings close to water tanks in the area, you've got to let us know."

The ranger seemed to have questions but considered his request all the same. Briggs finally put an index finger on Echo Canyon and a thumb on Williams. Then he dragged both away and converged them together over the area where he'd seen the symbols. "That's it," he said, tapping in the middle of a sea of green. "Wounded Ranger Tank."

Diego swallowed as he checked the map. "But there's nothing there."

"Sure there is," said Dan. "It's just not marked. That's how small it is. It's dry most of the time. That's why I'd forgotten about it. But with the downpours we've been having lately—"

"That's it," echoed Diego. "I can feel it."

Maxim eyed him carefully, perhaps feeling the same thing.

Chapter 47

Diego grumbled from the jeep's back seat. It was cramped and he couldn't hear the occasional remarks made between Maxim and Dan in the front. The biker had wanted to take his Scrambler, of course, but the ranger had pointed out how impractical that was. They were venturing into high country, through thick brush and two streams already, and his street bike wasn't built for that abuse. The open air was nice, at least. But this wasn't a pleasure drive.

After some time, Diego leaned forward to see Maxim studying pictures on his phone. As he scrolled through, Diego patted him on the shoulder.

"Wait. Go back."

Maxim swiped back a couple times until Diego nodded.

"That's the one," said the biker.

"What about it?"

"That kid. I've seen that kid before. In the forest."

Diego couldn't forget the golden hair, except in this

school picture, the locks were neatly combed.

"Well, yeah," said Maxim, slightly perplexed. "This is Todd Payton. Those were his bones you stumbled on."

"No, I mean I saw..." Diego trailed off, putting it together for the first time.

Maxim misread the biker's confusion and explained. "I worked up a new crime profile on Lachlan Munro last night after realizing there were many victims. That kilt you found? It wasn't the same one from the RV. Munro tried to burn the evidence in his possession. So I expanded the search parameters and looked for new matches. The task force has gotten multiple hits so far. Get this. Todd was confirmed missing six months ago out of Oklahoma City. The kilt in his grave was fake. Or cheap. It was just a costume kilt for Halloween. Todd Payton dressed in traditional Scottish attire that day. Except he never made it home from school."

Diego stared wordlessly at the digital image. He couldn't tell how old the boy was, but he was about Hazel's age. He had been, anyway. Something about the innocence in his expression tore at Diego. But something else didn't feel right.

"What's the link to Oklahoma City?"

Maxim nodded and tapped his phone to his temple. "You've got to remember. Munro lives in an RV. He's mobile. I've been trying to track his movements as best as possible, but the man lives off the grid. Even campsite records are lacking." Ranger Briggs glanced over with interest. "But Red's RV club is based out of Livingston,

Texas. As is his registration. And Texas requires a yearly vehicle inspection."

Dan cut in. "So Red leaves Arizona at least once a year."

"Not just once a year," said Maxim. "His renewal deadline is the end of October. He hit it right before Halloween. Oklahoma City is only six hours from Livingston. That would've given Red plenty of time to drive city to city scoping for targets of opportunity."

Dan whistled and shook his head. Diego couldn't even manage that sophisticated a reaction. There was no doubt anymore. The circumstantial evidence against Red had piled past any defense. The old man was a child killer.

Finally, the moment passed and Diego could work on the puzzle again. "So what did he do with Hazel?"

Maxim stretched his lips taut and put his phone back in his jacket pocket.

"What is it?" asked Diego.

Maxim sighed. "You're not going to like this."

"Like what?"

"Okay, here goes. Red's not a criminal mastermind or anything, but he's careful. Systematic. I believe he's abducted several children with this routine. He collects victims from out of state and disappears, nothing more than a passing blip on radar."

Diego knew what was coming. "Nobody's perfect, Maxim."

"I know that. I make my living from people's mistakes. But I don't think someone who takes the time to vary their hunting grounds would risk everything by shitting where they sleep. Look at Annabelle Hayes, or the other children who returned. They make no mention of Lachlan Munro, or any adults for that matter. I can't believe he'd be so sloppy as to let them get away and then so lucky as to remain unfingered."

Diego hissed, allowing his temper to come through. He knew what Maxim was saying. That everything they'd done so far had been wasted. That they'd been chasing the wrong lead the last four days.

Ranger Briggs, however, nodded in agreement. "You didn't mention one important fact, Detective."

They both waited for him to enlighten them.

Dan slowed the jeep and parked on the side of the small dirt road. He turned to them. "Well, it's obvious, isn't it? We're looking for a missing girl, but Red likes little boys."

Maxim raised his eyebrows, apparently satisfied with the reasoning. Diego leaned back, trying to process the possibility. Hazel and Annabelle went missing in too close a proximity to Red to be a coincidence. He had to be involved, all right. If law enforcement wanted to spin their wheels trying to make things more complicated than they needed to be, he wouldn't stop them.

Red wasn't his concern. Not yet, anyway. His only mission right now was the little girl.

"Why aren't we moving?" barked Diego, not disguising his annoyance with the men.

Dan Briggs hopped out of the jeep and hooked his hands on his belt. "Wounded Ranger Tank. We're here."

The biker scanned the area, not seeing anything

remotely resembling a lake.

The ranger read their confusion. "Something you need to know about the Sycamore Canyon Wilderness. It's one of the oldest such areas in Arizona. Even before the Wilderness Act, it was a designated Primitive Area. That means this land is as wild as it gets. There aren't any roads where we're going. This is as far as the jeep can take us. From here on out, we hike."

Chapter 48

Maxim wiped the sweat from his brow. It was cool within the forest—the grand canopy above smothered the sun like a dark storm cloud—but they had been hiking for more than an hour. It was a good thing Briggs had packed water bottles because the physical toll was greater than expected.

Much of the terrain was treacherous: uphill, downstream, through thickets and crevasses. It wasn't life threatening, but slow going all the same. The tree cover cast darker shadows than should have been possible during the day. Even worse, the sun was falling in the sky.

"I don't think an eight-year-old could've made it this way," complained Diego as he vaulted the rocky crest of the hill. The three men scanned the ground on the other side. Briggs squinted through the trees and Diego sat for a moment.

"There are easier ways to the tank," said the ranger.

"Really?" mocked Diego. "You don't think we could

have gone one of those ways then?"

Maxim chewed his lip. According to Briggs, they had almost reached Wounded Ranger Tank three times already. Instead, they were quickly losing the day.

"We're lost," said the detective matter-of-factly. "Aren't we?"

Dan Briggs kept his eyes on the lower ground. Maxim withdrew his phone and was surprised to see a faint signal.

Diego hissed. "What's the point of a park ranger escort if you don't know the way?"

"I know the way," assured Briggs. "I don't know what happened. I just... got turned around somehow. I've been to the tank many times before."

"Have you ever been here?" asked the biker.

Briggs nervously tapped his finger on his belt. "Not really."

"What about the dry creek we passed?" asked Maxim. "Shouldn't that have led us to it?"

The ranger shook his head. "The tank isn't a natural body of water. It's not connected to the river network. Don't worry, though. I think I got my bearings."

Maxim's phone finally loaded their GPS location. "You wanna check the map?"

"No need. It's this way. Let's go."

Ranger Briggs marched down the hill. Maxim nodded and put his phone away.

The biker frowned. "He has no idea where he's going."

"I don't know," returned Maxim. "He's headed straight to where the GPS says he should be going."

The biker heaved himself to his feet and let out a tired groan. "I'd be a lot more confident if he wasn't walking straight back the way we came."

Maxim smirked and the two men followed the eager ranger at a distance.

"Didn't you get lost in the woods for half a day?" joked the detective.

"I don't want to talk about it."

"Fine then." As they neared the bottom of the hill, Briggs pulled farther ahead. He was trying to beat the sun down. According to Google, a straight line to the tank would give them plenty of time. "As the crow flies," murmured Maxim.

Diego grumbled, "I don't think we'll be seeing any crows today." Maxim almost asked what the annoyed biker meant, but Diego moved on. "Look at him. He's practically running. He loves it out here."

"It's kind of nice," Maxim admitted. "It just needs better cell coverage."

"Doesn't bother me. I don't have mine with me."

"Big surprise."

"What gets me is all the walking and climbing. It's arduous. Slow. It's the opposite of the open road."

The detective couldn't disagree. They lived surrounded by nature. Sanctuary was nestled within the woods, but it was an oasis that held the wild at bay. Plus, it was connected to the rest of the world by asphalt and power lines. Well, maybe some of the roads were dirt, but it was nothing his TT couldn't manage.

"What do you think makes a person want to rough it out here?" asked Maxim.

His friend considered the question longer than small talk warranted. "You're talking about Red."

"I suppose. I mean, he had a mom and dad. Maybe siblings. He had to've been a part of society at one time. What makes a man up and disconnect like he did?"

"Besides his proclivities?" Diego swung his shotgun to his other hand. "He's running from something. If someone somewhere else had done their job, he'd already be in prison waiting for the needle."

"Or maybe he's far from home."

Diego didn't buy it. "Maybe, but he's running. I've seen it before. In his case, he probably killed somebody too close to him and had to take off. You've seen the news stories too. The media interviews the neighbor, who says, 'I don't know how this could've happened. He was always such a nice old man.' None of the friends ever suspect anything, but they should."

Maxim attempted to smile at the humor. "Well, let's hope he was old when he started this, anyway." Briggs was still in sight. Maxim and Diego kept to a brisk pace, and the ranger slowed to allow them to catch up.

"Do you think that's what makes a society?" asked Maxim. "Friends and neighbors?"

Diego cocked his head. "Do you?" he asked rhetorically. After a minute, he answered. "Living next to some other jackass doesn't make you social. It doesn't make you part of the greater whole. You need to actively *connect* to other people. That's why they call the opposite disconnected."

Maxim frowned, his thoughts directed inward. Here he was, judging Red's life, but the microscope didn't feel especially good on him either. Since his wife had died, Maxim had lost most of his social nature. His friends had really been *her* friends. Or coworkers. When it came down to it, Diego was his only friend. The irony was not lost on Maxim that a detective could only trust an outlaw.

But it was more than that. Ever since his wife, and a brief dalliance with Nithya Rao, Maxim hadn't involved himself with dating either.

The thought wasn't just uncomfortable. It burned him like an ant under a magnifying glass. He had to admit, the light of truth was harsh.

Good thing the sun didn't penetrate the Sycamore tree cover.

"I've been seeing Julia a lot these last few days," Diego blurted out.

Maxim shook his head clear and studied the biker. Diego had been analyzing himself as well. "Do you think that's wise? With Hazel missing?"

"Of course it isn't. But I've been taking it slow. I don't want to take advantage of her. She's..."

"Nice," finished Maxim.

The biker nodded. "You know, I've never met Hazel, but Julia's told me so much about her that I feel like I do. It's weird because I barely know her, but after my sister left town, I don't have anyone to look after. You know?"

Maxim frowned again. "You're ready for that? You want

a kid all of a sudden? How old are you again?"

"Oh, come on. You only got me by five years."

"Yeah, and I don't think I'm ready."

Diego chuckled. "It just feels right," he said. "I know we can find Hazel and move past this. Then we can see how things go when everything's stable."

"Nothing's ever stable for you, Diego."

"I'm serious. You know, I can tell there's something between you and Olivia too."

The flip of the lens was jarring. Immediately, Maxim soured. "Let's not get into that."

"Why not?" countered Diego. "I know her daughter didn't make it, bro. I'm so sorry about that. For her, but for you too." The man patted Maxim on the shoulder, but he brushed the arm away.

"That's not about me."

"But it is, Maxim. It's obvious to everybody except you." Diego quieted for a moment to let that stew. "You've been through a lot these last few years. It would be good for you to put yourself out there, even if it didn't work out. Make a connection."

All the wetness abandoned Maxim's mouth. He needed a chug from his water bottle before continuing. "It's not that I haven't thought about it," he said.

"But?"

"What do you want me to say? Something about the situation doesn't feel right. Something about Annabelle."

"You see? You know more about the girl than you let on." Maxim knew Diego was trying to lighten the mood, but he didn't see the reason for it. "Tell me something about her," the biker said.

"Who?"

"Annabelle. Tell me something about her."

Maxim dropped his eyes to his feet, comforted by the repetitive back and forth of their gait. He couldn't say how well he'd known Annabelle. During his limited visits, the girl hadn't spoken much. Like him, she'd been disconnected. She must have been happy one day, but something rotted the joy away until only emptiness remained. She hadn't talked because there was nothing left of herself to give.

"She was sad," professed Maxim. "Very, very sad." What else could he possibly say about her?

Diego shook his head. "No, bro. Tell me something about *her*. About who she was."

The detective released a heavy breath. He had to know more than that. It was his job to read people. Sometimes that was all he had to go on.

Vacant, lifeless eyes staring into nothingness.

Annabelle Hayes had put herself into that fountain. She'd taken her own life deliberately. The ME would say no different. That's what Maxim knew.

Only, the why was more perplexing.

"I know she believed in spirits," he finally said. He recalled the Ouija board, the kid's game in her room, meant for séances with the dead. Maxim stuck his hands in his jacket and retrieved her key chain, still there. Forgotten. He studied the eyes of the Day of the Dead skeleton. Another lifeless mask. "She believed in an afterlife."

Diego furrowed his brow. "Maxim, that's not quite what I had in mind."

"That's why she killed herself. I think that's why she ran off into the forest. She didn't want to be alive in this shitty world anymore."

The biker didn't have a response to that. Maxim was happy for the silence.

The key chain jingled in his hands. He thought about Annabelle leaving it behind at her father's house, a sign that she wouldn't need them again. Had she forgotten them in Maxim's car on purpose as well? Maybe she'd always planned on disappearing. Maybe it was a message to him.

It felt strange to have something of the girl's. He'd only found it the night before. There was never a chance to return it. Now that Annabelle was dead, it felt wrong to have it, like he had a part of her that she cherished. He clinked the metal in his hands absentmindedly.

Again he studied the alarm fob. He wondered what it was used for if Annabelle didn't drive. Then he read the labels above the buttons and realized the device didn't open or close doors. It didn't lock and unlock cars. It was an audio recorder.

Maxim pressed the playback button and heard a tinny voice through the speaker. Diego turned to him with a dark expression when they understood what they were listening to. Annabelle was singing. Maxim couldn't understand many of the words, but the song was sad and haunted.

He tried to turn the volume up but the track skipped.

The thing only had a few buttons so he didn't have very fine control over what he could do.

"I love you, Mom," came Annabelle's voice over the speaker. "I love you, Dad. It's not your fault, even if you don't love each other." Something unintelligible followed. Maxim moved the fob to his ear. There were strange clunking sounds and then he couldn't hear anything else. The track had ended.

He pushed the button again. This time there was a man's voice.

"Why are you always playing with that key chain?" Maxim didn't recognize him through the small speaker.

"I don't know," answered the girl. "You took away my cell phone."

"That's so we can talk privately, Annabelle. I want you focusing on my words."

Maxim realized it was Dr. Collins. Annabelle had recorded a session with him.

"You must stop doing this to your mother," he continued. "It really concerns her."

"She doesn't care about me," said Annabelle.

"That's not true. It hurts her. At your age, it's difficult to see the world through the eyes of others. You don't see what you're doing to her."

"It doesn't matter."

"You'll break her heart," he said firmly. "She still has affection for me. These cries for help cause more damage than simply bearing the burden yourself."

Maxim listened intently, getting the thrust of the

message while missing some of the specific references. It was standard psychoanalysis, as far as he knew, but it felt wrong. If simply having the key chain felt like an invasion of Annabelle's privacy, listening to her private songs and conversations was an outright violation.

"You are strong," repeated Bertrand several times. "Remember you told me that when you first ran away. I believed you Annabelle, then and now. You are strong enough for this."

As they hiked, Maxim had trouble focusing on the banalities of the therapy. Everything mentioned was about her feelings, her state of mind. The girl wasn't talkative and mostly just listened as the doctor dictated advice. Maxim listened and played with the key chain, walking in the dimming light, wondering how long the audio track was.

A faint smile crossed the detective's lips when he realized he was holding a mini-flashlight as well.

He squeezed the button and a sharp green light came on. Maxim waved it around but it was a useless gesture. The LED burned brightly, but it didn't cast any light on the dark surroundings. He moved closer to a tree to gauge just how close he needed to be to see the light against the bark. When he got closer, he saw it. A glyph, carved into the bark.

"Good job," said Diego sarcastically, sighing and squinting ahead in the fading light. "Now we just need a hundred more of those flashlights and we could see something out here."

Maxim didn't reply. In fact, he completely froze. With the press of a button, the audio cut out.

It wasn't the Celtic cross he was paying attention to anymore. Standing just a foot behind the brush, looking right at him, was Annabelle Hayes.

Chapter 49

"Holy shit," muttered Maxim under his breath. "Annabelle?"

Diego eyed him strangely. "What did you call me?"

"It's her," the detective answered.

The girl stood there, wearing the same ruffled dress she had drowned in. Her baby blue eyes shone against his dim LED. Just a few feet away, the girl waved at him and smiled at her key chain.

Maxim had to be dreaming, but everything felt so real. He released the flashlight button and jingled it. It sounded real. And Maxim remembered the entire day. He couldn't recall that ever happening in a dream. But there was one way to find out for sure. The detective reached for the girl.

Annabelle Hayes turned on her bare feet and sprinted away.

"Stop!" cried Maxim. He barreled through the low branches and gave chase. Diego yelled for him to wait but his words were muffled. Maxim crunched ahead through bushes and batted pine needles away from his face.

The woods weren't thick enough to impede him much, but the girl was fast. She dashed between trees with abandon, not even bothering to check on him. Maxim swore he saw Annabelle skip once or twice. She was carefree, almost. Playing.

"Maxim!" yelled Diego behind him. "Don't do it. Come back."

The detective didn't slow. She was getting away and he couldn't risk losing her.

Annabelle banked sharply and Maxim skidded in a patch of soft weeds. He didn't stop himself so much as ram his shoulder hard into the trunk of a large sycamore. He winced but ignored it and took off in the new direction, keys wildly jangling in his hand.

"Don't run, Annabelle!"

The girl darted from tree to bush to tree, partly obscured yet always in his sight. He noticed her haphazard path had no bearing. She was quicker than the detective but wasn't trying to outrun him. She took another turn and Maxim adjusted early, closing the gap between them.

"I just want to talk," he said, trying not the scare the girl.

A ribbon from her dress flapped in the air behind her. It brushed against Maxim's outstretched hands just as she leapt forward off the edge of an overhang. Too late Maxim realized the ground ran out beneath him. His gaze shot down when he felt nothing under his flailing feet.

The ledge wasn't high, or the fall dangerous. But it was

unexpected. Just six feet below, Maxim landed hard on his knee and tumbled to the ground. He did a full somersault, which he hadn't done in twenty years, and groaned as he scraped to a stop. He immediately shot his head up and turned to Annabelle.

Or, he turned to where she should've been. Whether she'd landed on her feet or not, her momentum would've carried her away from the small ledge. The tree cover had thinned on this lower ground, but the girl wasn't anywhere in sight.

Maybe he *was* dreaming.

"Maxim!" called Diego, who skidded to a stop before he could make the same fall. "You okay?"

The detective ignored the man and continued scanning the horizon.

The biker hopped down, boots thudding solidly beside Maxim. "What the fuck was that about?"

"Annabelle," repeated Maxim. "Haven't you been paying attention? Open your eyes."

Diego frowned at the pronouncement. "My eyes are open, Maxim, and I didn't see anyone."

"Come on."

"There's no one else here. Just you and me. At this point I don't even know where Dan is."

"I'm not crazy," insisted the detective, limping to his feet. "And I've never felt this much pain in a dream before, so this is happening."

"What's happening?"

"I saw Annabelle Hayes standing right in front of me,

Diego. It was her. Unmistakably. I was playing with the—" Maxim tapped his pockets, then searched the ground. "Where are they?"

Diego grew unusually silent. He watched Maxim pace back and forth as he looked for the keys.

"I was playing with the flashlight and making noise with the key chain, remember? They were in my hands. That's when I saw the glyph. That's when Annabelle showed up."

The biker ground his teeth and slowly approached a nearby tree. Maxim followed his gaze and saw yet another Celtic cross scrawled on the bark.

"It's not her," said Diego solemnly.

"It has to be," insisted Maxim. "You know what Olivia told me today? She told me her daughter was still out here. That the one that returned home to her was an impostor. She said she knew her real daughter was still alive."

Diego turned away and took a long breath. After a minute he hefted himself back up the ledge and sat upon it, feet dangling over the edge. "I don't mean like that, Maxim. If you say you saw Annabelle out here, I believe you. But it's not her. Not anymore."

"Meaning?"

"It's what used to be her."

Maxim's throat welled up. He knew what the biker was saying, but he didn't believe it. Not if there was still a chance to save Annabelle. The detective checked the trees again. He saw more carvings. They were close to something.

"Listen to me, Maxim," urged his friend. "Just stop for a second."

Maxim kept surveying the ground. "The keys. There was something in that audio. Something I was missing. There might be more. I need to find the keys."

Diego changed tack. "What was the name of that boy I found, again?"

Maxim rubbed his face. "What? Todd Payton. Why?"

"I told you I saw him before. It wasn't from a picture and it wasn't in the news. He was the one I saw in the woods that day." Maxim turned to the man. "He led me to his own bones."

Maxim didn't have the heart to protest. He paced back and forth, incredulous about dropping Annabelle's key chain. About Diego's statement.

"Kayda says this land is rife with spirits. She told me that before I ever mentioned anything about dead children. I didn't believe her at first, but it's the only way to make sense of this."

Maxim finally stopped searching the ground and leaned against a solid tree. His knee hurt anyway. "Children in the forest," he mumbled, remembering the reports from Lachlan Munro and Jason Bower. Red was compromised. He could've been lying or fucking with them. But Jason didn't have a reason to. "It wasn't Annabelle and her hoodlum friends. It was these..."

"I don't know what they are, Maxim. But Kayda has an idea."

The detective rubbed his eyes. He saw a sort of natural order in the explanation, even if it was supernatural. "If what you're saying is true, then it's too late to save Annabelle."

Diego nodded gravely. "Kayda said, 'Fay beget fay.' Annabelle's one of them now. The green children."

Maxim slid down the tree to the ground. He wanted to say it was ridiculous, but he couldn't. "She chose it," was his wistful reply.

Neither of them spoke for a bit. Their thoughts were clear. Annabelle had danced with the children of Sycamore. She had seen their carefree ways and wanted to stay with them. That's why she'd been restless. Why she'd run again at Echo Canyon. And, failing that, that's why she'd sought peace in the water.

"He doesn't kill them all," whispered Maxim.

Diego cocked his head at the announcement.

"Munro. He never abducted Annabelle. He never had anything to do with the local kids. He's too careful for that. But the kids he did kill—the Todd Paytons from hundreds of miles away—he dumped them here. He killed some of them, but he didn't kill them all."

The biker gasped. "The old man said the children continually pestered him. Maybe the ghosts from his past are gathering against him."

"Exactly."

"It explains the iron," said the biker. "Defense against the spirits. I've seen the danger firsthand."

Maxim shook his head. "But they're kids. All of them. Even the autistic daughter, Alice Radford, swore there were no adults involved. So the kids do what kids do. They play and sing and dance and find other kids to play with."

They heard some rustling behind them and spun around,

ready for anything. Ranger Briggs appeared. "There you are! I didn't see you stray off. Something the matter?"

"No," said Maxim. "I just slipped." The ranger contemplated them curiously. Maxim wondered if he saw through the lie. "Did you find a key chain on your way over?"

The ranger shook his head.

Diego ignored the interruption and suddenly became somber. "So even if we find Red, we don't know where Hazel is."

"She's with them," said Maxim. "The children. And we know they congregate by the water."

The park ranger climbed down the ledge and patted Maxim on the back. "Well, children and old men alike, they all need to drink. That's why we're out here, right?"

Diego and Maxim traded a conspiratorial look.

"I have to say," continued the ranger, "I'm pretty embarrassed to be outdone by you two."

Maxim lifted an eyebrow. "How do you mean, Briggs?"

He regarded them plainly. "Wounded Ranger Tank. I've been here twenty times and you were the ones that found it first." Maxim and Diego watched in confusion as the ranger marched past them. "You were right, Diego. You followed the carvings." He pointed at several trees with the symbols on the way. When they followed, it didn't take long to understand.

The ground banked lower as they moved along the crevice wall. They pushed through a pocket of ivy and landed in a small glen with a pool of brackish water.

Maxim swore in disbelief. Ranger Briggs would never believe them, but it wasn't the glyphs that they had followed.

Chapter 50

The peaceful glen was covered in shade. Surrounded by a hill and large pines with ivy snaking between branches, it was textbook beauty, if a bit creepy. The actual water tank was nothing more than natural drainage on sloping ground that sat against a twenty-foot overhang. The area was no wider than a baseball diamond.

"I don't understand," said Diego. He moved closer to the water but stopped short of jumping in. "There's nobody here."

Ranger Briggs crossed his arms. "After all the time it took to find, too. But don't worry, we've got other options."

"This has to be the place," stated Maxim.

Diego knew that to be true as well. What Maxim had seen wasn't an accident. They'd been led here by one of the dead. By one of the green children, who enchanted innocents and bedazzled intruders. This was their inner sanctum.

The ranger shrugged. He didn't know what they knew. "Well," said Dan, "I'd better radio out that we've cleared this tank. We can do that on the higher ground on the way out."

"I want to look around," said Diego.

"Suit yourself, but we're about to lose the sun. It's gonna get real dark real fast. I'll be back after I update them on our status."

Ranger Briggs hiked back up the way they had come to look for a signal.

"Maxim..."

"I know," said the detective. "We're missing something, right?"

"She's close."

"Maybe." Maxim scratched the scruff on his cheek. "Then again, Annabelle and Hazel never knew each other. We'd found Annabelle separated from everyone the same night Hazel Cunningham went missing. It's possible they never crossed paths."

"But the green children are the common link. They would be close together."

Maxim didn't answer.

"It's worth checking out," said the biker. Diego started around to the other side of the tank. "Since you hurt your knee, I'll climb the ledge on this side. I want to get an overwatch of the area."

Maxim circled the tank as well, examining the fresh shoreline where the water recently rose to after the storm. The long grass was flooded and sagged over.

"Why don't you use your green flashlight again?" asked Diego.

"I couldn't find it. It's like Annabelle took it back."

The biker stopped in his tracks. "Maybe that's the only reason she came back," he posited. "Maybe she wasn't helping us."

"I don't believe that."

Diego resumed his pace. It was a thought, anyway, but he wasn't sure what to think anymore. He hadn't said nice things about the girl when she was alive. Maybe he was right and maybe he was wrong about her then, but he had to believe she was on their side now.

He turned to say as much to the detective and found Maxim crouching beside the dark pool. He scooped water into a crushed plastic bottle. It wasn't one of those the ranger had supplied. Maxim held the half full bottle to his eyes and a stream of fluid leaked from a crack in the base.

"Or," suggested Maxim, "maybe Annabelle was here to lead us to Lachlan Munro." He held up the disposable bottle as evidence. "Aqua Vitae. I saw this same brand in the front cab of his RV. Someone had tried to fill it here and dumped it when they noticed the hole. Briggs said he'd need water."

Diego's face darkened. He wanted the old man, but Hazel needed him more. He shuffled away from the detective without a word. They were both just guessing at this point. Like the bottle of water, they could each surely poke holes into any theory. For Diego, this was past the point of debate. The only thing he knew now was his gut feeling, and he knew Hazel was close.

Halfway up the steep hillside, he glanced back and saw Maxim venturing away from the tank, searching the low ground. That was good. As long as he kept his eyes open, Hazel had a chance.

But Diego kept thinking about the key chain. Maybe he'd been right about Annabelle the whole time. Maybe she was a self-centered brat who didn't care about the welfare of others. Maybe she *had* only come back for her possession.

He scoffed as he remembered something Kayda had asked: Did Hazel want to be found? Then he wondered if she was distracted by the lights and the children, dancing carelessly. Unthinkingly. Was there an object of hers that Diego should have brought to get her attention? Maybe all he needed was a music box or childhood keepsake.

The biker scaled a steep boulder and made it to the top of the crevasse. It looked higher from this vantage than it did from below. He knew it was no more than a couple of stories. The lip of the rock jutted out so it was nearly above the water. The canopy was still above his head and he could see out between the tree trunks. After some searching, he noticed Maxim securing the perimeter. Diego scoped further out but concluded that no one else was close. He checked the high ground behind him as well. It appeared less promising. Desolate and cold, he didn't see any signs of life besides the foliage.

A hollow pit rose from his stomach as he imagined what he would say to Julia. He didn't know if he could bear to tell her, after he thought he was so close. He couldn't handle seeing her reaction to the news of another unsuccessful day.

Diego de la Torre sank to his haunches. All he'd wanted was a chance to meet the little girl. To see if Julia and Hazel were a fit for his life, and he for theirs. He didn't know that he'd be a good father figure. He damn well knew he wasn't perfect. But there was a light in Julia that warmed him. He imagined nurturing that warmth. And he imagined being happy.

Now Diego questioned his motivations entirely. The little girl in the picture with a self-conscious smile—had he ever really known her at all? The Hazel he knew was just a figment of his imagination. A secondhand ghost conveyed through a forlorn mother.

An image of Julia's face crossed his mind. It was a memory he cherished. The only one he had of her smiling. After Hazel had been missing for mere minutes, he'd assured her that she would be found. That all would be well. Julia had believed him, and she had smiled—a woman, a mother, perfectly contented. In truth, Diego had done everything for that smile, the only honest and pure one he'd seen since this all started.

Even after the hard reality had set in that she might never see Hazel again, Julia had lost herself in forgetful moments of happiness. She never smiled again, no, but the strain in her face eased. Her eyes clung to hope. When the cold truth of the world was absent, Julia's daughter filled her with joy and she hummed a sweet, soothing melody.

Diego laughed but it came out as a sob. He choked it away and tried to hum. A lullaby escaped his lips, just as

Julia had sung it. His eyes welled with tears, and he repeated the tune.

Somewhere below him, the melody echoed back.

Diego's eyes raced to the bottom of the glen. Standing on the edge of the shallow tank was a young girl. He'd never seen her before. Not in person. But he knew her.

"Hazel!" he called out.

Long black hair spun around as she faced the sky.

Diego didn't blink. He leapt off the edge of the rock and dove for the center of the tank.

Chapter 51

The night sky was peaceful, quiet, and full of stars. Even out here, in the middle of Sycamore, such beauty couldn't be masked by fear. The serenity was a reprieve from the arduous hiking they'd completed. Now, they waited back at the ranger's jeep with a new arrival.

Hazel Cunningham was safe. Barefoot, scratched, but unhurt. She was mostly silent but her curious eyes were a far cry from traumatized—Maxim figured she felt a mix of shock, joy, and relief. She was comforted by Diego's firm embrace, and she even giggled once or twice.

As heavenly as the moment was, the rumbling that sliced the air was a welcome interruption. The view was marred by a sharp streamer of light above. When the spotlight crossed over their crew, it temporarily blinded them. The airlift had arrived.

The three men instinctively ducked as the chopper set down on the dirt road. The sheriff's office Search and

Rescue Unit was a volunteer arm of the department that had been on standby since this began. The rotors of the chopper spun wildly, drowning out all other sounds. Maxim nodded to Diego and Briggs and they nodded back. There was no way not to be proud of the moment. Secretly, Maxim knew each of them had feared what they had just accomplished was impossible. Wins like this were few and far between.

"I'm going with them," yelled Diego over the noise.

Maxim understood. He'd stayed with Annabelle every step of the way until she was safely in the clinic, and even the whole night afterwards. He recognized Diego's investment. What the man chose to be a part of. Maxim couldn't begrudge the biker that. Hell, he respected him more for it.

Into the dense wilderness, in the direction they had come, Maxim noticed a white glow burning through the foliage. He pointed it out just as Diego was turning to go.

"There it is," said Maxim. His thoughts returned to the night he first met Annabelle. "I've seen that before."

Ranger Briggs squinted and shined a light at the blossom. Diego's eyes flashed and he stepped back to the detective.

"No, Maxim," he shouted over the helicopter. "You can't follow the lights. I tried it before."

Alice Radford had said something similar. Stay away from the water. Hide from the light. But there it was, gracefully moving on the wind. Flowing. Dancing. Growing in brilliance.

Maxim turned back to his friend. "Why not?"

The biker shook his head emphatically. It was difficult under the blare of the rotors, so his words were short. "It'll kill you."

The detective was about to protest when Ranger Briggs cut in.

"He's right, Maxim. There're a lot of things in these parks best avoided."

Maxim studied him inquisitively. "You mean Sycamore."

Briggs cleared his throat. "The Sycamore Canyon Wilderness. There are things out there we're not meant to understand."

"You said you didn't believe the stories."

The ranger shrugged. "Hell, if I told every person I met the things I've seen, they'd put me in a straitjacket. I've been patrolling these woods for years now. The little I know is to never stray from your path. That's how people get themselves killed. Those lights won't approach our vehicle."

For the first time, Diego and the ranger were in full agreement. Maxim understood the message. He knew it was a risk, but that was part of his job. "But Lachlan Munro's out there," he countered.

A rescue technician hopped off the helicopter and sprinted towards them. The three men huddled close to strategize.

"We can get him later," said Diego.

"He's right," said Briggs. "It's only gonna get darker and colder out here. We can pick this up in the morning."

Maxim worked his jaw. "Red was at Wounded Ranger Tank. And he's out there now. I know it. How easy will it be to get this close to him again?"

The chopper tech reached them and shone a small flashlight in Hazel's eyes. She responded as one would expect, and he didn't appear concerned. He leaned close to Diego's ear. "We need to get her loaded up."

Diego nodded. "Me too."

"One of you is okay," said the tech. Diego reluctantly handed him the girl and the tech split off towards the chopper.

The biker ran his fingers through his hair. "I can't leave her, Maxim. Not after all this." Maxim noticed that Diego avoided looking him in the eye. "I want Red. Bad. But I need to make sure Hazel's safe." Before Maxim could respond, Diego headed for the chopper.

Maxim cursed and followed the mysterious light with his eyes. Giving this up felt wrong. Maybe he could convince Briggs to back him up. Just then the ranger pointed out another flickering further south. Maxim saw it but thought his eyes were playing tricks on him. He rubbed them and scanned the surroundings.

No less than five wandering lights circled their position.

Maxim broke into a run for Diego, who had just boarded the helicopter.

"Something's happening," he bellowed. "It's now or never."

Diego pounded a fist against the helicopter cabin. "Don't you get it, Maxim? You could follow those beacons forever. You'll never catch them. They're not human."

"It's not me who's doing the catching."

Ranger Briggs remained by his jeep and was on the radio. The two techs in the chopper were confused by the magical sight. Maxim even saw fear on Diego's face.

The detective leaned in to the chopper so the man could hear him better. "Think about it. Wherever Munro goes, they follow."

"If you go out there," said Diego firmly, as one last warning, "you might never come back. Red is prepared. He has iron on his leg and in his hand."

That was true. Maxim had no idea what caused the strange fires in the forest. He wondered exactly what Diego had experienced when he'd encountered them. For all the old man's crazy ramblings, he surely knew more about these specters than any of them did, including Kayda. He thought about Munro, and what the autistic daughter had said, and then it hit him.

"Diego. If Red knows about the green children, then he knows about the lights." Diego studied the detective but didn't get it. Maxim explained it plainly and swiped his hand at the ghostly fires all around them. "Red knows to avoid the lights." As Maxim's arm circled the terrain, it stopped at a facing due north. The oblong moon shone down on them; the cardinal direction was notable because it was the only area devoid of the dancing torches.

Maxim and Diego exchanged knowing expressions.

"They're herding him," insisted Maxim. Immediately, and for the second time tonight, the detective bounded away from the others and headed into the wild north.

Chapter 52

Diego clenched his jaw as he watched the detective. He grimaced when Maxim disappeared into the brush. He may have had a magazine of lead and another of silver, but neither would do him any good against the orbs of light. The biker hefted his Benelli M4 over his shoulder, knowing his friend would need it.

"Strap in!" yelled the tech over the rotor noise. The man clicked a three-point belt across his shoulders. Hazel was already strapped to a gurney.

Diego's face contorted, but he relaxed as he considered the girl. She would be safe, at least. He squeezed her hand gently. "I'll be back, Hazel. I promise." Then the biker jumped off the chopper and waved them away.

The makeshift road wasn't a developed area, but there was enough open space to land the helicopter and get your bearings from the stars. All that disappeared twenty yards into the trees. There, the canopy took over. The vegetation crept together. The headlights from Dan's jeep faded behind him, and the darkness closed in.

Except, of course, for the incandescent ghosts that drifted around them.

The flares were on all sides of him except ahead. As Diego ran, he checked behind him. Somehow, the lights had gained on him. Had they crossed the road already? Had the ranger seen them pass?

The biker pressed ahead, a feeling of anxiety sweeping over him. He'd had a close call with one of these things before. Simply being near one was gut-wrenching. He sprinted harder to keep ahead of them, and a dark thought crossed his mind: what if he and Maxim were the ones being herded?

The outlaw raced further. He didn't see Maxim, but he moved where his gut told him to, where the lights weren't. Finally, after what seemed like ten minutes of full-press running, he heard the detective shout.

"Sanctuary Marshal's Office! Don't move."

As Diego had predicted, Maxim was straight ahead. But there was still a bramble of trees in the way; he didn't yet have eyes on the detective. The biker swapped his shotgun to his firing hand and surged ahead.

"I said don't move you bastard!"

Diego finally crested a hill and could see the forest ahead. The canopy was thinner and allowed the moonlight through. At the end of a small dip, another hill rose in their path, this one much steeper. From his vantage, he could see Red clambering up the side. The iron on his leg must have been slowing him down, but he was still limber for his age. He made good time up the steep ledge, using his pike for support.

At the bottom of the valley, Maxim sprinted after him, pistol in hand. The biker was still two minutes behind him.

Diego scanned his surroundings and noticed the hill he was on ran along the right side of the canyon. The route was more circular, but it led to the top of the distant hill without a change in elevation. It was easier than climbing the ledge, and he might beat Red to the punch.

Diego turned on his heel and raced tangentially to the action. He went over how this would go down in his head. Given that he successfully flanked Red, the old man would need to deal with threats from both sides. The key was to keep Red at a safe distance, out of reach of his pole. As far as Diego figured, that was the only trick left in Red's bag.

That didn't mean he wouldn't be careful. Diego wouldn't hesitate to fill the old man with buckshot. It would only take one wrong move. And Diego wouldn't be sorry.

As the biker circled the men, he realized the fault in his plan. Ahead of him, a fluttering glow grew in intensity. The men were being corralled, and Diego was running straight for the fences. Straight at the threat. He squinted against the oncoming light and hastened to the bend, where he turned and galloped ahead. Once he cleared the valley, he'd be heading away from the blooms again. He should be safe then, at least from them.

The woods grew thick again. Diego lost sight of the other men. But he was making great progress, and he had no doubt he would beat the old man. He banked around the turn, hopped up a couple of rocks, and found himself on the far hill.

He saw the old man still navigating the incline now. Red was almost at the top, where he would head down a trail alongside the rock face. Diego burst ahead when he saw he could skirt around from the other side and cut him off.

The ground became rockier, the dirt sandy. Diego's leather boots lost purchase a couple of times and he slowed down. It wasn't about being careful as much as being silent. His ambush wouldn't work if Red heard him coming.

When Diego reached the large boulder, he understood the terrain he was dealing with. As it lowered to the adjoining path that Red was on, he saw the stark drop-off on the other side. They'd be confronting the old man along a ridge. Diego decided to press his back against the rock and wait for Red, lest he risk falling into the canyon below.

The Benelli was ready in his hand. Diego took care to hold it up so it wouldn't peek out past the edge where Red could see. The biker considered how easy it would be to take Red out from here. He simply needed to wait for the man to pass and he could shoot him in the back and watch him tumble to his death. It would be so easy.

As much as he wanted to, Diego told himself to let Red make the first move. Maybe he was inspired by what he thought Maxim would do, but it felt right to let Red decide his own fate. The biker patted his wrist and felt his knife under the sleeve of his heavy jacket. The blade was silver, and it might work in a pinch, but he thought about what

Kayda had said. It was ironic, but this was a case where a plain-old steel knife would have served him better.

A silent breath to calm his nerves. A wiggle of his hand to loosen his trigger finger. A shift in posture to trade the weight between his feet. Diego waited, and it wasn't long before he knew something was wrong.

Red wasn't advancing up the trail. Given his hatred for the things in the forest, it was the only path that made sense. Diego had risked approaching them, but they were only getting closer. It was only getting more risky.

Diego rounded the corner and jutted his shotgun out. The ridge was clear. The biker stepped ahead on the rocky ground and listened. The crunch under his boots was all he could make out until he heard the gunshots.

Instead of Red walking into an ambush, he'd set one up himself.

Diego charged toward the reports. He heard three more pops, and some yelling. When he cleared the cliff wall, he saw Maxim sprawled out on the ground. He wasn't holding his weapon.

Red advanced on the detective and swung his heavy weapon. The pole arced overhead and Maxim rolled away just in time. The metal hit solid ground with unusual strength and rang like a tuning fork.

Diego didn't hesitate. He lined up his ghost ring sight and fired the 12-gauge at Red's back.

The old man twisted around from the impact. His eyes went wide as he recognized that he'd been cut off. Surrounded. With Maxim still on the ground favoring his right hand, Diego silently begged the old man to give him a reason to fire again. Red's eyes glinted in the moonlight, and he took a menacing step towards Diego.

The autoloader released another round. This one impacted the old man in the chest. He lost his footing and fell to his knee. His right leg, the one supported by the metal brace, jutted out stiffly to the side.

That wasn't exactly the reaction Diego had hoped for.

12-gauge buckshot wasn't for hobbyists. It wasn't for shooting pheasants or sporting clays. This was for wild game, and Diego would happily depend on it to take down a bear. While Red didn't exactly shrug off the blow, somehow he'd found the strength to stay mostly upright.

"You're right, Diego," said Maxim, rising to his feet. "He's immune to lead. I wasn't sure if I'd hit him back at Echo Canyon, but he took three to the chest and acted like nothing happened."

Diego stepped forward, keeping careful aim on the wild man. "You should come out hunting with us more often, Maxim."

The detective narrowed his eyes.

Diego explained. "You've heard about lead poisoning. It's awful for the environment. And for your body. Who wants to shoot a deer and accidentally eat a lead pellet? Not to mention all the metal that gets left behind in the forest."

Red clutched his pike with his left hand and his chest with the other. His head faced the floor, and he rasped heavily.

"What the hell are you talking about, Diego?"

"Lead isn't iron," he answered. "These things—these creatures of the forest—it's iron and steel that poison them. Silver and lead won't get the job done."

Maxim turned a skeptical eye to Red. "What's that got to do with hunting?"

"Lead buckshot's not the only alternative anymore, Maxim. My M4's loaded with pure steel." The outlaw took another step towards the downed man. "Okay, Red. Drop the pole."

The old man chuckled, a rumbling deep from his belly, and he lifted his head. His eyes were bloodshot and filled with hate.

"Idiot," he coughed, spittle on his lips. "I am of the highlands, not the forest."

Diego snorted. "Tell it to someone who gives a fuck."

The biker's boot upended the pole planted in the dirt. Without the support, Red fell forward on his face. He grunted and lay motionless, still gripping the pike tightly. Diego moved forward to step on his hand. And that's when Red surprised them both.

The old man swung his arm along the floor, swiping the pole at the biker's legs. Diego, unprepared to defend the blow, had his legs swept out beneath him. He fell to his side as Red pounced to his feet.

"I am not like *them*," he boomed. "I keep the metal for them, but I cannot be hurt by it, iron or otherwise."

Red expertly swung his weapon around. Diego aborted his plan of firing the Benelli and instead held it with both hands to counter the blow. The crash of metal jarred the shotgun loose, and Diego fell back again.

"It's you who's going to die out here," said Red to both of them. "If not by my hand, then by them." His pike pointed to the beacons of light that cut through the darkness and converged on them. They'd stopped their advance, though, as if afraid to approach.

The old man readied another blow but Maxim jumped on his back, clasping him in a bear hug, pulling the pole close to his body where it couldn't be freely swung. The hermit tried to wriggle away but Maxim held strong.

Diego lurched forward and tugged his knife loose from its sheath. Red elbowed Maxim hard enough to force the detective to the floor, but the distraction was good enough. Diego plunged his blade between Red's ribs.

The old man roared. He grasped for Diego, but the biker ducked under his arms and went for the pike. Red swung it wildly with both arms, knife protruding from his chest.

It was Maxim's turn again. He kicked Red's back, pushing him off balance and toward the edge of the ridge. The man was too strong, however. He kept his balance and backed away. He pulled the knife from his chest and flung it to the ground, then readied another swing of his iron.

Diego lowered his shoulder and barreled forward, striking Red in his wounded chest. The man backed precariously closer to the ledge. He panicked and spun around, switching places with Diego. The biker ducked to the ground to brace himself against slipping and grabbed the iron pike. At the same time, Maxim mimicked Diego's move and put his shoulder into Red's side. Again the old man spun away from the edge of the hill.

Only this time, his grip on the pole came loose.

Diego yanked so hard he thought to throw Red off the cliff. Instead, the old man released his weapon and watched as it careened over the ledge, tumbling down the rocks which they had climbed.

His eyes widened. "You fools!"

Diego searched the ground for his M4 and saw it past Red. He lunged and skidded in the dirt to grab it. Meanwhile, Maxim backed away as the old man swiped at him.

Somewhere on the fringes of the hill, the lights danced closer.

Diego snatched up his shotty in one hand and spun around, expecting to see Red engaged with Maxim. Instead, the spry man was swinging a large fist his way. The biker couldn't get the gun up to block the attack in time, so he raised his right arm.

Diego had taken many punches in his lifetime. None like this. His arm pressed into his chest and the continued force slammed him into the ground. One second he was readying his M4 one-handed, the next he was catching his breath on the ground. If it wasn't for the steel reinforcement in his motorcycle jacket, he was sure his arm would have snapped in half.

Diego rolled to his stomach and saw Red scamper down the trail that he'd planned on ambushing him on. The biker turned to his friend and saw him wincing in pain from a similar blow.

"He's running from us," said Maxim in disbelief.

"No," said Diego, forcing himself to his feet and recovering his bloody knife. He waved it at the converging flares, once again brightening. "He's running from them. And I think we should, too."

Chapter 53

The old man was fast. Even with the brace on his leg, he outran them.

Diego remembered something Maxim had said about Red having a wheelchair and a bad leg. Something about him faking it. Diego hadn't considered whether that was true or not, but it was obvious Red didn't need the devices. Like the heavy pike he once held, the iron leg brace was protection against the green children, if not a sword, then perhaps a shield.

With the man half-disarmed, the ghostly fires of the forest were emboldened.

Diego's legs pumped back and forth, their dial turned to maximum. That was enough to keep Red in sight for now. Maxim followed behind, sprinting with his hand on his panama hat. It was ridiculous, and the biker would've left him behind if they didn't have trouble on their tail.

"Pick up the pace!" yelled Diego, skidding to a halt.

Maxim's silhouette was a sharp outline against a white star. Diego lifted his Benelli M4 and aimed for the center of the looming mass. The steel may not have been effective against Red, but Diego knew the lights didn't like it. The second the detective whisked by him, Diego fired and continued running.

"What are those things?" screamed Maxim.

"You're asking that now?" returned the biker.

They sprinted side by side, watching helplessly as Red disappeared ahead.

"He's too fast, Diego."

The biker nodded and continued running. He was becoming increasingly worried about the two of them. They'd done their job. They'd found Hazel. Now Diego wondered whether he would live to see the girl and her mother again.

At least they'd be happy together.

The two men descended the slope of the hill. It wasn't as steep on this side but, at their speed, it was just as dangerous. They wildly swung their arms as they rapidly slid down the gravel.

A dead branch rapped Diego's face as he navigated the decline. To the far left, the terrain became much smoother, but it would be hard to cut over to it with his momentum. Even worse, a flat rock jutted up and out ahead of them, and Diego couldn't see the ground past it.

The biker instinctively pitched to the side to avoid the crevice. He turned to motion for Maxim to follow. The detective panicked and tumbled out of control towards the edge.

"Maxim!"

Diego chucked his shotgun to his off hand and reached for his friend. He snatched a handful of jacket and worked to stabilize the man, but his footing slipped as well. His waist scraped the ground and slammed against the stone.

Maxim rolled past him and over the side. Diego hugged the ledge and squeezed his grip on the jacket, unwilling to let go. The weight of the detective hurled his chest into the rock, but they skidded to a stop, Maxim hanging out of sight.

Diego's arm muscles strained at the extension. His head circled back and he squinted at the oncoming glow. The brilliance forced his gaze to shy away, and he felt the heat on his back rising.

Below, Maxim began jerking and bucking. Diego only had him with one hand—his other pressed the M4 to the ground and stabilized the awkward contortion. He couldn't lose the weapon, he realized. It might be the only defense they had.

Maxim tugged again, almost pulling Diego down.

"Stay still, Maxim."

"Would you let go already?" he shouted in a voice more irritated than afraid.

Curious, Diego slid towards the edge and peeked, lowering Maxim another foot. The detective rose to his feet and rolled his eyes at the biker. Then Maxim grabbed Diego and heaved him down.

They both landed on their hands and knees. Diego could

see the large boulder towering above them, leaving a cavernous gap beneath. He immediately pulled Maxim and his shotgun underneath and pressed his back to the rock.

The detective was about to say something, but Diego put his finger to his lips. He got the message.

The unnatural shine on the hillside bobbed and swayed, leaving them in heavy shadow. Maxim tucked his legs back, and Diego followed suit.

A blinding flash forced Diego to shut his eyes. His face burned horribly and he hefted his shotgun outward to fire, but Maxim shoved it aside. Diego almost snapped before barely making out the detective with his finger on his lips. Instead, he shielded his eyes against the glare and breathed easier as the luminance dimmed.

"They want him, not us," whispered Maxim once they were alone.

It was hard to argue with the statement. Whether or not the dancing fires had seen them, they were hot on Red's trail. The tree cover below Maxim and Diego lit up, fingers of light stretching into the sky above.

They were no longer encircled by ghosts.

"Fuck it," said Diego. "I say good riddance."

"But his leg irons," mentioned the detective.

The biker nodded. "His shield."

Maxim stood and limped down the hillside again, this time pursuing the lights. "I'm not gonna let him get out of this one," he called back.

Diego shook his head and hopped to his feet. He shouldn't have expected anything less.

Back on the flat ground, it was easy to pick a direction. The lights that had been herding them were now converging with the one ahead. They all zeroed in on their target. The darkness couldn't hide Red from them.

Still, another interminable amount of time passed as they ran. The old man was giving it his all. Diego wondered if Red could escape the blazes, but then he heard the man cursing ahead.

Diego and Maxim slowed as they entered a brightly lit span of forest. The bluish-light cast a cold glow on the surroundings, creating a shifting and shimmering world. The haze instilled a dreamlike quality to the scene. Diego became lightheaded at the sight.

Red hooted and hollered in a small clearing of artificial daylight. The presences around him were so close that they melded with each other. As Red attacked them, he appeared completely mad, swiping at invisible bees. Diego knew better and wondered if fists had any power.

Maxim caught Diego's attention with a hand gesture before breaking off to flank the old man. The biker answered with nod but was unsure what the detective had planned. He'd lost his pistol back on the ridge.

"Come at me you little bastards!" cried Red, swiping at the air. His chest was soiled with blood and his red hair appeared whiter in the cold light. "If you think you can!"

Red was an enigma. Old but vigorous. Brittle but strong. There was something to fear in his calloused eyes, but he didn't look all powerful. Especially not now. Kayda had said something about a man in between life and death, feeding on the living. Powered by the children he killed. His cannibalism sustained him, then. Whatever he was. Now that it had been some time since the old man had a victim, it was possible he was weakening.

The old man flinched away from something closing in on his back, then swung his metal leg in a roundhouse. The glow flared in his face and he laughed. These actions repeated in a cycle, with Red getting a nip or two from the enemies that surrounded him, yet able to fend them off with heavy blows.

"It'll be a cold day in hell when you get the best of me!" he challenged.

Red's foot seemed to connect, if that was possible, and the clearing flashed a brilliant blue. Diego spun away. He felt the heat on his face as the fires drew away. When he could see, Red was hurrying away, and the chase was on again.

"Damn it," said Maxim, joining Diego's stride.

"They can't quite touch him," said the biker.

Maxim's face was grim. "I saw."

The men continued their pursuit. Diego tried not to talk anymore. He hated to admit it, but he was out of breath. If he couldn't change the situation soon, he'd be forced to bow out.

Before he could figure a plan, a dense fog crept onto the low ground. The air was rife with humidity again. It became more difficult to exert himself. And to see Red.

Even worse, the shadows around them grew like a plague that infected the land. Diego rubbed his eyes in disbelief as the lights dimmed, then was shocked to see them snuffed out completely.

As they ran, his vision adjusted back to the raw light of the partial moon. Within seconds, he figured out why.

The tree cover abruptly ended and Maxim and Diego flew out into an open field. A huge lane of grass cut through the wilderness from east to west. Only it wasn't grass now. The low fog hugged the ground and gave the impression they were atop a giant cloud. The only break in the smoke was a line running down the center of the wild alley like a spine—the iron train tracks that led back to Williams.

Maxim pointed to Red. He wasn't hiding in the woods anymore. He was between the iron rails, charging down the tracks.

"Old iron," exclaimed Diego.

"He's gonna make it," spat Maxim, and bolted after him. "Stay where you are, Red!" he ordered. "You're under arrest!"

Diego took a deep gulp of clean air and joined the pursuit. Along the tracks, he searched the tree lines on both sides. The lights were strangely absent. This worried Diego. If the fires weren't going to stop the old man, that meant it was up to Diego and Maxim. With buckshot and blade proving ineffective, the biker was out of ideas.

He considered Kayda's tale of a man immune to metal. The only thing that killed him was a great flood. The man had metal strapped to his leg. He could sure as hell run, but could he swim?

The three men raced along the tracks. The only good

news was that Red appeared to be limping. Diego couldn't tell if the man was hurt or if the wooden railroad ties proved difficult to navigate, but he was slowed either way. They at least managed to keep up with the old timer.

Still, at this pace, Red might make it to Williams. What would a monster like him do out in the open, with so many easy targets around?

They pressed forward and Diego could feel his lungs giving out. Maxim didn't look too hot either. They were so close to the old man, with no obstructions between him and them. Diego took a chance. He came to a stop and fired a blast towards Red. He didn't see a reaction, and then Maxim entered his line of sight. Diego jogged hard to keep up, knowing he wasn't going to make it.

In the distance, past Maxim, past Red, and further than any of them could make out, a sharp, single light cut through the fog. The old man slowed his stride and checked the trees.

"Impossible!"

Maxim pressed harder. Red noticed and stomped onward.

Diego kept running too, but he was getting lightheaded again. He could swear he felt a rumbling in his chest. His leg muscles began to tremble as they threatened to go on strike.

The sharp effulgence ahead flowed closer. Red charged right ahead, yelling obscenities, daring to be confronted again. Diego spun around, expecting to see themselves surrounded again, but nothing was out there. The woods were quiet and cold and dark.

Up ahead, the old man suddenly collapsed.

"Red," yelled Maxim. "Stop where you are!"

The two men rushed toward the downed man. And the light. The vibration in the ground continued. Diego realized what was happening.

A loud horn screamed over the wind, a sound that was made by man, not spirit. Ahead, the spotlight rushed straight towards them, warning them out of its path. The iron horse would not stop easily, and it was almost on top of them.

"Maxim," he yelled. "It's a train."

His friend glanced backwards as Diego pulled off the tracks. Maxim did a double-take before understanding, and he hopped away himself.

Red was a different matter. He understood the situation. At least, Diego thought he did. But he was stuck on his knees, yanking his leg away from the wood. His leg brace had caught on the tracks, and he was frantically trying to correct the predicament.

Maxim moved towards Red.

"You can't get to him in time," said Diego, tugging his friend back.

"The hell I can't."

"You can't do it! We need to move away. If that thing derails then who knows which way it'll careen."

The detective paused and turned to him. "Can a little leg brace derail a whole train?"

Diego simply shrugged and retreated from the tracks.

The horn blared again, this time on and off with a lazy urgency. Brakes squealed to life and sparks shot out like fireworks and bounced in the fog, looking like a thousand dying fireflies. The rumbling roared over their voices and they covered their ears.

Red tugged at his leg, stood to face his judgment, and cursed so loud that Diego could hear him above the onslaught of sound. Then the iron train slammed into him.

The abrasive scraping against the tracks sped past them, slowing but still carrying a monster's momentum. Diego saw Maxim wince but wondered if his face showed any reaction at all. He certainly didn't feel anything for the man.

Since it was apparent the train would not skip off the tracks, they moved closer and watched the juggernaut finally come to a halt.

"How's that for old iron?" asked Maxim.

Diego shook his head. "Iron. Steel. He said no metal could hurt him." The biker hurried to Red's position under the train.

"Come on. No one can survive that."

Diego didn't answer. He ducked under the train car where Red had been. Half a twisted leg brace stuck out from the wheel. A red sheen of fresh blood spattered the metal. On the other side of the train was the other half of the brace.

Diego tried to pass under the train but it was too low. He backed up and followed Maxim between the train cars.

"Shit," said the detective.

Diego emerged and saw the other piece of metal and the

rest of the blood. It was exactly what he would have expected, sans the actual body.

"No way," uttered the detective.

A quick motion caught his eye at the northern tree line. Red peered back at them, limping, awash in his own blood. His face contorted as he saw them. The old man's grin twisted into something evil, and his long, spindly arms braced against the tree trunks. He shoved himself inward and vanished into the brush.

Diego sighed, thankful at least for the short respite. He heaved his shotgun and started forward, but Maxim held him back.

"Look," he said, pointing to the expanse of woods ahead.

Diego saw it. The bluish-white fires returned to life within the trees. A mass of them, all on top of each other. All on top of Red.

A scream pierced the air.

Diego crossed his arms over his chest. "He lost his iron."

Wild rays of light escaped the trees, cutting back and forth. The leaves bustled violently. Red howled now. Gone were the taunts, the curses, and even the words in the end. The only sounds that escaped his lips were gurgles, and even that cacophony withered away with the unnatural, dying light.

A soft wind blew over the canopy and lifted the fog. It rolled through the grass and washed against Diego's face as it escaped to higher ground. Then Sycamore became still. And for the first time in five days, it was truly beautiful.

Epilogue – Last Rites

Chapter 54

Maxim fixed his collar and hurried through the black iron gates of Sanctuary Memory Lawn. He didn't like cemeteries. The dead spoke to him through clues, through the desperation of their killers. He didn't see anything meaningful or peaceful about funerals. Yet every day, crowds shared uplifting stories about those that had passed on.

The ugly truth never entered those tales.

Many people were gathered around the grave. Olivia Hayes had a larger circle of influence than Maxim had expected. She stood front and center by the casket. Although the priest was reading from the bible directly opposite, the mother's eyes were lowered, staring at the hard ground, whispering one last goodbye to her Annabelle.

Maxim wondered if he'd be able to get through this without her noticing him. It was a fantasy, of course. Wishful thinking that the inevitable could be avoided. But the detective knew better. Olivia would be expecting him.

Beside her, Bertrand Collins stared past the proceedings, a melancholy look on his face. Maxim scanned the rest of the group and was surprised to see Annabelle's father in attendance. He, like Maxim, was a man on the outskirts. Afraid to mingle outside his element. Afraid to confront the truths of what this day meant.

Finally, Maxim settled on a smaller group paying their respects in the back. Diego held a strong arm around Julia Cunningham. At his other side, he gripped Hazel's hand tightly. None of them had known Annabelle. Not really. But each of them understood in different ways the tragedy that had occurred.

The detective shook his head. Diego may have been an outlaw, but he had a lot of heart. Maybe that was why Maxim overlooked the legal missteps the biker often made. Sometimes Maxim wondered what it would be like to let loose completely. To uproot and turn his life on a dime. But the detective knew that would never be in his cards. More and more, he was a slave to his calling. More and more, he wanted to be.

Maxim quietly stepped behind them and tapped the biker's back. "Didn't expect to see you here."

Diego de la Torre smiled. "Yes you did."

Maxim didn't have a rejoinder. He returned Julia's wave and removed his white panama hat from his head. They listened to the eulogy for a few moments, then he pointed out the perimeter. "You ever look closely at cemetery gates?"

The biker furrowed his brow and checked. Maxim noticed the second Diego realized.

"The bastard's pike," said Diego. "He stole it from a cemetery."

Maxim nodded. "That explains the fleur-de-lis. You know, it's funny. Red used the old iron to keep his ghosts at bay, but the gates were meant to keep them in. This whole place is a trap."

"Not for her, Maxim. She's free now. You know that more than anybody."

Again, the detective didn't know what to say. He was comfortable with death, but funerals were awkward. If it were up to him, he'd be chugging a bottle of bourbon right now. But it wouldn't be that kind of day. He had business to attend to.

Maxim changed the subject. "They're still finding pieces of Red."

Julia turned to him with a horrified gasp. Diego narrowed his eyes. The biker shoved Maxim away from his girls with a whisper of apology.

After they distanced themselves from the others, Diego shook his head. "What's wrong with you, bro?"

"Sorry. I'm not used to kids."

"Or civilians, it seems. Julia doesn't need to know those details either."

"Fair enough," said Maxim, zipping his finger across his lips. Maybe that hadn't been the smartest time to relay the information.

His friend sighed. "Really? You're gonna make me work

to get it out of you now?"

"Ah, hell," Maxim snapped. "I would but I'm not in the mood. The dogs worked through the night. Lachlan Munro was ripped apart. They're saying wild animals. Bears."

"Smarter than saying 'wolves' in this town."

Maxim agreed. "Anyway, that was some creepy shit out there. I'm thinking about seeing Kayda after I organize my thoughts. See what she knows. See if we can get a handle on what's going on around here."

"Sounds like a plan," said Diego.

Maxim noticed Julia checking on them. It was just a quick glance, and not an overbearing one. She had a smile on her face and probably missed having Diego by her side. After recent events, Maxim couldn't blame her. As far as he was concerned, they'd all earned it.

His eyes subconsciously fluttered to Olivia Hayes in the front. He wished they hadn't, because she was looking right at him. He smiled weakly. It must have been easy to see through, but she waved anyway. Maxim nodded and put his finger up to signal that he needed a minute.

"I can't do this," he said, turning back to Diego. "I don't know how you can."

His friend took a deep breath. "It's as easy as it looks," he said. "You just go with it."

"You know Lola left me before she died. You're one of the few who do. What am I supposed to do after that?" Maxim motioned at Julia. "How do you know she's right for you?"

Diego braced Maxim's shoulders. "You're thinking too

hard. You know, for days I stared at that class picture of Hazel. The smile was off. I realized it was a pose for a picture, a response to 'cheese,' and not genuine. Now check out her smile. Look at them both. Those are real, and they're worth the world to me."

"So one smile from Julia and you know she's the one?"

Diego dismissed the skepticism. "You want the honest answer? I have no fucking idea if she's right for me. But she's beautiful, and her heart is even more so. And Hazel? She's got a lot of spunk. She wants to be a biker like me now."

"Already?"

Diego laughed. "Already." They faced the crowd again and Diego left his arm around Maxim. "Just look at them," he said. "That little girl needs close watching. She's trying to be tough, but she has stuff to work through. And Julia's just as fragile. I can't tell you what will happen six months or six years from now, but I can say this: I'm gonna keep an eye on them. At least for now."

Maxim cleared his throat. He couldn't help admitting it sounded nice. Maybe some good did come from bad situations after all.

The eulogy finished and the gathered crowd began to disperse. It was now or never.

"So what of it?" asked Diego. "Olivia keeps checking you out. She's in a much worse situation. It won't be easy on her. Probably not for the rest of her life. She needs someone looking after her."

Maxim's words caught in his throat. He wasn't big on

setups, but he was already past that with Olivia. He could let the chips fall and see where they landed—it wouldn't be a hard thing to do—but inside, he already knew.

"It wasn't her that needed looking after."

Maxim put his hat back on, tipped the brim at his friend, and strolled away. He headed straight for the center of the proceedings, beside the casket of Annabelle Hayes.

Olivia welcomed him with a smile and tears. "Oh, Maxim," she sobbed, burying her face in his chest. He put his arm around her and patted gently.

"I'm sorry, Olivia. I'm sorry I couldn't save her. I did my best."

"Shush," she cried. "It's not about blame."

Maxim gritted his teeth. Yes it was, he thought. Everything was cause and effect. It was easy to talk a good game, to wish well, but actions needed to go into motion for it to count. A little added attention here and there could have made all the difference.

When he pushed Olivia away, Maxim was surprised that he felt guilty. That didn't stop him from walking past her.

The psychologist was heading to the exit. Maxim called for him to wait and jogged to catch up.

"What are you doing here?" asked the detective.

Dr. Collins turned to him and pressed his wire frames to his face. He appeared annoyed. "Paying my respects, of course. It was nice of you to show up, too. However late."

"Yeah. I'm a little slow sometimes. But I keep at it until the job's done."

Bertrand crossed his arms over his chest and lifted an

eyebrow. "Yes, I heard. Congratulations on the case, Detective. Isn't that the lucky little girl over there?" He pointed out Hazel Cunningham, and Maxim noticed Diego eyeing them.

"Concerned about another victim, huh? I've got news for you, buddy. You're not getting anywhere near that little girl. But that's not the case I'm finishing up. Right now, I'm speaking for Annabelle Hayes."

The doctor's nostril's flared. It was quick, but Maxim picked up the tell.

"It's unfortunate," said Bertrand. "It's common for men in your position to burn out after extended stress. Time off is the most important thing. It's vital you don't carry the burden of guilt for events beyond your control." The psychologist took a heavy breath and gazed longingly at the casket as it lowered into the ground. "This didn't end the way any of us wanted."

Maxim slipped his cuffs from their case. "Who said this was over?"

He saw panic in Bertrand's eyes, the classic moment of fight or flight. But there were too many people here, and he was too distinguished to run. Within seconds, the panic transformed to indignation.

"What do you think—"

"You fucking dirtbag," exclaimed Maxim. "You're the reason she's in the ground at all."

The doctor was startled by the accusation.

"Look familiar?" asked Maxim. From his pocket he produced Annabelle's key chain. The same one he'd lost in

Sycamore. Somehow, it had turned up in his car again. And this time, when he'd listened to the recordings, he understood the subtext. "You made her turn off her cell phone," explained Maxim, "to make sure she couldn't record anything incriminating. But you never realized she had an audio recorder on her key chain." He spun the man around. Just as he did, Olivia Hayes approached them.

"Maxim?"

He shot her a stop gesture with his hand while keeping his eyes on the doctor. He knew this would hurt Olivia. It had been what Bertrand meant by Annabelle making her mother jealous. If she had found out. If Annabelle had told her. The doctor had been convincing Annabelle to bear the burden of what he did to her by herself. He had instructed her to be strong.

Now, Maxim had to let the truth out.

"Bertrand Collins, I'm arresting you for sexual contact with a minor. You have the right to remain silent." Maxim cinched the doctor's hands behind his back, making sure the lock was extra tight. He didn't normally read Miranda this early, but he wanted to put on a show. "Anything you say or do can and will be used against you in a court of law."

Once Dr. Collins was safely secured, Maxim continued announcing his rights, but his glare turned to Olivia. The woman trembled, mouth open but at a loss for words.

If Maxim had to guess, the mother had never known. She wasn't evil. She had just been caught up in family politics. She'd moved on from her husband and moved up in the world, but she never figured out how to make Annabelle fit.

Over and over, Annabelle had tried to expose the truth. She'd left her key chain behind at her father's house. Her mom made mention of the same thing. Even Maxim hadn't seen it until it was too late. It was a tough thing to live with, and he would ponder it for a long time.

But Olivia Hayes had years to see the truth. Maxim knew her failure was in not being vigilant enough, and he could never forgive her for it.

"What is this?" demanded the doctor. He'd been silent, but now that a crowd had gathered he was obligated to play a part. "This is a ridiculous mistake! You'll make me late for my appointment."

"It might do your patients some good to take a day off," snarked Maxim.

"Oh, no. If you think I'll spend more than a minute in a cell, you're sorely mistaken." Bertrand wriggled in Maxim's tight grip but didn't dare resist. "I want my lawyer. I'm going to be back to work in time for lunch."

Maxim laughed coldly. He turned away from the crowd and shoved the man towards the grand iron gate. "That's not gonna happen, Doctor. You and me are in for a long day." The detective even managed a smile. "Trust me. We're just getting started."

-Finn

Connect

If you're reading this, it means you demand more from your urban fantasy. Dark forest monsters are good for a scare, but they're nothing without a layered cast of characters and realistic plot drivers. *Sycamore Moon* is my stab at a cut above the rest: driving mystery, true friends banding against impossible odds, and themes that hopefully make you put the book down and ponder, if even for only a minute.

My writing process demands quality control at every step of development. I hope you agree *Sycamore Moon* is the premium product I strive to make it. Unfortunately, doubling down on originality and quality in an on-demand world has drawbacks. It's simply not possible for me to get you a brand-new novel every month or two. The process takes time.

That's where you come in. Together we can build a better book.
All you need to do is connect.

- Join the Outlaw Underground, our private Facebook group. (www.facebook.com/groups/dominofinnfans/)

- Leave an all-too-important review where you bought the book. Each one helps more than you know.

- Recommend this book to your friends. Link it on social media.

- Join my reader group newsletter, get a free story, and hear from me only when I have new releases or important news. You'll never miss another launch sale again. (dominofinn.com/newsletter/)

Simple, right? Five minutes of your time makes a world of difference to me, Maxim, and Diego. Thank you for your heartfelt support. I'll keep writing as long as you keep reading.

- Domino Finn

Also Try:
Black Magic Outlaw

Did you know Maxim and Diego aren't the only ones standing up to the supernatural?

Did you know they're part of a wider shared universe of everyday heroes?

Did you know that sometimes the good guys use a little magic too?

If you're into bullets, black magic, and an extra helping of action, check out Cisco Suarez, a too-cocky-for-his-own-good necromancer in a tank top.

Dead Man
Black Magic Outlaw Book One

Waking up dead is the worst. Trust me. I know these things.

The last time I woke up this hungover I was naked, soaking wet, and wrapped in a Cuban flag.

This time, at least, I had clothes on. I couldn't see them in the pitch black, but I could feel them. I could feel other things too. Raw pounding in my head. Enough tightness in my chest to make every breath a chore. I was in ten kinds of pain. Apparently that wasn't enough because my leg was asleep too.

There was more. Cold, wet, grimy more. Flies buzzed around my face, circling the stench of death. My arm was slimy. I shifted my weight and something crunched beneath me. My hands and feet pressed against the tight confines of a box.

Smell of death and decay. Check. Some kind of giant coffin. Check. I'm no mathematician but things were starting to add up.

Despite the evidence of my apparent death, I didn't panic. You see, I'm a necromancer (among other things) so I know a little about the subject. I couldn't tell you where I was or what happened the day before to get me here, but I had an inkling I was still alive. Even if just barely.

I tried to sit up. A stabbing pain pulsed through my body until I relaxed again. Request denied.

Okay, deep breath time. I focused inward to calm myself, then reopened my eyes. A thin sliver of light crept through the seam of my crypt overhead, but it was too weak to illuminate the interior.

Good thing I knew a trick or two.

I stared into the darkness, more deeply than before. Not into the box or any physical place, but into a place within me. The pupils of my eyes leaked and my green irises filled with black, and with a blink I could see.

And you thought the necromancer thing was all about wearing black and growing your hair long. I hate to burst your bubble but I'm not a walking death metal stereotype. I don't wear a trench coat and I have a crew cut. I live in Miami, for fuck's sake. It's hot and humid *in the winter*. No sense getting a heatstroke to appeal to northern sensibilities.

Not only that but Cisco Suarez (that's me) isn't just a necromancer. He's a shadow charmer too. That's the magic I just called on. The darkness all around me, it was still there—I could just see through it now.

The thin razorblade of light now stung my eyes. I avoided looking directly at it and checked the rest of the tomb. Crushed cardboard boxes. Stuffed plastic bags. My accommodations weren't as morbid as I'd feared. This wasn't a coffin but a dumpster.

Maybe I wasn't dead after all. Just down for a nap. A bed made of beer bottles. My pillow? A dead sewer rat.

That would've made most men jump, but remember: necromancer. I scrunched my nose and reached for it.

The simple act of limberness was a battle of pain. My muscles were sore. Dry and withered like the old husks of a toppled tree. My bones creaked and my joints were half-dried cement. I stirred up more dust than the Mummy. But I pushed through the agony until I dangled the dead rat by its tail.

It had been decapitated. A tribute. Sacrificial magic, and not mine. That spelled trouble.

I checked for other signs of ritual or binding. Charms. Runes. Burnt sacraments. Scanning the contents of the dumpster, I spied a couple of dark-red cowboy boots on my feet and literally hopped in place. (I almost knocked my head on the dumpster lid.) You see, the rat I could handle. My wearing a bona fide pair of alligator boots was unacceptable.

Don't get me wrong. There was nothing magic or cursed about them. It's just that the modern Cuban doesn't wear cowboy boots. Cisco Suarez doesn't wear cowboy boots.

That's me again, by the way. Shorter and catchier than Francisco, it always reminded me of a comic book name. What kid didn't want to be a superhero? I liked the sound of it so much I picked up referring to myself in the third person. My fatal flaw.

Enough about my name. Let's talk spellcraft. I'm what you call an animist: an everyday human who happens to tap into spirits for magical energy. Wild, huh?

I know what you're thinking: A cleric deals with gods and a wizard with books, right? Well, put the Player's Handbook away and forget everything you think you know. Gods and books have plenty of overlap. (The most famous book in all history is a notable example.)

Fact is, magic is a universal force in the world, pure energies known as the Intrinsics. They're the building blocks of all creation. People like you or me can only manipulate them through spirits. That makes us animists.

Everything else is just a title. Wizard. Cleric. Learned men like to use mage (it's more sophisticated). You see shaman or witch doctor applied to primitive peoples. Or if you wanna vilify animists, call them witches and warlocks. You get the idea. I'm sure some academic somewhere compiled a list of unofficial "official" definitions—but you'd have a hard time running into that terminology on the street. And the street is where the real stuff happens.

Case in point: the dumpster I was lying in.

Some alarm in my head screamed that I was hurt. Maybe fatally. The thing was, besides stiffness, there wasn't anything wrong with me. I wasn't dying, anyway. I kinda felt like a homeless vampire more than anything else. Which would be a lot funnier if I didn't know vampires actually existed. After all, right now I had a hangover from hell—maybe hell was where I came from.

You're probably bored by now, right? Sorry. I think too

much. It's a problem I'm trying to address.

With a strained kick of an alligator boot, the lid of the dumpster flew open. Blinding light engulfed me and seared my senses. I literally hissed and uselessly threw my hands up in defense. Maybe I was a vampire after all.

But I didn't burst into flames. After I took another second to get my head on straight, I realized I was still drawing upon my shadow sight. I drained the darkness from my eyes, my lids pushing out black tears, until it was safe to look.

A blue sky. Fluffy clouds. Palm trees.

I was in South Beach.

Not the pretty coastline with white sand they show on TV during football games. That was never far in Miami Beach, of course, but the back alleys were far less picturesque. I was just off Washington Avenue somewhere, outside a dive bar. The alley was empty. I heaved myself over the dumpster wall and landed on the concrete with a thud. I wouldn't win any vaulting medals but it got the job done. Standing and walking involved entirely new kinds of pain, but either it was wearing off or I was getting used to it.

Normally I'd assume this predicament was my doing—it wouldn't be me if I didn't go big—but the dead rat was a bit much. It was also a dead giveaway that someone else was involved.

I padded at my jean pockets. I had a cell phone but no wallet. Was I robbed? It seemed unlikely given the evidence of spellcraft. A beatdown, then?

I frowned. I'd annoyed people, sure. I'd had minor run-ins with gang tough guys and stirred up the local talent, but that was life as a small-time hustler. I was too young for real enemies. No reason anyone should wish me dead.

The preternatural fog in my head wasn't going away. I couldn't think clearly. No amount of head-scratching helped.

With my head on a swivel for danger, I staggered to the pink sidewalk. (Miami Beach, remember?) I was ready for anything. What I didn't expect was to be ignored.

Small groups of shoppers strolled up and down Washington Avenue. Horns honked and cars inched forward and came to a stop at the light. I got a few odd looks but nobody confronted me or threw any blood curses my way. It was just your average whatever-day-it-was in South Beach.

A man strolled by and held his hand out to me. While trying (and failing) to make eye contact, I accepted his offering. A nickel and two pennies. He avoided my puzzled expression and continued on his way.

That was random, but I couldn't be accountable for the South Beach crazies. Cisco Suarez needed to stay on task. Since everything appeared normal outside, I considered pumping the bar employees for information.

The car that was stopped on the road in front of me clicked its doors locked. I looked and the woman in the passenger seat averted her eyes. Bitch. Then I got a glimpse of myself in the window reflection.

I would've locked the doors too.

Besides my healthy tan, nothing of my disheveled appearance was recognizable. My usually close-cropped hair hung over my shoulders in a wild mane. My eyes were permanently frantic, sporting the raised-by-wolves look. The full-on homeless beard didn't help. And my clothes. Besides my jeans and red cowboy boots, of all things I wore a yellowed and bloodied tank top.

Tank tops were never really my look but, to my surprise, I actually filled this one out. My chest strained against the thin fabric and my bare arms looked carved from marble. Still in disbelief, I flexed a bicep at my reflection. Maybe the car windows were made from magic fun-house mirrors.

This warrants an explanation. I may be a little cocky and reckless at times, but one thing I'm not is a gym rat. I was always that scrappy skinny kid who was too stupid to stay down. Yes, that means I lost a lot of fights. I wanted to be a superhero but lacked the dedication. What animist would spend time working out anyway? The power of the world at your fingertips, wasted by repeatedly picking up and putting down heavy things.

No, I was never out of shape, but I was supposed to be thin. Now I suddenly felt like Peter Parker after running into that radioactive spider. I was straight buff, is what I'm saying.

My jaw glued to the floor, I stared like a lunatic. The driver floored the gas at his first opportunity. In their place, a matte-black jeep slammed on its brakes. Which was weird since the light was green and the cars behind it honked. I snapped out of my shock as the group of Haitians in the jeep focused on me, anger in their eyes.

They yelled, "Dead man!" and dismounted, brandishing light automatic weapons.

I threw seven cents at them.

Pick up DEAD MAN
where Domino Finn books are sold

Also by Domino Finn

SYCAMORE MOON
The Seventh Sons
The Blood of Brothers
The Green Children

BLACK MAGIC OUTLAW
Dead Man
Shadow Play
Heart Strings
Powder Trade
Fire Water
Death March
Blood Craft
Open Season

SUMMONER FOR HIRE
Tooth and Nail
Hell and High Water

AFTERLIFE ONLINE
Reboot
Black Hat
Trojan
Deadline

Shade City

About the Author

Domino Finn is an award-winning game industry veteran, a media rebel, and a werewolf junkie. As a grizzled author of urban fantasy and litRPG, his stories are equal parts spit, beer, and blood, and are notable for treating weighty issues with a supernatural veneer. If Domino has one rallying cry for the world, it's that fantasy is serious business.

Take a stand at DominoFinn.com